Fingerprints
In The
Water

OTHER BOOKS BY LAWRENCE NAULT

STANDALONE NOVELS
Political & Economic Fiction
Leviticus 25: Jubilee
Speculative Fiction
Inversion‡
RePHleXions: Echoes of Existence

THE DRACONIM SERIES
Young Adult Contemporary Eco-Fantasy
Draconim Lacrima Mortis: Tear of the Dragon
Feeding the Fires
THE MACIVER KIDS ADVENTURES
Young Adult Science Fiction
Loma
Diversion
Titan's Song
THE ANIMAL TALES
Early Chapter Books/Transitional Readers
Squirrel Tales*
Wolf Tales*
Bear Tales*
The Mountain Hermit's Animal Tales†

---

* Available as e-book only
† Includes the complete Animal Tales trilogy
‡ Contains mature content - suitable for readers 18+

Fingerprints In The Water

By
Lawrence Nault

Our Workshop
Publishing Div.

FINGERPRINTS IN THE WATER

ISBN: 978-1-997568-03-2

FINGERPRINTS IN THE WATER

Content Note

Content Note: This novel explores real-world environmental issues through the lens of teen-led activism and dragon-human bonds. While appropriate for a YA audience (ages 12+), readers should be aware that the story includes:

- Themes of **ecological destruction**, including **ocean pollution, wildlife harm**, and **toxic waste**
- Instances of **environmental injustice, corporate negligence**, and **community displacement**
- Scenes depicting **near-drowning, physical collapse**, and **emotional distress**
- References to **colonial history** and **intergenerational trauma** through Indigenous and multicultural characters
- Moments of **grief, fear, and resilience** in the face of overwhelming environmental crises

This book aims to empower young readers while remaining honest about the challenges we face in protecting our planet. It emphasizes hope, collaboration, and the strength of youth-led change.

Reading Community Notice:

Upon completion of this printed edition, readers are welcome to participate in book-sharing initiatives such as Little Free Libraries® or BookCrossing®, provided the book remains in its complete and original form.

Chapter 1

Uranus was drained, physically and mentally. The Tear of the Dragon, held so delicately within the coils of his tail, was still smoky grey. Others would not have seen the last flicker of life deep in the heart of the crystal, but Uranus could. He could feel it more than see it. There was something left of Nessie in there, hanging on. She was not giving up, and if Nessie wasn't giving up, neither was he.

The other dragons listened to Uranus, as he willed life back into the Tear of the Dragon. He had truly loved Nessie, and since returning to Earth, Uranus had gone through a gamut of emotions from hatred to anger, to loss, and was now grasping at holding onto hope. The other dragons knew that if the last flicker of life left the tear of the dragon, the ties that bound Uranus to his promise to Nessie would be broken, and the people of Earth would pay. Humans had led to the separation of Uranus and Nessie before, and it was only Nessie that had prevented him from destroying all of their kind. If their acts took her completely away from him, there would be no holding back his anger. Their existence would be revealed as Uranus rained down terror on any man or machine that crossed his path, and Uranus would go looking for more. Jupiter communed with the animals in Algonquin Park. This was her refuge on Earth. She had been the first to find her people. Jacob and Hannah made her whole on this planet, and they championed the cause of the dragons, but while she wanted to share with them through the crystals, she needed to keep them sheltered from the sounds of Uranus. To do this, she had to remain disconnected from her people, because both Jacob and Hannah were able to read her intimately.

Mars slept, exhausted from the energy he had expended in creating the fire tornado. His body was now buried under the sands of the Chukchi Sea. He listened to the voices of the dragons, and like the others, worried that his efforts were in vain if the life drained from the Tear of the Dragon. Kyle, Mars' person, would reach out often, genuinely concerned for Mars. Occasionally, Mars would wake enough to let Kyle know he was well before closing his mind again and returning to rest.

Saturn did not rest. Her search for her person, Zara, had taken her to the Nakivale settlement in southwestern Uganda, where remaining hidden was a constant challenge. Saturn had tracked Zara from South Sudan, where she had left after her father had disappeared. She had left in the night with her mother and two younger siblings after her mother had heard rumors of militants about to raid their village to "recruit" more fighters.

Their path had taken them off the paths they knew, through familiar territory now turned treacherous. Saturn followed their path for three days, sensing their fear in each hurried footprint pressed into soft earth and each snapped branch where they fled off known trails as they avoided main roads, sleeping in abandoned buildings under the stars. She could sense where Zara and her family had dove into the bush to hide. Saturn used many of the same hiding spots as vehicles approached.

Circling the Nakivale settlement, Saturn knew that while they may have found shelter and food, it was not a safe place for a young woman of Zara's age. During the nights, sounds echoed endlessly. Muffled sobbing from tents, whispers exchanged anxiously between families, and the distant hum of generators could be heard even without the sensitive hearing of a dragon. During the days, the air was thick with smoke from cooking fires, mingled with the sour scent of unwashed bodies and refuse. Saturn's scales brushed against dry grass and dusty soil as she cautiously circled the settlement, every rustle and noise tightening her muscles in readiness to flee or hide. Her person was so close, yet untouchable within the massive camp of more than 100,000 refugees, so Saturn kept moving, sleeplessly vigilant under the cold, indifferent stars.

Pluto basked in the Southern lights, letting the waves of the aurora wash over her. This had become a ritual for him since he was on Earth. Unlike the others, there were few people or eyes on the sky that would see him each time he emerged from the ice. The aurora amplified the voice of the dragons, and Pluto could feel Uranus' quiet prayers, as much as he could hear them. Pluto had called out to Uranus to join her, but Uranus did not heed the call.

Mercury boldly ventured from her resting place on the floor of the ocean in the Bermuda Triangle, to visit her person in Northern Ontario, quite often. The others had cautioned Mercury about the risk, but Mercury was unconcerned. He knew how fast he was, and any near enough to see his passing would only feel the breeze of movement, their eyes never catching the source of the breeze. He felt an inexorable pull to Anne, a young girl who others only saw as a person unable to communicate with others. To Mercury, Anne had a brilliant mind, and the conversations the two of them had were intelligent and stimulating with a child-like innocence that gave Mercury hope.

Neptune watched from his perch high in the Himalayas, where he had been watching for months as people challenged the mountains, and in particular the mountain they called Everest. He didn't understand the motivation of people to conquer something just because it was there. He understood even less why they ignored the destruction they were causing as they fed their egos. In their pursuit of personal glory, they left their waste behind, and all too often, their dead.

There were some among those he observed who were there not because of their egos, but because of a connection to Mother Earth and a need to commune with her and understand her, so they could understand themselves. Long before the dragons had left the earth, they communed with people. That is where Neptune learned the Buddhist concept of "kusala" which describes actions done with pure intention and wisdom, free from ego. Neptune had never seen any man act free from ego, but some were close, and among the hundreds of climbers and the people that supported them were those acting with kusala. One of these was a boy whose family earned their living supporting climbing teams, and whose father guided people up the mountain. This boy was Neptune's person, though the boy did not know it yet.

After taking some time to recharge with Pluto, Venus decided to explore the world she was trying to save. This day found her in Brazil in a paleotoca, the ancient cave of a giant ground sloth. As she entered the almost hidden tunnel, despite being as wide as it was, in the red Brazilian soil, Venus could smell the ground sloth still, though they had been gone for thousands of years. Ancient claw marks scored the ceiling in long parallel grooves, a testament to the massive ground sloths that excavated this labyrinth thousands of years ago. As she descended the gentle slope, Venus could see and feel the pressed and smoothed soil, evidence of the giant mammals moving through the tunnel over centuries. Since that time, the wall had hardened to an almost ceramic-like consistency.

When Venus stepped out of the narrow (to her) tunnel into the first chamber, she stretched a little. The floor was covered in a fine, powdery sediment that had filtered down through tiny fissures in the ceiling. Secondary tunnels branched off at regular intervals, most too small for Venus to enter, so she continued down the main tunnel that spiraled deeper into the earth, punctuated by more chambers of varying sizes. Some of the chambers showed evidence of different construction phases, where generations of animals had made the caves their own home long after the last giant sloth had left.

At the bottom of the system, the largest of the chambers spread out. The floor in this chamber was noticeably different, compacted to an almost stone-like hardness by countless massive bodies that had once rested there. Small alcoves ringed the chamber, each sized perfectly for a giant ground sloth to back into, letting them keep their defensive claws oriented towards the chamber's center. This is where Venus stopped to

5

rest and commune with the current occupants of the chamber, the bats and spiders, and insects. Among these creatures were tiny spiders, as big as a grain of rice is wide. Paleotoca Diminas, the humans were calling them, after only recently discovering the pale, blind, spiny creatures. There were more creatures down here that man had yet to discover, but man thought they knew everything.

While the dragons watched and explored and rested, the dragon-bound continued on their own paths. Jacob, Hannah, Kyle, and Anne all felt what their dragons were experiencing, and heard their thoughts, at least those the dragons chose to share. While those connections influenced them, their lives continued as the world moved around them. Teenagers and kids, lost in an ocean of humanity, trying to find their place in the world.

Anne sat in her living room watching television with her family, sketchbook in hand as usual. She had been making extensive use of the color pencils Jacob had given her on his last visit, and the sketch she was working on showed skills well beyond her age. Aggressive circular strokes that left small flecks of paper showing through had transformed into dark indigo and slate gray clouds roiling against each other. Below the darker clouds were subtle layers of dark chartreuse, capturing the peculiar yellow-green light that precedes severe storms. The ocean itself was deepening layers of Prussian and cerulean blues, with whites worked in for the foam caps. The waves showed sophisticated dimensionality, each one carefully constructed through burnished layers of colored pencil, darker at the troughs and lighter at the crests. She used the white paper strategically, letting it show through in places to create highlights on the water's surface, and pressing so with the pencils in some areas that the paper had a waxy, almost metallic sheen.

This wasn't the first ocean scene Anne had drawn, which may not seem unusual, but Anne had never seen or been near a real ocean. Despite that, many of her sketches in recent days were dramatic ocean scenes, striking in their sense of movement. After her fire images, Anne's parents knew that her drawings were not just the works of a savant, but a warning. Jane, Anne's mother, shared Anne's drawings with Jacob and Hannah, emailing them pictures, hoping Jacob and Hannah could tell them what was coming next.

Kyle sat in his great-aunt's kitchen. This was his first visit to her home since meeting her. The house smelled of sage and cedar, so different from the artificial pine cleaners in his house. He sat at a wooden table, his fingers tracing the grain of wood while his aunt moved around the kitchen, her silver-streaked braids swaying as she prepared tea. He tried not to stare at her profile. She had the same strong nose and determined chin as in the photograph of his father he had seen.

"Your father," said his great-aunt, setting down two mugs of deep amber teas, "he used to drive me crazy, always tapping rhythms on every surface. Table, walls, trees. Everything was a drum to him." Her voice was warm with memory.

Kyle stilled his fingers, suddenly aware he'd been doing the same thing. His great-aunt sat down across from him, her movements unhurried.

"Your grandfather's spirit is strong in you, nephew. The way you move your hands. The way you talk to the spirits through that stone."

"Not spirits," said Kyle, hesitating for a moment, considering his next words. "Not spirits. Dragons."

"That is what your grandfather used to say." His great-aunt reached across the table and squeezed his hand. "Drink your tea. It's raspberry leaf. Your father and I used to pick it with our mother every fall. And I have stories to tell you about a young man who would talk to the birds and the bears...and dragons."

Jacob sat at his easel, his phone in his hand, looking at the pictures Jane had emailed. His first reaction was to be impressed. Anne's skills as an artist were well on their way to surpassing his own. In the short time since he had met her on the shores of the lake in Algonquin Park, she had developed skills that had taken him years to learn. As he scrolled through the pictures, his admiration became concern. Every sketch was the ocean, and there was no still water in any of the drawings. Jacob didn't know whether to describe Anne's foresight as pre-cognitive or visionary, or even if those were the right terms. Anne saw the world through different eyes than the rest of the world, and Jacob suspected her dragon did the same. He thought about walking over to see Hannah, to talk about the pictures, but he could feel her and he knew that she already knew what he was thinking.

Hannah sat in her bed, her hand clasped around the crystal she always wore around her neck. She could feel Jupiter's presence, and it was reassuring. She could also feel Jacob and the joy and concern he was feeling as he looked at the pictures of Anne's most recent sketches that her parents had sent. She could feel Kyle, a person she had never met in person, but she knew he was in a safe place, fighting almost overwhelming emotions of loss and confusion. She could sense Anne, and she knew that the young girl was standing at her window, talking to Mercury, her dragon. But there were more now.

Three of them. She couldn't sense them the way she did the others though. It was like they were standing on the other side of a glass wall, waiting to come in. A girl, so far away. A boy who exuded peace. And another boy, much clearer than the others. To Hannah, he looked Chinese, but where was he? Where were the others?

Kai Chen sat at the top of the grassy hill overlooking the harbor. He had spent many hours in this exact spot watching the fishing boats come and go from the harbor below, much of that time spent wishing he were somewhere else. This small Cape Breton town wasn't exactly a hive of activity for a fifteen-year-old boy. He often found himself wondering what it would be like to live in Halifax, or Toronto, or Vancouver...anywhere but where he was now. At least in one of those big cities he would blend in. That was almost impossible here.

Having their children grow up in this small fishing community had not been the plan for Kai's parents when they immigrated to Canada from Hong Kong. Kai's father had been a doctor in Hong Kong, and his mother had a doctorate in marine biology. They immigrated to Canada with great hopes of having a much better future, only to find that it would take years for his father to be licensed as a doctor in Canada, and his mother's PhD meant nothing to the jobs she applied for. To earn a living they had to fall back on what they knew, and that was fishing. Both of them grew up in a fishing village outside of Hong Kong, where their families worked in the fishing industry. That was where they first met. They fell in love during their university years.

Rather than spending years re-qualifying as a doctor in Canada, they drew on their fishing village background. They started small, moving to Cape Breton and working on fishing boats, gradually building up to owning a market/processing facility. His mother's biology knowledge proved crucial for quality control, and his father's medical precision applied well to business management. Kai worked summers helping process catch, a job that he hated, and in his free time, he volunteered at a marine mammal rescue center. As vital as the processing plant was to the local community, he and his family were still outsiders.

Kai hoped this would be his last summer here. If it was a good fishing season, and market prices held, his parents had agreed to let him go stay with his aunt in Vancouver and attend school there for his final year before university. When he had first suggested this idea to his parents, he expected a lot of push-back, but his parents knew the value of a good education, and there were opportunities he would find in a bigger city that he would not find locally. They also knew that fishing didn't hold much of a future. They understood and respected the hard work and sometimes lives, given by fishermen and others, and they had strived to teach Kai that work ethic, but they wanted their son's life to be easier.

Kai's state of solitude as he watched the boats come and go was interrupted by the buzzing of his cell phone. He reluctantly checked his text messages to find his mother was reminding him that he needed to be part of the shore clean-up that was happening that afternoon. He lifted himself from the ground and took a last look at the harbor before hopping on his bike and heading down to the shore.

Chapter 2

Uranus could feel it more than hear it. His person, calling to him.

He ignored it at first, but as the call got stronger, something else happened. That faint flicker of light in the heart of the Tear of the Dragon became brighter. It wasn't enough of a change to be noticed by any other, but it was noticed by Uranus, and it stirred something deep within him. It was the last thread of hope, and that flicker of life in the Tear gave Uranus the motivation to reach out and grab that thread and pull it back.

As Uranus gripped that hope, the other dragons felt it, and they too grasped onto it for all they were worth. It wasn't just the dragons, though. Hannah, Jacob, Anne, and Kyle all felt that glimmer of hope, and they clung to it, and as they did, Uranus was reminded of the words of Nessie before he last left Earth. "Hope doesn't grow on its own. It's strengthened by those who cling to it, until it becomes so powerful that it no longer needs to be hope because it has become reality."

As this memory of Nessie's voice and words filled the thoughts of the dragons, the Tear of the Dragon grew brighter, the light filling the cavern. "Venus," Uranus called out, the joy he felt carried in his call. "It is time for you to return. I have work to do."

Venus burst from the tunnels of the ancient ground sloths and took to the sky. When she had left the Tear with Uranus, she was not sure she would ever see it again, fully expecting that if she did, she would find no life in it. Uranus was the only one among them strong enough to hold on to the hope that the Tear contained, and though she left it in his care, none of the dragons were confident that Uranus had the will to do what was necessary. They were wrong.

Kai knelt on the rocky sand of the Cape Breton beach, his gloved fingers wrapped around a half-buried plastic bottle, bleached almost white by sun and salt. He tugged it free, the motion sending up a small cloud of sand and the scent of seaweed. The bottle joined a growing pile at his feet. In that pile were nests of discarded fishing lines, broken buoys, and a cluster of battered plastic bags. The air was cool, tinged with salt, and the sea stretched out, blue and vast, as if it too were watching the group comb through the shoreline.

Around him, other volunteers scoured the beach, their garbage bags already filling. Beside Kai, an older volunteer whom he worked with at the marine mammal rescue center held up a tattered strip of netting and shook his head.

"This stuff? It's brutal for the sea creatures," he said, gesturing to the tangled, brittle net. "Fish get trapped in it, birds too. Even whales, if it drifts back out to sea."

Kai nodded, his eyes flicking to the horizon where he imagined sea turtles and seals, creatures that could mistake the garbage for food or shelter. He thought about the animals he had seen at the rescue, and a documentary he'd seen in school that showed images of young turtles caught in plastic rings, and fish with bellies full of microplastics. It hadn't seemed real back then, something from faraway places. Now, looking around, the extent of the trash felt overwhelming.

"Look what I found." Another volunteer, a girl about Kai's age, held up a fistful of plastic straws and bottle caps, many covered in slime and bits of shell. "This stuff could choke anything that tries to eat it. I heard seabirds eat these, thinking they're fish eggs."

Kai took one of the bottle caps, flipping it over in his palm. It looked harmless, small and ordinary. But he knew better now; just a few of these could fill a bird's stomach with nothing but waste.

Working methodically, he began picking up cigarette butts littered around a patch of dried kelp, frowning at how many were scattered over such a small area. He'd heard these contained toxic chemicals that could leach into the sand and water, poisoning tiny creatures and disrupting the delicate marine ecosystem.

Further down the beach, a volunteer pulled up a long, frayed fishing rope tangled in seaweed. It was heavy, encrusted with barnacles and sand, and it took two people to wrestle it loose. "Ghost gear," the volunteer said, exhaling as they added it to a pile. "This stuff just floats out there, catching anything in its path. Fish, dolphins, even sharks."

Kai shuddered at the thought. He glanced back at his own pile, now a jumbled mound of plastic scraps, cans, fishing gear, and even an old shoe. Some items had been so deeply buried it was clear they'd been there for years, hidden and breaking down into microplastics that would never truly disappear. With every item he pulled free, he thought about the creatures out there whose lives were constantly at risk from this debris.

As he straightened up to stretch his back, he caught sight of a small, transparent bag snagged on a rock near the waterline. It looked like a jellyfish as it waved gently in the water, and he could imagine a sea turtle mistaking it for food. Quickly, he jogged down and plucked it up, feeling a swell of relief as he stashed it safely in his trash bag.

As the sun set, several of the volunteers sat around a bonfire on the beach talking about what they had found, sharing food, and it didn't take long for a few instruments to come out and the music to start. Kai had heard workers at the fish plant talk about ceilidhs all the time. Random kitchen parties that broke out in storytelling, music, and even dancing. He had never been part of one, but he imagined this must be what it was like. He sat on a piece of driftwood near the fire, listening, watching the embers pop off the fire and float on the cool breeze of the ocean as their glow faded.

As the fire crackled, the voices around him blurred into the background noise of the waves sweeping up onto the shore, highlighted by the sharp clap as the water struck a nearby rocky outcropping. The sandpipers' high-pitched chatter was punctuated occasionally with the plaintive cry of a seagull, all to the background sound of the clang of the buoy bell out in the distance, its bright color reflecting the shine of the lighthouse light that swept across it every few minutes. Something triggered in him as he stared off into the distance, seeing everything and nothing at the same time. A loud pop from the fire caught his attention, and he watched one particularly bright ember drift towards him, refusing to go out

14

as it floated, then fell as though it had a purpose, landing at Kai's feet. As it hit the ground, Kai noticed an unusual reflection below it.

Kai reached down and picked up a shard of something from the sand. It felt strangely warm to his touch, and he could not tell what it was in the dim light of the fire. He turned it over in his hands, seeing shades of many colors, while he listened to the others talk about everything they found on the shore that day.

"What did you find, Kai?"

Kai looked up, a little uncomfortable to see everyone's attention on him. He thought for a moment, then realized he was among people who probably thought like he did or they wouldn't have been at the shore clean-up. "Too much. But I also think I found what I want to do. I want to go to school and find a way to stop this. Not just clean it up but stop it before it happens. I didn't know that before now."

"That is a marvelous goal," said Rob, the director of the marine mammal rescue center. "I think that is perfect for you!"

The others around the fire joined in agreement, and then more music broke out. Kai realized it was getting late, and while they all joined the song, he took the opportunity to slip away and head home. His mother was waiting with some warm food which Kai eagerly sat down to. He reached into his pocket and handed his mother the shard he found by the fire. "Do you know what this is?"

Kai's mother took the shard and held it under the light. "This is beautiful," she said quietly, admiring the deep purple hues. "See these shades of purple, with these dark purple bands?" Kai looked closer as his mother pointed out the lines. "That tells me this shell comes from a very old shellfish."

15

She held the shard close to her face, admiring how the bands of dark purple blended into smoky gray and nearly black tones. She adjusted her glasses to get a better look, and she could see concentric lines and faint ripples running through the nature polished shell. They were numerous and tightly packed, reflecting slow growth over many years. The shard felt dense for its size in her hands. Under the light, the natural patina appeared to give off a soft glow and had a subtle iridescence.

"I think what you have is a piece of the shell of a quahog," she said, setting it down on the table near her son. "One that was very old. And that piece itself has spent many years being shaped and polished by the oceans."

"Why is it warm?" asked Kai.

His mother put her hand on it, but she couldn't feel any warmth. "Your hand must have been cold."

Kai reached out and touched the shard. It still felt warm to him.

"The daughter of one of the women at the plant makes things out of pieces of shell like that. She is Mi'kmaw, and it means something special to them. A connection to the sea, I think. I can ask her to do something with it for you."

Kai picked the shard up, feeling its warmth, and thinking for a minute before handing it to his mother. "Thanks, Mom. But something manly, please."

Kai's mother laughed gently. "Of course."

Mei sat down and had tea while her son ate and told her about his day. She looked at the list he had written down of everything he found on the shore, which was typical for Kai. He liked to document everything. As she looked at the list she shook her head. She was more surprised that they hadn't found more than they had, though the regular clean-ups were obviously helping. Her attention was pulled from the list when Kai asked a question.

"What does a person study to get a job that could stop all this garbage from going in the ocean, or find ways to clean it up?"

Mei thought for a moment. "I don't know."

Kai looked at his mother with an exaggerated look of shock. "Wait till Dad hears you said those three words."

"It's not recorded, so it never happened," replied his mother. "But finish your food, and let's see if we can figure out what you would study. I am guessing you are thinking about university."

Kai nodded. Mei smiled. She and Kai's father had been encouraging Kai to pick a path for his future, but tried to let him find his own way. He was a smart boy, and she expected he could get into any program he wanted. She thought, given his work with the rescue, that he might study biology, but this was the first time he had actually said he knew what he wanted to do. She was going to do everything she could to help him.

The two of them sat up late into the evening, researching careers and courses. They found several in different fields, from environmental science and research to engineering, conservation, and even business and innovation. Kai was so involved in the process that he didn't even notice his father had come home and was watching them from the kitchen door.

"Can I do both of these?" Kai asked, pointing at the laptop screen.

"Marine biology and environmental engineer? Lot's of work, but you can do it." Mei tried to not sound too excited. She wanted Kai to be confident that it was his choice.

"That's what I am going to do then," said Kai confidently.

"Not a doctor?" Kai heard his father shout from the kitchen.

"Not a doctor," his mother replied. "A biologist!"

Kai closed the laptop and shook his head as his father joined them. "Good choice. You will have our full support as long as you put in your full effort, like you always do."

Kai's father was a man of few words. For some, these words would have been what was expected. Kai though, recognized the words as the high praise they were coming from his father.

Chapter 3

"Are you Kai?"

Kai looked up. He hadn't noticed a young woman approach him, his attention on the boats returning to the harbor.

"Sorry to disturb you. Your mother said I would probably find you here. I am Amy. Your mother asked if I could make something with that shell you found."

The mention of the shard of quahog shell got Kai's full attention. It had been a couple of weeks since he gave it to his mother, but it was constantly on his mind.

"Can I sit with you?"

"Yeah, of course," replied Kai awkwardly. "I have seen you before. At school, I think."

"I am a year ahead of you, but we probably crossed paths in the halls a million times. This is a beautiful spot."

"You can see everything from here. All the boats come and go. Ships on the horizon. All the life on the shores. On a calm day, you can sometimes see whales breach the surface," said Kai as a seagull called overhead. "Look down at the dock. See those men arguing. That boat captain does the same thing every time he returns. He is never happy when he gets back."

"My family knows him," said Amy. "He is just never happy. He was different a few years ago, but his son died and his wife left him, and Dad says he got lost in a bottle."

Kai felt a tinge of guilt. He had been judging the man's behavior from his perch on the hill, "I didn't know that. I should probably be less judgmental."

"No, you weren't wrong. You were working with what you see, but sometimes it's what you don't see that tells the story."

Kai looked at Amy thoughtfully. She wasn't wrong.

"Look at the end of the dock. What do you see?" asked Kai.

Amy watched the people at the end of the dock for a while. She recognized the boat, which was one of the oldest in the harbour. She also recognized the boat's captain, who was also one of the oldest in the harbor. Everyone knew him as Ernest and as a bit of a recluse and hermit who lived in a shanty that looked like a good wind might blow it over.

"A mother who has brought her children along to buy some fresh fish?"

"Close," said Kai. "That's Mrs. James. Her husband got cancer real bad and hasn't worked in a long time. She doesn't work cause she stays home to take care of him. Her son is in my class."

"That's sad," said Amy.

"Yeah. They don't have much, but Ernest there gives them some of his catch every day. He doesn't charge them. When he leaves his boat, he actually drops some of his catch off to a few homes. Never charges them a dime."

"Really! You see a lot, don't you?"

"I am kind of an odd person out around here, so I don't talk a lot, but I see everything," Kai replied, a note of sadness in his voice.

"I can relate, I think," said Amy as she reached into her pocket and pulled out an amulet.

Kai was shocked as he looked at the piece she had in her hand. He recognized it as his shard of shell, even though it no longer looked like it had when he found it. He knew what it was though, because he could feel it.

"May I?" asked Kai.

Amy handed him the pendant, and Kai felt its warmth as soon as it touched his hand. The warmth felt welcoming and seemed to touch his whole body. It was as though the carved piece of the shard was a part of him.

The shard of shell had been carved into a stylized shape of a turtle, not overly detailed, but intentionally shaped with a rounded shell, distinct head, and four strong limbs extending outward. It was polished to a smooth, glass-like finish, which heightened the deep purple tones contrasted with white bands. There were traces of the shell's striations, preserving the organic patterns formed over centuries, and the edges were rounded, but slightly uneven.

"It's amazing," Kai murmured. "Did you…carve all of this?"

Amy watched as Kai slowly traced the smooth shell. He seemed almost mesmerized by it. "Can I tell you about what I did?"

"Yes, please," Kai said softly, enthralled by the look and feel of the amulet.

Amy shifted over so she was right beside him, almost against him. This would have had Kai feeling embarrassed and nervous and completely awkward at any other time, but he barely noticed as he held the amulet in his palm so Amy could see it better.

"My grandmother helped me with this. She said it was a very special shell, from a very old animal and it carried a power."

"A power?" Kai wondered if that was why it felt warm to him.

"In our traditions, objects made from the ocean carry a connection to the ocean. A polished quahog shard, especially from an ancient clam, symbolizes endurance, wisdom, and the passage of time. I think that is what my grandmother meant."

Kai nodded his head, a little disappointed that the power wasn't more than that, but the connection to the ocean meant something to him. It reminded him of what he was feeling sitting by the fire after the shore clean-up. That connection was his drive to pursue marine biology and environmental engineering now. He had a connection to the ocean.

"Grandma is the one who suggested I make a turtle."

Kai looked up. "Why a turtle?"

Amy tucked her hair behind her ear, choosing her words carefully. " The turtle represents a lot in my culture. Longevity, wisdom…endurance. My grandmother said those things would be important to you soon."

"Important to me?" Kai's brow furrowed. "What did she mean?"

Amy shrugged. "She didn't explain, exactly. Sometimes she speaks in riddles. But turtles are tied to creation stories too, like Turtle Island, Earth itself."

Kai turned the amulet in his palm, noticing faint lines etched across the turtle's back. "What's this pattern?"

Amy shifted closer, pointing to the design. "The circles symbolize the earth's growth and expansion. The other lines are waves. They connect the turtle to the ocean, a reminder of the water's strength, but also its calm. The ocean's always moving, always changing, but it endures."

Kai nodded slowly. The water's persistence, never stopping, never giving up, reminded him of the endless plastic and debris they kept finding during shore clean-ups.

"What about these dots?" he asked. Pointing to the seven tiny circles.

Amy's smile widened. "I was hoping you'd ask. Those are for our seven sacred teachings. Love, respect, courage, honesty, wisdom, humility, and truth."

Amy picked up the amulet from Kai's hand. "The turtle represents Turtle Island, Earth. I used this simple braided leather to hang it on because your mother did say you wanted it to be suitable for a man."

Kai blushed a little which brought a smile to Amy's face.

"The wooden bead on each side of the turtle ground the oceanic energy with elements from the land."

"It is beautiful," said Kai. "I don't know what to say, or how to thank you. Did my mom pay you? If she did, I am sure it wasn't enough."

"My grandmother said I can not take any money for this. She says it is there is something special attached to this, and you."

"But…"

"Nobody argues with my grandma, Kai."

Kai wanted to object, but he didn't want to offend Amy or her grandmother.

"Can I ask you a question? Does it feel warm to you?"

Amy wrapped her hand around the amulet. It felt cool to the touch. She shook her head. Kai reached for the amulet, and as he picked it up from her palm, she felt something and jumped a little. Kai quickly drew his hand back.

"Sorry." Kai didn't know what he had done, but he was still sorry.

Amy reached out and took Kai's hand, placing it over the amulet as she held it. It felt warm.

"It's cool when I touch and hold it, but as soon as you touch it, it warms up." Amy lifted Kai's hand and set it back down on the amulet a few times, testing the reaction, until they both broke out in laughter at what they were doing.

Amy shifted herself onto her knees so she could place the amulet over Kai's head. He let it fall against his chest, tucking it into his shirt. As soon as the cool shell touched his skin, warmth radiated outward. It wasn't just warmth, but something deeper. It seeped into his chest, his ribs, and his arms, like sunlight stretching through his veins.

Then everything shifted.

The sound of the ocean swelled, louder than before. The crash of the waves seemed to echo inside his head, each one striking harder than the last. The wind rose, cutting through his shirt and biting at his skin.

Then came the voice, faint but unmistakable.

"Kai..."

He jerked his head up, scanning the shoreline. His breath hitched as the world around him seemed to blur. The beach stretched away from him, the horizon curling in like a rolling wave. For a heartbeat, it felt as if he were standing in two places at once, here on the grassy hill, and somewhere else…like the bottom of the ocean.

The voice came again, louder now.

24

"Kai…"

It wasn't just a sound, but a feeling. A tug deep in his chest, as though something unseen had reached inside him and was pulling him forward.

"Kai?" Amy's voice was soft, cautious.

He blinked hard, the world snapping back into focus. The beach was just a beach again, the waves steady, the air calm. But the warmth in his chest lingered, pulsing faintly beneath his ribs.

"You okay?" Amy asked, watching him carefully.

"I…thought I heard someone calling my name," Kai said slowly, still feeling the pull. "It was…weird."

"Amy's brow furrowed. "Weird how?"

"Like…like the ocean was calling me," he said finally.

Amy gave him a curious look, but she didn't laugh. "Maybe my grandmother was right," she said quietly. "Maybe you're going to need that turtle more than you know."

"Would you like to stay a while? People watch from my mountain top?"

Kai was surprised at himself for asking, but he felt odd at the moment and didn't want to be alone.

"Under one condition," said Amy. "You promise to come join me and my grandmother for supper one night. She would love to meet you."

Kai stammered a little. "Ummm…you mean, like a date?"

Amy smiled. It wasn't what she was thinking when she asked him to come for supper, but it worked. "Sure, a date."

"Okay," Kai replied.

Amy sat down, right next to him, and they sat like that for a couple of hours. There was very little talking. Kai spent most of the time watching out to the ocean, and Amy spent most of the time watching Kai. They both lost track of how long they had been sitting there.

"My grandmother says the turtle reminds us that everything takes time," Amy said finally. "That no matter how hard things get, if you keep going…you'll get where you're supposed to be."

It wasn't until someone else came along walking their dog that they realized what time it was.

"I need to get home, Kai. Can I drive you home?"

"I have my bike," said Kai. "Thanks for staying. And really, I can't thank you enough for the turtle."

Kai stood up, brushing the grass from his pants, then offering Amy a hand. "About our date. When would you like to do that? And what should I bring for your grandma and parents?"

"Just my grandma," said Amy. "I live with her." Amy handed Kai her cell phone. "Put your number in there. We will figure it out."

Kai entered his number into her phone and handed it back. Amy turned to go but stopped. "You know, it doesn't have to be a date, if you don't want."

Kai was feeling unusually confident. "And if I do want?"

Amy found herself blushing. "I guess it is a date."

As Amy drove off, Kai climbed onto his bike and pedaled slowly home. As soon as he stepped into the house, his mother asked if Amy had found him. Kai showed her the amulet and told her the details of the carving that Amy had told him. His mother loved the amulet, but his father wasn't quite as impressed.

"You know you will be going away to school soon. Not a good time to be starting a new relationship," said his father, not unkindly. "School, your volunteer work, and a relationship

26

is a lot. You don't want to break your friend's heart when you leave."

"What?" Kai was confused.

"Your dad saw you and Amy sitting on the hill together," whispered Mei.

"What! Really dad? We were just sitting."

His father pounded his fists together. "Sitting like this. The wind couldn't get between the two of you."

"Oh my god! I am going to my room," Kai said as he stomped off down the hall to his room. He thought about slamming his bedroom door, but that would not have ended well. Instead, he closed it properly, then flopped down loudly on his bed. He wanted to be angry, but he could still hear someone calling to him. It was more than just calling him, though. It was as though he was feeling a strength and emotions that weren't his own. On his own, he would never have agreed to a date with Amy, let alone ask her to stay and sit with him. It was the amulet that gave him the confidence. At least that was his theory.

Kai drifted off to sleep, hearing his name called. It was faint at first, but growing louder. In his dream, a dragon swam deep beneath the ocean, its wings cutting through the water like blades through the air. The currents bent around it, following its path as though the ocean itself answered to the dragon's will. The dragon turned its head, and its voice, low and endless like the rolling tide, spoke his name...

Lawrence Nault

Chapter 4

It would have been easy to take to the sky. The thought of bursting forth from Loch Ness and flying out over Scotland to the nearby sea appealed to Uranus. He longed to feel the stretch of his wings. There was too much risk of him being seen, so that left him with three other alternatives. His size made following the waterways to the sea just as much of a risk. One path would take him through the Caledonian Canal, but that was a series of man-made locks where he was sure to be seen. The second would be to travel the River Ness, but it was shallow in areas, and Uranus did not relish the idea of sneaking along shaded riverbanks or waiting for a fog to roll in. That left only one option for him.

The Great Glen Fault was a major geological fault line that ran diagonally across the Scottish Highlands from northeast to the southwest. It had shaped the landscape of the region, and part of the shaping created a series of fissures and caverns far below the surface, like the cavern Nessie had called home. Some of these fissures ran parallel to the River Ness that Nessie had used as a tunnel when she wanted to escape the confines of Loch Ness and explore her world. Those tunnels would be a tight fit for Uranus, which made him uncomfortable and nervous, but it was the only path available to him.

The sides of the tunnel were polished smooth, evidence of the number of times Nessie had made this journey herself. Along the top of the tunnel there was one distinct line carved into the rock. Uranus knew what left that mark, and he let the memory of that occupy his mind while he squeezed through the narrow passages.

His mind drifted to the games he used to play with Nessie. Chases through the skies and oceans, across and through the depths of Earth. In one very exuberant chase, Uranus had tackled Nessie, but it was a careless moment, and his misplaced claw lifted a large scale from Nessie's back. She did not cry out or complain. In fact, she quickly turned Uranus' shock at hurting his friend to her advantage and pinned him to the ground. They laughed about it after, but that one scale never did heal properly. It stood up from her back like a spike on a stegosaurus for the rest of her life, leaving an exposed area of flesh that always made her vulnerable. It was that one scale that left the scar in the ceiling of the tunnel.

The tunnel ended and Uranus found himself in the depths of the Moray Firth. He burst out of the narrow passage, into a spin as he extended his wings and felt the freedom of the space around him. From the Moray Firth he headed straight for the North Sea, where he turned south. As Uranus glided effortlessly through the depths the sense of freedom he felt turned sour. The water clung to his scales like a film of grease, stinging as if the sea itself was sick. The taste of oil and iron lingered on his tongue, sharp, bitter, and unnatural. He understood now why Nessie had rarely left her loch in recent years. There was a time when this area was teeming with life under the surface of the water, but the poisons of industrial runoff had changed the North Sea's occupants. They didn't create new life as abundantly as they once did, and the shells that once protected mussels and oysters had become soft. The deep seagrass beds that Uranus could remember hiding in while playing games with Nessie, once full of so much life, were now smothered by algae, feasting off the nutrients running from the land into the sea, a result of modern agricultural practices.

Uranus continued down through the English Channel and past the Bay of Biscay, his sensitive ears assaulted by the numerous ships travelling on the surface above him. Their massive propellers turned up the waters as creatures below and above the surface of the water followed their wake, picking at the food the propellers' turbulence had exposed, unaware that in the wash of those giant blades, the pollutants were stirred up as well.

From here, it would have been quick and easy to bolt across the Atlantic Ocean and find his person, but Uranus needed to understand his task before that. He had made this journey through the oceans before he took over care of the Tear of the dragon, but when he made that trip, it was with anger and rage blurring his vision. His time spent in meditation with the Tear had changed him and he was seeing the world through clearer eyes now. Instead of heading west, Uranus continued south, through the Straight of Gibraltar to the Mediterranean Sea.

As he entered the waters of the Mediterranean Sea, he contemplated turning back around. The Mediterranean clung to him like a poisoned fog. Plastics drifted like dead jellyfish, their shred forms tangled with filth. The water was heavy, not just with waste, but with silence. It was a silence that pressed against Uranus like a tomb, a sea no longer singing. Uranus forced himself to swim through the sea, and his heart broke as he did. The other dragons felt what Uranus did, all of them feeling not just the deep sadness, but the fear that it was too late. A thousand years ago, when Uranus had travelled this sea, it was teeming with life, a thriving, complex ecosystem. What was there now was almost lifeless in contrast. A body holding onto its last bits of life and losing the battle, soon to be dead.

Uranus ventured to the surface, lifting his head out of the water just enough to see the shores. It did not take the eyes of a dragon to see the problems. The shores of the Mediterranean Sea were crowded with people and buildings, packed tighter than a school of fish, but unlike that school of fish which moved in unison as a single entity, the people moved against each other and the world around them. Their waste from their homes and factories emptied straight into the ocean. Their garbage and plastics, poorly stored and unintentionally dropped, were carried by the winds into the waters. In many instances, it was intentionally dumped into the sea, not to be seen by people on the surface again, but consumed by marine creatures, and capturing life in the bindings they could not escape.

Uranus could not leave the Mediterranean fast enough. He bolted for the Suez Canal. He moved so fast that, even as deep as he was, he left a wake behind him that drew in all the garbage in the area and left a path like the contrail of a jet flying through the sky. Uranus did not notice. He needed out of these poisoned waters. He did not slow until he reached the Canal where he slowed and walked along the bottom of the man-made waterway, hiding in the shadow of the ship above him.

The waters of the Red Sea felt clean compared to the Mediterranean, but it was hardly clean by Uranus' standards. Numerous oil spills had contaminated the waters, and along the coasts, coral reefs that once supported so much life were destroyed or dying, and seagrass meadows were buried as humans developed the coastlines. Raw sewage and plastics were becoming a problem in this sea as well, and Uranus knew it wasn't far behind the Mediterranean. He did not linger in these waters.

The Indian Sea was like a breath of fresh air, but Uranus did not breathe it. As massive as Uranus was, his eyes could see the smallest things. The last time he was on Earth, those small things were tiny life forms, some just a single cell, and they gave him joy. Now, he saw tiny fragments a fibers floating everywhere, some as small as the single-cell organisms. There was no way the creatures that called these waters home could avoid ingesting them. Uranus dove deep, hoping that he would find waters clear of this material he did not understand, and while there was less of it, those microplastics were still there.

At almost seven thousand feet under the surface of the ocean, in the inky darkness, Uranus noticed a creature stalking him. This humored the dragon because despite its almost 20-foot length, and stealth approach, it was no threat to him. He turned to face the shark, noticing its wide, flattened head and blunt snout, and the extra gill slit it had. "You aren't that hungry my friend."

The shark approached cautiously, and Uranus could make out its gray-brown color and pale underside. He recognized it as a bluntnose sixgill shark, a rare creature with roots dating back millions of years. The shark moved closer, circling Uranus but not threatening him.

"I have heard tales of your kind but have never seen you in these waters."

"My kind is more rare than yours," Uranus replied. "I am rediscovering these waters after a long absence."

The shark brushed against Uranus, and the creatures felt a connection.

"There is little to find here, dragon. Sickness. Disease. It consumes all in these waters. It is not so bad here, and deeper, but we all feel it." The shark swam away but returned shortly, pushing a fragment of net with its blunt nose. "This, and smaller pieces, are everywhere. We can not escape it."

Uranus didn't reply. He didn't have to. The shark could feel the dragon's sadness and concern.

"I must move on," said the shark. "Food is not as plentiful as it once was, and I am hungry. We all hope the dragons can restore our homes."

"Good hunting my friend," replied Uranus. "We will do what we can. I promise."

Uranus moved on as well, heading deeper to the Diamantina Trench off the coast of Western Australia. At twenty-six thousand feet deep, the dragon found a bed of rocks and rested on them, breathing deeply. These weren't just any rocks, but lumps of metals like manganese, nickel, copper, and cobalt. These metals reacted with the salt water, splitting it into hydrogen and oxygen. There were several of these spots throughout the oceans, but humans had only discovered one near Hawaii recently. They called the oxygen "dark oxygen". It didn't matter what humans called it to Uranus, the dragons had discovered it long before them and had their own word for it. It was pure. So pure that it filled him like breath after drowning. The cold, oxygen-rich water moved through him, clearing the poison from his scales and the ache from his bones.

There was life down here, at these deep, dark depths. Life that had not felt the eyes of humans look on them yet, but they still felt the impact of them on their home. Uranus communed with them, and creatures came to him, feeling his presence. Deep-sea jellyfish with their bioluminescent displays floated around the dragon, riding the currents of nearby vents in the ocean floor, and rising on the bubbles of dark oxygen. Snailfish swam around the dragon, their elongated, soft, tadpole shapes, and almost translucent color, appearing like stars in the night sky to the dragon on the floor of the ocean. Giant amphipods moved along the ocean floor around the dragon, feeling the dragon's presence, but also taking advantage of the food the dragon had kicked up. Other creatures joined the dragon as well. Many had not been given a name by humans, but the dragon knew them well.

While Uranus rested, he reached out to his person. He knew their name now. Kai. And he called to him. Uranus had felt the moment Kai found the shard, and he felt the time the shard was not with Kai. He also knew Kai had the shard once again, but something had changed. The connection was more clear, more direct, than it had been. As he called, he could hear the boy's confusion and feel his fear, so he waited for him to fall asleep, then he visited him in his dreams, showing him the visions of an ocean only a dragon could see. As Kai slept, Uranus did his best to prepare him. Meeting a dragon for the first time did not always go well.

Rested, refreshed, and a new strength fueled by his newfound bond with Kai, Uranus headed eastward, through the Timor and Arafura seas, and into the Coral Sea. He slowed as he passed the Great Barrier Reef, not because he wanted to, but his passing was knocking over large patches of the stark white coral skeletons. As he slowly passed the reef, he recalled the vibrant, dense coral colonies that once occupied this area. Brain corals, staghorn corals, and so many others, making a kaleidoscope of vivid colors. Uranus closed his eyes and could picture the pinks and oranges and blues and greens, much of it covered in seagrasses and plants, with an abundant variety of life living in the crystal-clear waters, among the coral. Opening his eyes, what he saw now were dull hues with browning, grey, and stark white, all through cloudy waters. There was still life there, but the Great Barrier Reef was a shadow of what it once was.

Uranus turned towards Canada's west coast. His intention was to pass under the Arctic ice in the North and meet Kai the next morning, but his travel plans changed as he entered an area of the ocean littered with plastics. The humans called this the Great Pacific Garbage Patch, but Uranus called it death. This garbage hadn't been dumped here intentionally, at least not most of it. The ocean's natural currents swept this plastic debris from the lands surrounding this ocean, swept into the waters, and then gathered by the currents in this area of the ocean. Uranus could see the plastics floating on the surface, which was bad enough, but in the top level of water, where the sunlight reached, there were so many minute particles of plastic that they could not be avoided by any creature in those waters. Uranus plunged to the ocean's bottom, where he found not only plastics but the rotting carcasses of creatures that had become entangled in the debris or filled their stomachs with the undigestible material.

Like a submarine-launched ballistic missile, Uranus burst out of the ocean and into the sky, high above the earth. Looking down, he saw an island of debris almost as large as

South America. The humans and their cameras and satellites wouldn't see the island. It wasn't dense enough to be seen by even the most advanced satellite cameras, and most of it hid just below the surface, but to the eyes of a dragon, it was an island. A floating island of garbage that destroyed the life that occupied it. From his position, high above the earth, Uranus could see other garbage patches as well. They were nowhere near as large, but the currents in those regions gathered the humans' plastics just as efficiently as they had in the Great Pacific Garbage Patch.

Uranus folded his wings in tight to his body and dove down. He may have been seen, but any eyes that caught sight of him would only have seen a falling meteor or piece of space debris that crashed into the Pacific Ocean. An explosive plume of water reached higher than the Eiffel Tower, punctuated by a deafening boom. Massive waves rippled out in all directions, the energy of some of them reaching distant shores. In the water, Uranus stopped to look around. The shockwave he had created in the water had killed many of the creatures nearby. The dragon had felt their life force leave them, but his act was intentional. These creatures were all suffering, and as cruel as it seemed, it was an act of compassion, and it wasn't taken by him alone. He had spoken with the other dragons before making his plunge into the water.

Uranus turned South. He would have to move faster now to meet Kai the next morning, and the route was longer, but he had more ocean to explore.

He raced through the South Pacific, avoiding the South Pacific Gyre, another vortex of polluted waste. His path took him under the ice of Antarctica, where he could see channels in the microplastic-embedded ice, carved as the ice melted at a rate that it should not have been. Embedded in one of those

37

channels was Ran, an unmanned research submersible that the ice refused to release. Uranus wanted to be angry about this as well, but he understood that this was the humans' way of trying to understand what was happening to their world.

Turning North into the Atlantic, Uranus followed the coast of South America. He didn't need to slow down because these waters had the same problems as the others, just not as bad, yet. The dragon did slow for a while, taking some time to swim with an oarfish. It was a unique sight to other creatures that swam nearby as the massive dragon moved slowly alongside the thirty-foot ribbonfish, which swam vertically in the water, like watching a ribbon dance in the wind through the air. Uranus admired the silver and shimmering color of the oarfish, its scales reflecting ambient light, giving it an almost ethereal glow in the dim depths of the ocean.

"We have heard the dragons have returned. That is a good omen," said the oarfish.

"Dragons, a good omen!" Replied Uranus. "Those are kind words coming from the sea serpent of legend."

They laughed together, and others around them took part in the joy. The rare appearance of oarfish near the surface after storms fueled the myths among men of giant sea creatures. Some even called them "Messengers from the Sea God's Palace" and saw them as harbingers of earthquakes and tsunamis.

The oarfish drifted closer, its striking red, spiky head crests and scarlet red dorsal fin that pulsed in ripples capturing the dragon's attention. Uranus found himself slightly jealous of the oarfish's colors. The long flowing tendrils that resembled whiskers gave the oarfish the appearance of a wise old man, though its life was but a moment to that of a dragon.

"Your return is welcome by all in the oceans. You were but a tale told to us by the last remaining dragon of Earth. That dragon spoke well of you, Uranus."

Uranus stopped, shifting himself to a vertical position in the water, matching the oarfish.

"We all knew her voice," continued the oarfish. "Even though we never met her. Just as we all know your voice now, and that of the other dragons. There is a note of hope in your voice in recent days, and that gives us all hope."

Uranus bowed his head in thanks and left to meet his person. He followed the Gulf Stream, witnessing the relentless flow of plastic waste driving northward to gather in the North Atlantic Garbage Patch, settling off the coast of Cape Breton. This had always been one of the richest ecosystems in the world, supported by the Atlantic's nutrient-rich currents. The scars of pollution were visible here as well. Discarded fishing gear, oil spills, plastic fragments. They were all here, but so was Kai, and Uranus knew the resilience of life would endure.

Uranus settled on the ocean floor and closed his eyes. He reached out to Kai, not with words, but with memories. He showed the boy the seas as they had once been, teeming with life, bright with color, singing with movement and possibility. Then he showed him the world as it was now. Choked, clouded, and dying. And in that dying world, Uranus whispered one word to Kai, a word carried by wind and water, through dream and memory.

"Help."

Lawrence Nault

Chapter 5

A damp chill filled the air as a heavy fog rolled in off the ocean. Kai sat on a large boulder near the cliff face, listening to the waves lap at the shore as an orange orb rose into the sky behind the fog.

"Did you bring me to this isolated beach to kill me and get rid of my body?" Amy joked. She was sitting beside Kai, watching the sun rise behind the fog and listening to birds she could not see.

"I know it is weird," said Kai. "You barely know me. Honestly, I can't believe you agreed to meet me here this early in the morning."

"I just wanted to see what kind of crazy you are."

Kai forced out a gentle laugh.

"I am some kind of crazy, since you put this amulet around my neck," Kai said seriously. "I hear voices. I have the most vivid dreams. But if I am right, and it is real, you will want to be here. Just don't panic."

"Seriously, Kai. You are getting me more worried."

They were distracted by a sound that became a constant hum. They looked through the fog towards the sound as it slowly transitioned from a hum to the flutter of wings blending with the sharp, high-pitched calls of terns. As the sounds got closer, Kai and Amy could make out a vague shape in the fog. The shape became clearer as the sound got even closer. It was a flock of birds shifting and moving together as one, creating fast-changing shapes against the backdrop of the fog. The sound of their wings was both calming and elusive, fading in and out like the rustle of leaves in the wind.

"I think they call that a murmuration," said Kai quietly. "I have never seen terns do that."

The birds moved in unison, a restless, shifting shape. Amy's eyes narrowed. Something about it felt…wrong. A pattern too purposeful, too unnatural.

"I don't like this," she muttered. "Kai…what's happening?"

"Just…trust me," Kai said quietly. But his voice wavered, not with fear, but something else. Something closer to awe. "Don't panic."

The flock of birds scattered like dry leaves in the wind, revealing something vast and shadowed in the fog. A hulking shape rose from the water, droplets streaming off scales the color of storm clouds. Uranus stepped forward, the sand shifting beneath his massive claws. The ground trembled slightly with each step, a deep, steady thrum that Kai felt in his ribs. The dragon's head lowered, and in the dim light, his eyes gleamed like molten gold.

"Holy shit!" exclaimed Amy, moving to get up.

Kai reached a hand out and set it on her leg to calm her down and get her attention. He lifted the amulet from behind the heavy sweater he was wearing and showed it to Amy. "It told me it was coming. We have nothing to fear."

Amy fought the instinct to bolt, but she was frozen in place as she looked at the large dragon standing at the water's edge, water dripping off its body as it looked at them. Colossal was the only way Amy could describe the size of the dragon. Its scales shimmered in shades of pale blue and turquoise, the soft glow of the colors barely visible through the dense fog. Hints of green flickered across its body. The dragon's wings were vast membranes of translucent canvas of silver and faint blue-green hues, reflecting the rising sun's light as the rays struggled through the fog. The sunlight filtered through the wings like a translucent curtain. The wings shook quickly, shedding the salt water from them, before they folded in.

Kai slipped down off the rock he was sitting on and approached Uranus. Amy reached out to hold him back, but she moved too slow.

"You are real," said Kai as he approached Uranus. The dragon lowered himself to the ground to appear less intimidating as the boy stood in front of him.

Amy watched as the dragon reached forward slowly with one of its wings and gently lifted the amulet Kai was wearing. She couldn't believe Kai had just stood there.

"Did you make this?"

Amy looked around to see where the voice came from.

"It's the dragon," said Kai. "His name is Uranus."

Amy slowly slid down from the rock. She moved slowly towards Kai and the dragon.

"I did," Amy said nervously. "With some help."

The dragon held the amulet, still on a leather string around Kai's neck, surprisingly delicately, admiring it.

43

"It is beautiful. And I can see and feel you treated it with respect."

Amy wasn't sure what the dragon meant by treating it with respect. "Ummm, thank you."

Uranus closed his eyes as his claw rested against the amulet. A deep rumble rose from his chest. It wasn't a growl, but something softer, like distant thunder. His breathing slowed, and for a moment, Kai swore he could see the image of a giant quahog, its massive, rigid shell covered in barnacles and seaweed, shimmer in the air, the ghost of Uranus' friend. The dragon's expression softened.

"This shell, was once a life I knew," said Uranus without opening his eyes. "She kept me company on the ocean floor for a couple of hundred years before I left. She was a stubborn old thing," Uranus murmured, his voice low and fond. "I would rest on the ocean floor, and she would sit beside me, never moving, never giving up. I told her once she was the most determined creature I'd ever met.

He smiled faintly, though the smile looked a little terrifying to Amy and Kai, and as he did, a ripple ran down his massive form. "She kept me company when the world above me seemed too cruel to return to. And now…she is still here."

Uranus opened his eyes, and there was a warmth in them. They were glowing with an intense, almost liquid green color, making the gold color even more intense, but soft. He let the amulet fall back against Kai's chest and looked directly at Kai. "That is why you can hear my voice through it."

Amy swallowed hard. She had carved that shell with steady hands and careful thought, but she hadn't expected it to mean this. Had she unknowingly shaped a memory that wasn't hers to touch? "I didn't know," she whispered. "I didn't know it meant so much."

44

Uranus looked at Amy. He looked almost gentle.

"You did not hurt her, Amy," Uranus rumbled. "She has long since left this world. Yet her essence lingers still, a whisper in the currents, a memory in the tides. By shaping her shell into something of meaning, you gave her purpose once more."

Amy moved closer, standing next to Kai, her fear gone.

"You know my name."

"I told him," said Kai.

Amy thought for a moment. "Did your friend have a name?"

Uranus lifted his head high. "Names are a human artifice. The other creatures have no need for names. We recognize each other as the unique life they are."

"But you have a name," said Amy.

Uranus chuckled the way only a dragon can.

"So I do. Given to me by humans. I have had many names, most of which you could not pronounce."

Amy reached out to touch Uranus, but stopped when his head turned towards her hand.

"You are a bold young woman," Uranus said, his golden eyes narrowing. "Brave…or foolish?"

Amy froze, unsure how to answer.

Then the dragon's mouth curled slightly, in what appeared to be a smile. "I suspect a little of both," Uranus rumbled, amused. "That's a good thing."

He lowered his head to the ground, resting it close to Amy and Kai. They both reached out, their small hands landing on the same scale, and barely covering it.

"It is warm," said Amy in wonder. "And it almost feels soft. I thought it would be cold like steel."

She looked over at Kai, who stood with his eyes closed as his hand rested on the dragon, a look on his face much like

Uranus had when he held the Amulet. The world shifted when Kai touched the dragon. He felt warmth, not just against his palm, but inside him as a pulse of energy seemed to fill his bones. In his mind's eye, he glimpsed flashes of memories that weren't his. He staggered back, breathing hard. "I saw...I felt..." Kai stammered. His voice shook. "I felt the whole ocean dying."

Uranus' gaze was heavy with sorrow. "That is what we are fighting for."

Amy looked at Kai curiously. There was something happening between him and the dragon that she did not understand. The two of them were communicating at an entirely different level.

"Come, let's move higher to dry ground."

Uranus moved past Kai and Amy towards the cliff wall, where the ground was dry. He reached out with his massive wings and pulled them in close, wrapping his wings around them. They were warm, sheltered from damp fog and cool breeze off the water, and anyone passing close enough to see them would only see a large rock outcropping from the cliff face.

Uranus told them the reason he and the other dragons had returned to Earth. He went into great detail about the things Hannah and Jacob had accomplished working with Jupiter, and Kyle with Mars, and Anne's bond not just with Mercury, but all the dragons. It was important for Kai to understand his connection with dragons.

"But why am I here?" asked Amy."

"You are here because Kai wanted you here," rumbled Uranus. "You may not have the bond to myself or the dragons that he has, but I sense there is more to you two coming together than just chance. You have a role to play, but only time will reveal it."

Amy tried to hide her disappointment, but Kai noticed.

"This amulet is more than just a carving, Amy. It is a nexus between Uranus and I, and the other dragons and their people. It lets us communicate and feel what each other are feeling, and understand each other better. But it is more. I can't explain it, but you are part of it. I can feel your presence in it."

"You are important to Kai, so you are important to the dragons," Uranus said. His gaze softened. "But I believe there is more to your place in this than either of you yet knows."

Amy was still confused, and a little disappointed, but also very curious about what Kai meant. "I will help in whatever way I can. The ocean is important to my people, but I did not understand just how bad things have become."

Kai reached for Amy's hand, and she took it and held it firm. It was comforting.

They talked longer as the fog lifted, and the sun rose into the sky. Uranus shared so much information about what he had found in the waters that Kai and Amy could have been easily overwhelmed, but there was a calm and peacefulness that filled that space under the dragon's wings.

"I must leave now," Uranus said. "We will speak more."

He didn't wait for a response. Standing up and opening his wings wide. Kai and Amy squinted at the sudden assault from the bright sun. With a single leap, Uranus cleared the beach and disappeared into the ocean. Moments later, a family came down the path that led to the top of the cliff. Amy looked at Kai, her wide eyes conveying the message about how close the family had come to seeing Uranus. Her eyes dropped to her hand, which Kai was still holding. He noticed and quickly tried to release her, but she held tight, a playful smile on her face.

"I guess this means tonight is date night. I can't be holding the hand of a boy my grandmother hasn't met."

"Tonight?"

"I will pick you up at five," said Amy. "Can't have you being all sweaty from biking out to my place."

"Okay, but fair warning. My Dad will probably want to meet you."

Amy laughed, then looked at Kai seriously.

"Thank you for making me part of this. I still don't understand why, or what I am supposed to do, but you have made me part of an experience only a chosen few know. That's special."

"If it helps, I still don't understand why, or what I am supposed to do," said Kai. "But I am glad to have you help me figure it out."

They finally let go of each other's hands as they climbed the path to the top of the cliff, but only because the path was too narrow for them to walk side by side. Amy reminded Kai about picking him up at five as she got in her car and left. As Amy drove off, Kai lingered on the cliff. The ocean stretched before him, a vast, restless thing, powerful, yet fragile. He closed his eyes, listening. In the distance, he swore he heard the low rumble of wings.

"We will make things better," Kai thought.

"Yes," came the whisper in his mind. "We will."

Chapter 6

"There is someone new here," Kyle thought. I can feel him.

"I feel him too," said Hannah.

There were thousands of miles between them, but Kyle, Hannah, Jacob, and Anne, all checked in with each other through their dragon-bound artifacts.

"You only have to think the thoughts to speak with us, just as you do with your dragon," encouraged Jacob.

"I am Kai. I have just heard the stories about all of you."

"Kai, I am Kyle. Which dragon are you bound to? My dragon half is Mars."

"My…dragon half…" The term felt awkward to Kai. "I am bound to Uranus."

"Yikes," thought Jacob before quickly catching himself. "Sorry. Nothing bad. He has not been in the best of moods since returning to Earth from what we know. Hannah and I are bound to Jupiter, and Anne is attached to Mercury who seems to be an interesting character."

49

"Can I ask, what am I supposed to do now?" asked Kai.

All of them saw one of Anne's recent ocean drawings in their minds.

"Yes," said Kai excitedly. "The ocean is why Uranus and I are here."

"Anne has known that is why you were coming for months," said Hannah. "She may be quiet, but I think she is smarter than all of us."

Anne showed them another drawing. It was a massive dragon walking out of the water, a flock of birds in the background, and two people on the shore holding hands. Kai went quiet, but the others could feel what he was feeling.

"That is how you met your dragon, isn't it?" asked Jacob.

"Yes, but it just happened this morning. How…"

"Anne sees and understands things before we all do," replied Hannah. "That is the strength she brings to us."

"Who is the girl, though?" asked Kyle.

Kai didn't respond.

"Dude, there is good and bad to how scales and crystals and stuff help us communicate. You didn't have to say anything, but we can feel how nervous you are about your date tonight." Kyle was kind as he spoke to Kai. He didn't want to embarrass him.

"Oh…"

"You should get ready for your dinner," said Hannah. "There isn't any of us that weren't nervous about a first date or meeting their parents."

"You said scales and crystals and stuff," said Kai. "Do we all have something different?"

"I have a dragon scale which I keep in a medicine bag. The others have crystals formed by dragon fire if I remember right," said Kyle.

"What do you have?" asked Hannah.

Kai held his pendant in his hand and looked at it. He heard Hannan take a sharp breath in. "That is beautiful!"

"Wow," they hear Anne whisper.

"Amy, the girl I am having supper with, carved it. Uranus said it is a shell from an old friend from before he left Earth."

"So, your artifact isn't just dragon-bound," said Jacob. "It binds you to another person as well. That's new."

The conversation was interrupted as Kai's mother came into his room. She was holding a bouquet of flowers. "This is not for your girlfriend. This is for her grandmother."

"Mom..."

Mei laughed. "Trust me. Maybe you can take that pretty one in the center and give it to Amy."

Kai shook his head as his mother came and sat on the foot of his bed.

"Amy is a good girl. I like her grandmother, too. But you should know that your father knew her parents, and that might make him a little cautious."

"I don't understand," said Kai.

Mei looked at her son lovingly. "Only Amy can help you understand. That is not my place. Just don't judge your father too harshly. I have already reminded him to be kind."

Amy arrived shortly before five, and she came straight to the front door. She seemed unphased when Kai opened the door and let her in, both of his parents standing right behind him.

"Amy, so good to see you again," said Mei. "You made a very beautiful piece of art from that old shell."

"Thank you," said Amy. "My grandmother helped me."
"How is your grandmother? I have not seen her for a long

time."

"She is well. She doesn't get out as much as she used to."

Amy reached her hand out to Kai's father. "Nice to meet you, sir."

Kai's father shook her hand quickly and looked out the window over Amy's shoulder. "I can't believe that old car is still running."

"Oh, don't say that," Amy joked. "You will curse it."

Kai's father forced a smile onto his face.

"Here, don't forget these for Amy's grandmother," said Mei, quickly interrupting. "Kai got them for your grandmother." She reached into the center of the bouquet and pulled out a single red rose. "Except for this one. He picked that one for you."

Amy blushed.

"Now go, go, go. Don't make your grandmother wait, or you will be eating cold food with a cranky woman."

Mei ushered them out the door, quickly shutting the door behind them. She turned and gave her husband a harsh look before heading to the kitchen.

"You didn't get the flowers, did you?" asked Amy as they walked towards the car.

"I did not," said Kai.

Amy laughed. "That's okay. My grandma doesn't have to know that. She will love them. Your mother is very nice."

"She tries too hard," said Kai. "But she means well. My Dad is hard to understand sometimes."

"Honestly," said Amy. "If someone was picking my kid up in a car that looked like this, I would ask questions too."

"Ummm, maybe I should ride my bike."

"Maybe you should get your butt in the car."

"Your dad knew her parents," his mother had said.

Kai thought about that as they drove. His father's brief handshake, the quick glance away…whatever had happened, it wasn't just caution, it was something deeper. Something he didn't understand yet.

Kai was welcomed with a hug from Amy's grandmother. He was quickly ushered to a seat at the kitchen table, where Amy's grandmother sat down as well. The kitchen smelled like frying onions and sizzling beef, warm and inviting. The wooden table at the center of the kitchen was well worn with the marks of the many people who had gathered there over the years. "You can bring in the food, Amy. My old legs are tired from cooking."

"Thank you for cooking and having me over for supper," said Kai. "I hope you didn't go to too much trouble."

"It's just burgers and fries. Nothing fancy. Bet you were expecting something like bannock and moose meat, weren't you? I suppose if I went to your house for supper, I would get Chinese food."

"Grandma, stop it," said Amy as she set the plates of food on the table. The plates were mismatched as were the faded floral placemats they were set down on. It wasn't fancy, but to Kai it felt…homey. "She is just messing with you."

Amy's grandmother broke out in a roar of laughter, to the point she started choking. "You should have seen your face," she said as she started laughing again.

Kai joined in on the laughter, as did Amy.

"I have to tell you," said Kai. "If you came to my house, you probably would get Chinese food, but better than the restaurant food."

Amy's grandmother laughed again.

"I will bring you some next time."

Amy's grandmother stopped laughing and looked at Kai seriously. "Next time, eh. That's good to hear. If a young man is going to hold Amy's hand, he better plan on sticking around a while."

Kai felt the heat in his face as he blushed. Amy's grandmother broke out in laughter again.

"Just eat," said Amy. "If you wait for her to stop giving you a rough time, you will go home hungry."

The burger was good. It was a nice change for Kai. Everything at his house was either seafood or some version of Chinese food. His family never ate out.

"I wanted to thank you for helping Amy with my pendant," Kai offered as they ate.

Amy's grandmother once again got a serious look on her face. "I have held and carved many shells over my years. Yours was different. It had an energy in it," she said softly. "It's old…older than you know. It's like it contains the power of Turtle Island in it."

Kai felt the pendant warm against his skin, the faintest pulse beating in rhythm with his heart. There was no laughter this time. The old woman looked deep into Kai's eyes as though she were looking for something.

"It feels…alive, doesn't it," Amy's grandmother whispered. "There is something special about you, young man. You are destined for something great. I know this sounds like the ramblings of some crazy old woman, but there is a life force in that pendant, and I am guessing it makes you whole."

Kai and Amy exchanged looks. He didn't know how to respond.

"See. See," said Amy's grandmother. "You two know something about it already. I can see it. You can have your secrets, but there is one secret you can't have." She leaned forward, once again staring into Kai's eyes. "What are your intentions with my granddaughter?"

"Grandma!"

Amy's grandmother broke out in another fit of laughter. "I have not had this much fun in years! But seriously, I don't know what that pendant means to you, or Amy, but both of you can always talk to me about it if you need to. I am an old lady. I will soon be taking my secrets to the grave anyway."

Amy gave her grandmother a dirty look.

"Oh, you know I am right, child. We can't live forever. Now finish your food so we can have dessert."

Kai helped Amy clear the plates from the table when supper was over. Despite Amy's objections, he insisted on helping her wash the dishes and clean up. Amy's grandmother moved a short distance from the kitchen table to a threadbare lounge chair where she appeared to nod off. Kai started to talk as he washed the dishes, handing them to Amy to put away, but Amy interrupted him.

"Don't let her fool you. She is only pretending to be asleep."

Amy's grandmother laughed. "I hear everything." Amy just shook her head as she rolled her eyes at Kai.

With the dishes done, Amy invited Kai to sit for a while. An invitation he happily accepted. They sat down on the couch, and as they did, Amy's grandmother attempted to lift herself out of her chair. Amy hopped up and helped her, holding on to her hand until she was sure her grandmother was steady on her feet.

"I think it is time for this old lady to go to bed. Don't get ideas, young man. I hear everything. Thank you for the lovely flowers."

Kai quickly got up from the couch. "Thank you for supper and having me in your home. It was delicious," he said, meaning every word of it."

Amy's grandmother looked around her home. "It isn't much. Everything in here is old, including me. She looked at Kai softly. It's not the things we have that are important. It's the people we have in our lives, and I was happy to have you in my home," she said as she reached out with her arms wide.

Kai met her offer of a hug. It was a quick one, and when they released each other, Amy's grandmother placed her hand on Kai's chest, directly over where the turtle pendant hung under his shirt. "It's warm…" Her hand stayed there for a minute, then she turned and headed towards her bedroom. "Goodnight."

Amy watched her grandmother shuffle towards her room.

"Did I pass the test?" Kai asked playfully.

Amy gave him a jab in the arm. Her grandmother turned halfway so she could see them. "Young man, if you intend to court my granddaughter, every day will be a test. Treat her well and with respect."

"I will."

Before turning back towards her room, Amy's grandmother looked lost in thought for a moment.

"You okay?" Amy asked, concerned.

"Keep her safe too, please," Amy's grandmother added. "I don't know what the two of you are involved in, but I am trusting you Kai, to protect her."

Kai wanted to promise he could protect her. But how could he? He barely understood what was happening to him with the dreams and the dragon and the pull of the ocean. What if he wasn't strong enough? What if he failed?

"I'll do my best," he said softly. It didn't feel like enough, but it was all he had to offer.

Amy's grandmother nodded and turned away. They watched as she entered her bedroom and shut the door. They returned to the couch.

"She is wonderful," said Kai. "Fun."

"She is getting old. Moving slower and not so steady anymore," replied Amy, a little lost in thought. "But her mind is still sharp," she said cheerfully. "Oh my god, you should have seen your face when she asked if you expected bannock and moose meat! And when she said she knew you held my hand."

"I can't believe you told her," said Kai, his face flushing with embarrassment again.

"I don't keep any secrets from her. It's no use, cause she always knows. Just like she knows that we are involved in something, and she knows about the life in that pendant you wear."

Kai unconsciously moved his hand to his chest, feeling the pendant. "What are we involved in?" he said quietly.

Amy shook her head. "No idea. All I know is, thanks to you, I met a dragon. I talked to a dragon. A real fricken' dragon."

The two sat and talked for a while, until Kai heard the familiar tone of a text message from his mother. He looked at his phone quickly before returning it to his pocket. "That is my signal to get home."

Amy laughed. "My grandmother still has a landline. She refuses to get a cell phone."

"A landline?"

Amy pointed at the faded black phone hanging on the wall in the kitchen, the long, coiled cord hanging from it, twisted in knots.

"Wow…"

"That's one way to put it," said Amy as she got up from the couch and offered Kai a hand to help him up. He ended up standing directly in front of her. "I won't do this at your house, so I am going to do it now."

Kai barely had time to process what was happening before Amy leaned in, pressing a soft kiss to his lips. It wasn't just a kiss. It felt like an anchor, something grounding him in a world of dragons and so much that seemed impossible to control.

"Thank you," she murmured, taking hold of his hand. "For the dragon. For coming to supper. For helping with the dishes. And for being kind to my grandmother. Now let's get you home before your Mom comes looking for you."

Chapter 7

Titan's Haul was an aging behemoth of steel and rust. The massive ship was built in the 1990s during the boom in global shipping expansion. It was once considered state-of-the-art, but it now showed the wear of decades spent crossing oceans. It had changed hands a few times and was destined for scrap until its most recent owners acquired it and kept it operational and profitable by less than scrupulous means.

With a length of three hundred and fifty meters and a width of fifty meters, Titan's Haul was one of the largest ships to dock at Halifax Port. Now anchored outside of Halifax harbor, smaller ships and fishing vessels went out of their way to get a closer look, keeping a safe distance. Its hull was a dull slate-grey, streaked with rust blooms, particularly around the waterline. Oxidized orange stains bled across its flanks, and patches of discolored paint revealed hastily applied repairs. Faded white block letters spelling Titan's Haul were across the bow, barely legible beneath layers of grime, but obviously covering up the previous name of the ship.

A towering white block rose above the stern, the superstructure standing starkly against the rust-streaked hull. Radar domes and communication antennas bristled from the top, massive compared to the technology of more modern vessels, but impressive to observers all the same, even if many didn't even work. Along the ship's spine sat endless stacks of multicolored containers. The stacks of red and blue and grey building blocks stood six and seven containers high. Some were brightly colored, but many of them bore the evidence of many ocean crossings, their paint peeling and exteriors battered.

The captain of the ship was a Russian man, and his crew a mix of poorly paid sailors from Southeast Asia, Eastern Europe, and West Africa, but the ship flew under a Liberian flag. This flag of convenience allowed the ship's owners, a group hidden behind layers of offshore companies and shell corporations, to bypass stricter labor laws, safety regulations, and environmental standards.

The captain was anxious to be on his way. Every hour he was anchored was just more opportunity for the Coast Guard to focus on his ship and find a problem. The Titan's haul had a reputation among port authorities as a troublesome visitor. It had been detained in Rotterdam for leaking bilge oil and in Singapore for structural concerns. It always managed to avoid serious consequences and return to operation after minor repairs. It wasn't just the condition of the ship that was a concern to authorities, though. Altered cargo manifests and dodged inspections had led to many eyes on the ship.

"We just got the call," the second mate informed the captain." Rybaka is in place and ready to drop its nets. There is a storm rolling in though."

The captain had been watching the sky and the limited tools he had access to. He didn't have access to modern satellite imagery, specifically because they had gone out of their way to limit the ability of the ship being tracked by satellite signals. He had to rely on the navigational telex and METAREA reports. He saw the storm coming in, but he was confident the ship could handle it. He needed to leave now to make use of the distraction provided by the Rybaka.

"Call the crew to stations," the captain ordered.

The second mate grabbed the ship's intercom mic and barked the order. His voice buzzed from the crackling speakers in the crew quarters below.

"Stations for departure! Crew to anchor windlass. Standby to weigh anchor!"

The second mate glanced at the weather radar. The screen flickered, showing a messy cluster of green and yellow. The captain switched the radar screen off, and the second mate got the message.

"Engines ahead slow," he ordered.

The third mate, standing at the throttle controls, eased the leavers forward. The deck beneath them vibrated as the ship's massive engines growled to life, sluggish, but still responsive. The vibration deepened, a steady thrum that reverberated through the steel walls.

"Anchor's aweigh!" crackled the voice from the radio.

The captain moved to the forward window, watching the massive chain rattle up from the black water. The winch clanked and screeched as metal ground against metal, until the last of the chain vanished into the deck housing. The crew below gave a wave, confirming the anchor was secure.

"Rudder ten degrees port," the captain called out. "Bring her around."

The helmsman grunted in reply, gripping the oversized wheel with both hands. The Titan's Haul groaned as the rudder bit into the water. Through the forward window, the coastline of Halifax drifted slowly into view, a chain of flickering lights along the horizon.

"Hold this course," he muttered, lighting a crumpled cigarette with a battered brass lighter. Smoke curled around his face as he exhaled, eyes still fixed on the rolling horizon.

"Tell the Rybaka to drop its nets," the captain grumbled quietly to the second mate.

To the North, off the coast of Cape Breton, another Russian captain barked orders. The Volya Rybaka was a toy compared to Titan's Haul, a thirty-meter fishing trawler, but it too had some notoriety, mostly for skirting maritime laws, exploiting loopholes, and pushing the boundaries of international fishing regulations. It had been fined, flagged, and even detained before slipping back into operation under revised paperwork. It was currently registered to a loosely regulated fishing outfit out of Murmansk.

The captain looked out over the deck of his ship. His crew was at the wait. They knew just how ruthless their captain could be. There was more than one former crew member "lost at sea" in the calmest of weather. The deck was cluttered with equipment like winches and pulleys and tangled nets, two-hundred meters long, double what was legal, piled high on the deck. Grease-stained tarps covered portions of the gear, while empty fuel drums rattled in the corners.

The call came from Titan's haul, and the captain of the Rybaka hit a concealed switch. This switch was not standard equipment. It was connected to the ship's Automatic Identification System, which transmitted its location. He had learned from past experience that simply turning off the AIS tended to draw unwanted attention, and put his vessel at more risk. This switch allowed the AIS to operate at random intervals, not only concealing his exact location, but if observed by authorities would look like a system malfunction and not an intentional act.

The captain dragged a calloused hand down his face, then grabbed the radio mic.

"Get the nets ready." His voice was low and clipped like a man who knew his orders would be followed without argument.

Down on the deck, the crew slid their oil-streaked gloves on and snapped into motion.

"Let's go! Move it!" barked one of the senior deckhands, a wiry man with a face like worn leather. He knew the drill. They all did.

The nets were coiled along the stern, damp and heavy from the last haul. The steel rollers were already slick with seawater, and the air was sharp with the metallic tang of rust. Salt-encrusted pulleys clattered as they prepared the lines. The oversized trawl net lay stretched out like a coiled serpent, tangled in places, but ready.

"Check the cables!" someone shouted.

A deckhand scrambled to the side rail, ensuring the winch cables were clear. The Rybaka's winch system, a rust-streaked beast that shrieked like a wounded animal when engaged, was temperamental at the best of times. Tonight, they'd be pushing it harder than usual.

The captain's voice crackled over the deck speakers. "We're going deep. I want those nets scraping the bottom. I don't care what you hit."

This operation was intended to attract the attention of authorities so Titan's Haul could slip out of the main shipping lanes on an altered course unnoticed, but the captain wasn't going to give up the opportunity to haul in as much fish as possible. Two paydays were better than one.

The crew moved fast. One man stood by the winch controls, sweat beading on his forehead despite the chill. The others worked the net, dragging it to the stern's edge. The heavy steel weights clanked against the deck as they hauled the sprawling mesh into position.

"Lower away!" someone called.

The winch groaned as the cable spooled out, feeding the net over the stern. The weights splashed down first, steel spheres the size of bowling balls, designed to drag the net low and deep along the seafloor. The net itself followed, unspooling in slow, steady waves.

"Keep it steady!" the winch operator barked. The net's sheer length made it dangerous, if the current caught it wrong, the ship could list hard to one side. Already, the trawler leaned subtly starboard, its low freeboard just inches from the water line. It was all the more dangerous in waves of the storm quickly rolling in.

The captain appeared at the deck railing, watching the net vanish beneath the waves. His eyes narrowed as he scanned the horizon for patrol boats or signs of Coast Guard vessels.

"Run it slow. Give it time." His voice was gruff. "I want the big ones."

Below, the net dragged through the cold, murky depths. The steel weights carved deep scars across the seabed, tearing up coral clusters and sponge beds. Sediment rose in plumes, clouding the water like smoke. Crabs scuttled from the destruction, and fish darted in crevices, their hiding spots now stripped bare.

The net's expanding maw swept wide, scooping up halibut, scallops, and anything else too slow to escape. The mesh strained under the growing weight, bulging as stones, seaweed, and debris tangled in its folds.

Kai watched the destruction through Uranus' eyes. He couldn't believe what he was seeing. He had read about the destruction caused by these nets, and seen movies and documentaries, but watching it through the eyes of his dragon gave him a new perspective. Kai felt the water shudder around him and heard the sound of metal scraping the ocean floor. It felt like a wound ripping open.

"Is this what you feel when this happens, Uranus?"

"It is a fraction of what all the dragons feel. It is a sliver of the pain that drained Nessie of her life. If I let you feel any more than the sliver I am giving you, I would be responsible for your death."

Kai fought his own anger, wanting Uranus to drag the net and the boat, dropping them to the bottom of the ocean. Uranus understood that emotion. It wasn't long ago that he might have done just that. Instead, he called out to the creatures around the net to move to safety.

The trawl cable stretched taut as the Rybaka pushed forward at low speed, dragging the oversized net. The ship groaned, metal flexing under the strain. The crew struggled to keep their footing as rising waves washed over the deck. They had seen the storm coming in, but it was getting worse than any of them expected, as they found themselves racing to grab a railing or something secure, catching another wave rising over them as the deck lights reflected off it. Waves pounded the hull like battering rams, each thud reverberating through the ship's steel bones. The wind screamed, a banshee howl that swallowed orders across the deck. The Rybaka lurched, tipping just far enough that the winch operator swore under his breath.

"Easy…easy…" the winch operator yelled over the wind, his fingers twitching over the controls. The net strained harder than usual, a warning sign.

What the winch operator didn't know was that on the other side of the waves, running dark and driven off course by the storm, was Titan's Haul, its massive propellers captured by the Rybaka's nets, its rudder rendered useless.

Through Uranus' eyes, Kai glimpsed something vast and shadowed moving behind the trawler, dark water swirling in its wake. The dragon stirred uneasily. "Something's wrong," Uranus rumbled in Kai's mind. "Something big."

For hours, the Rybaka's engine had pulsed beneath the deck, a low, constant throb that vibrated through the walls and floor, a heartbeat of worn metal and grinding pistons. The sound was ugly but steady. It was the kind of noise the crew barely noticed anymore, like background static in their bones.

But now…something shifted.

The throb faltered, and there was a sudden hiccup, sharp and jarring. The crew on deck glanced toward the wheelhouse, expecting the captain to adjust the throttle or correct the ship's heading. Instead, the engine coughed again, a harsh metallic choke, then staggered into silence.

The sudden absence of sound was deafening. The familiar pulse that had kept time with the crew's every movement gone. For a heartbeat, there was nothing but the rush of wind and the roar of the ocean.

Then the Rybaka shuddered.

Without propulsion, the ship lost momentum almost instantly. The stern, weighed down by the two-hundred-meter trawl net caught in the rudder and propellers of Titan's haul, lurched hard to one side. The deck tilted beneath the crew's boots, sending loose gear clattering. The overloaded net, now an anchor in its own right, kept pulling, dragging the ship into a dangerous yaw, the bow singing wide as the stern strained against the weighted cables.

"Get the winch!" someone shouted. Boots hammered across the deck, splashing through seawater as crew members raced for the controls.

The trawl cables stretched taut, groaning under the strain. Metal pulleys shrieked as the windlass tried to reel the net back in, but the ship's failing hydraulics sputtered and stalled. The Rybaka was dragging deadweight now, a drowning beast fighting to pull itself free.

"Cut it loose! CUT IT!" someone screamed.

In that moment, everything went still. The wind dropped, the rain softened, and the waves seemed to hesitate. The trawl cables went slack, and a flash of hope crossed the eyes of the crew waiting for the nets to be cut loose. Then, like a breath drawn too long, the storm roared back with a vengeance, the deck tilting as the bow of the Titan's Haul loomed overhead.

Lawrence Nault

Chapter 8

As the wave lifted the Titan's Haul high, the cargo ship seemed to hang for a moment, teetering at its peak. Then gravity claimed her. The massive cargo ship came down hard, not on empty ocean, but on the Rybaka.

The fishing trawler vanished beneath Titan's Haul's steel hull. The impact was instant, brutal, and the smaller vessel crumpled like tin, driven deep beneath the waves. The crew aboard Titan's Haul never knew. They never felt the shudder of twisted metal or heard the cries of men lost beneath them.

But the storm knew.

The cargo ship lurched hard to starboard. The cables holding the stacked containers, already strained by wind and water, snapped with sharp, metallic cracks. The containers broke free, crashing like boulders into the raging sea. Some struck the deck, hammering the ship's battered hull. Others vanished into the blackness.

The sudden shift in weight was too much. Titan's Haul wrenched violently to port, pitching hard. The deck tilted steeply, and for a sickening second, the ship seemed frozen, caught between capsizing and righting itself.

Then the waves took over.

The next swell rolled Titan's Haul onto her side, her rusted steel skin screaming as she twisted. The weakened hull gave way with a deep, shuddering groan, the ship snapping apart in three jagged pieces before vanishing beneath the storm's fury.

There was no call for help. There would be no rescue. The Rybaka's AIS, with its intermittent signal, would trigger no emergency if anyone was paying attention, because the natural assumption would be that the system just failed completely. Those near the radio were shielded by the cabin roof and never saw Titan's haul come down on them. Titan's haul was running dark. No radios. No lights. No AIS. Not that it would have mattered. The crew had been tossed about so violently, none of them would have been physically capable of getting to the radio.

On the ocean bottom, Uranus screamed. It was a deep, dark, terrifying roar that sent waves of sound crashing through the water that surrounded him. It wasn't just a scream, it was a wave of sorrow, an endless ache rolling through Kai's chest. His lungs felt like they were filling with water. The grief wasn't just Uranus'. It was the ocean itself, a wounded beast crying out in pain, and the other dragons joined in. Kai screamed with his dragon, though he didn't know why. Anne, Hannah, Jacob, and Kyle felt the fear of their dragons in their bones.

Kai's mother burst into his bedroom. She looked relieved to see him sitting up in the bed, but she could see he was covered in sweat. "You had a bad dream," she said reassuringly, putting a hand on his forehead. "I think you have a fever. I will go get a cold cloth and some medicine."

Kai didn't respond to his mother. He was still caught in Uranus' scream. She left the room and returned quickly with a cold cloth in hand, and Kai's father close behind.

"You okay?"

Kai looked up at his father. He recognized the look. It was his father's doctor look, where he examined a person in great detail, without ever examining them. "I think you are okay. Must have been a really bad dream. Too much of that junk food before bed maybe."

Mei shot her husband a stern look as she put the damp cloth on Kai's forehead.

"Take the medicine your mother has. It can't hurt," his father said.

"I think a ship and a fishing boat crashed," Kai murmured.

"In your dream?" Mei asked.

"No. For real. I think people are dead. Not far from us."

"No boats out in this storm. Not from here," said his father, who paid close attention to the weather and movement of boats and ships in the area. It was vital to his keeping the fish plant running smoothly.

Kai wanted to convince his parents, but he knew he couldn't. They wouldn't understand. They would never believe the story of his dragon. If he told them, they would probably go rifling through his drawers looking for drugs or alcohol.

"Yeah. Just a dream, I guess," Kai said as he lay back down. "I am going to try and get some more sleep."

Mei tucked her son in as he closed his eyes. He was surprised to feel the touch of his father's hand on his forehead before they both left the room. He noticed they didn't shut the bedroom door tight.

71

"Uranus, are you okay?" Kai asked, deeply concerned.

Kai glimpsed a sea can bobbing in the waves above him through Uranus' eyes. Something black and oily seeped from the torn metal, slicking the waves like a stain. The water shimmered strangely, the color wrong, almost bruised. The current twisted the slick in sluggish spirals as it sank into the ocean. "That's poison," Kai thought.

"That is death," Uranus rumbled. "Not just for the ocean, but for your kind as well. So much death."

Hanging on to another of the sea cans was a person. Kai couldn't tell if they were hanging on or if they were just caught on it.

"Is he still alive?"

"Barely," said Uranus.

"You have to get him to shore," said Kai. "He will die out there. No one is coming in this storm."

"No."

Kai thought for a moment.

"I know you can't reveal yourself. I know you don't think he deserves to be saved, but I can't watch somebody die like that."

Uranus' voice rumbled low, a sound that vibrated in Kai's bones. "You don't know what men like him have done," the dragon growled. "He's no innocent."

"I know," Kai whispered. "But he's still human."

Uranus had no desire to rescue the man, but he felt Kai's compassion, and he understood. "I will push the can to shore, where we met. It will be up to you from there."

Kai sat back up. He couldn't get to that beach now. His parents would never let him out of the house, and even if he got out, he wouldn't have made it on his bicycle. He grabbed his phone and texted Amy. "Please tell me you are awake."

Amy wasn't awake, but she heard the distinctive ring she had given Kai's text messages.

"Do you know what time it is?" she replied.

"I need your help. A ship sunk. Uranus is bringing a survivor back to our beach."

"I will pick you up." Amy didn't have to think twice about her response.

"No. Can't get out of the house. This is your part."

Those words meant something to Amy. She knew what Kai meant when he said it was her part. She quickly got dressed and drove to the lot over the beach where they met Uranus. She had to move slowly down the trail to the beach, the narrow path slick from the rain. As she stepped onto the shore, she thought she saw Uranus, but it could have just been a trick played on her eyes by the mist of the waves crashing and the sun coming over the horizon. The clouds had started to break up, and the rain was slowing.

There was a sea can pushed partway onto the shore, and Amy found a man hanging from the side of it, his vest caught up on a shard of metal. She reached into her pocket and pulled out the pocketknife she always carried, cutting the man down. There was a thud as he hit the ground, and Amy worried that she was too late. Using all her strength, she dragged the man up and away from the water, laying him flat on the ground. His face was pale, his lips blue, and his fingers barely twitched when Amy dragged him higher up the shore. His eyes flickered open, glazed and unfocused, but he let out a faint cough. It was a fragile sound that felt more like a whisper than a breath.

"Hold on," Amy murmured, unsure if he could even hear her. She took off her coat and made a pillow for the man.

Amy quickly took in the situation. There was nothing she could do for the man herself, and she could not carry him up to her car. There was only one choice, so she pulled out her phone and dialed 911, then tried to make the man comfortable while she waited for the police and ambulance to arrive. It didn't take long.

The ambulance arrived first, quickly followed by some members of the volunteer fire department. By the time the RCMP officer arrived, they had bundled up the man and had him on a stretcher, ready to start up the path to the top. The police officer quickly took in the situation, but his first question was not about the man or how he was doing. "What are you doing out here at this hour?"

Amy had prepared for this. As an Indigenous person, she was all too familiar with police jumping to conclusions.

"Storms bring in driftwood that we use to make crafts we sell. I try to get out here before the other collectors."

The police officer looked over to one of the volunteer firefighters. He was an older man, and the two of them obviously knew each other.

"Early bird gets the worm," said the firefighter. He at least believed Amy's story. "What you need to be worried about is where that sea can and the guy attached to it came from. There is a ship in trouble out there somewhere."

Amy watched the realization hit the police officer, who quickly got on his radio and walked over to the sea can to find a container number.

"He got transferred here from Saskatoon. Doesn't have a clue," said the old firefighter. "I think this coat belongs to you."

"Oh, thank you," said Amy, taking the balled-up coat from him.

"Follow me back up to the top. You can wait in your car where it's warm. Pretty sure he will want to get your name and stuff, but you'll be good. Lucky thing you came along."

The old man started for the trail, then stopped. "One minute," he said as he jogged off towards the water. He came back holding a beautiful piece of driftwood."

"You should have something for your troubles," he said, handing it to her. "I'll go up first. That way, you can give me the push I need when we get to the steep part."

Amy laughed. She knew he was going out of his way to distract her from finding the man, and dealing with the RCMP officer, but she appreciated it. The firefighter waited while she started her car.

"You going to be okay?" he asked kindly.

"I think so. I am just going to phone my friend."

"Good plan. Old guy like me ain't much help to a young woman in situations like this. I come from that generation where we were all told to suck it up and deal with it."

"Thank you," Amy said. "You really have helped."

Amy sat in her car, her fingers still numb from dragging the man across the beach. She hadn't really stopped to think until now. The man's face, pale, cold, barely breathing, stuck in her mind. "He almost died," she whispered to herself. She exhaled, long and slow, before picking up her phone to text Kai.

"Found him. He is alive. The ambulance came and got him."

"Are you alright?" asked Kai.

"Think so…"

There was a knock on Amy's window before she could finish typing in her reply. She looked up to see another RCMP officer there, but she recognized this one.

"Amy, right?"

"Yes, sir."

"You found the sailor?"

"Yes, sir."

"Great work getting him help. They are going to take him by helicopter to one of the bigger hospitals, but they think he will be okay. How are you doing?" The officer asked the question like he meant it. A totally different attitude than the first one, who she thought figured she was out there doing something suspicious.

"I am okay. Just a little cold and wet."

"See you still managed to find a nice piece of driftwood," the officer said, noticing the wood she had put in the back seat.

"Not really. You know that crazy old guy in the volunteer fire department? He grabbed it for me before bringing me up here to warm up in my car."

"Don't let him fool you," said the officer. "He may have a few years on him, but he is smarter than all of us, I think."

A few more vehicles pulled into the lot.

"It's going to get busy here pretty quick. Why don't you head home? We will come by and get a statement from you later."

"Thank you, Sir."

The officer gave the roof of her car a gentle tap. "Love this old car. Drive safe."

Amy didn't go home. She went to Kai's instead. It was Kai's father who answered the door.

"Amy! Come in. Come in. I heard you found the sailor," he said. Amy was surprised by the warm welcome.

"Mei. Mei. Amy is here. Come, help her find some dry clothes," Lu called out loudly. Amy found it odd to hear him speak with an accent. Everyone talked about his perfect English. "I just heard the Coast Guard did a flyover and found a lot of sea cans and debris, so they think a pretty big ship went down. We are getting the word out for boats to stay in today, so they don't run into any of that stuff."

"Amy! You're here."

Lu turned to see his son. "I called your mother, not you. This girl needs dry clothes. Ugh...I will go wake her up."

Kai watched as his father rushed away, puzzled. For years, his dad had been closed off, quiet, and distant. Now, seeing him fuss over Amy and hearing him talk with an accent in the presence of someone who wasn't family, felt different. Warmer. But strange, too.

When he rounded the corner, Amy leaned close to Kai and whispered, "He has an accent."

Kai laughed. "Only when he is excited and at home. Never in public."

Kai looked over his shoulder, then gave Amy a quick hug.

"Hey, hey, hey," said Mei, coming around the corner. "You are sick, and Amy is wet and cold. You are going to get her sick too."

Kai blushed, embarrassed to be caught by his mother. Mei didn't pay any attention. She took Amy's hand and pulled her along to another room. "I set out a pair of Lu's sweat pants and one of Kai's hoodies for you, and some socks. I hope that's okay. You change and bring me your wet clothes, and I will wash them."

"You don't have to do that," said Amy.

"Hush. You are a guest in my house. My rules."

Amy got changed, glad to be in some warm clothes. She brought her wet clothes out and handed them shyly to Kai's mother. "Thank you."

Mei smiled, then handed her son some money.

"Your Dad is busy, and I have to help him. The whole town is going to be busy today. Take Amy for breakfast. Make sure she eats well. Besides, she didn't come here to see us, did she?"

Amy giggled nervously.

"I called your grandma to let her know you were here safe," said Mei. "She said she can't wait to hear the story."

Amy looked nervously at Kai. She had never told her grandmother she was leaving. Mei poked Amy's arm. "You should tell your grandmother when you are leaving and where you are going. Don't let Kai set a bad example for you. My son is trouble."

"Mom…"

"I will remember that," said Amy, embarrassed a little at being called out for sneaking out of her house.

"You do that," said Mei. "Now go get breakfast."

As they walked out to the car, Kai noticed it was his hoodie she was wearing. "You look kind of sexy in my shirt."

"Don't you be setting a bad example for me, Kai," Amy quickly responded. The two of them laughed out loud at the comment.

As Kai climbed into her car, he shifted over her damp jacket that she had set down on the passenger seat. A clear plastic envelope of papers fell out of the jacket as he lifted it.

"What's that?" asked Amy.

Kai shut the car door and looked at the top paper. "Looks like a manifest or something."

"That's not mine," said Amy, taking the envelope from him. "You don't think that sailor had it on him, do you?"

Amy checked, and the plastic envelope was sealed tightly. A little water had leaked in, but not much. She handed it back to Kai. "Breakfast first. Your mother told you to feed me."

Chapter 9

There were some strange looks from people in the small-town café as Kai and Amy found a booth off in the corner. Word had already spread about the man Amy had found and the Coast Guard's discovery of all the containers, as well as a quickly spreading oil slick. Neither of them was sure if the eyes were on them because they were together, or because of Amy's involvement in the events. Kai remembered the words of Amy's grandmother about protecting her well, though, and when he noticed someone inviting themselves over to talk to them, he subtly but kindly gestured for them to stop. Thankfully, they understood and respected that boundary.

Amy took a few moments to call her grandmother, wishing she could just text, because she hated hearing the sound in her grandmother's voice when she disappointed her. She was surprised when she didn't hear disappointment, but encouragement.

"I heard you go out. I know it was because you were needed. Told you there was something about that boy," she heard her grandmother say.

"Grandma…" Amy spoke in a loud whisper, confident that everyone in the café was listening to her conversation.

"I called Mei because I was a little worried. I heard what you did. I am proud of you."

"Sorry for worrying you," said Amy. "I didn't want to wake you."

"You don't realize it yet, but you are your own young woman now. I haven't had to watch over you in years. I keep you around to watch over me." Amy's grandmother laughed, and Kai could hear her chuckle in the phone from across the table.

Amy smiled and relaxed. "I am having breakfast with Kai. I thought maybe I would bring him home after. His parents are busy with this shipwreck stuff."

"I imagine they are. Everyone is speculating. Will they find more people?"

Amy looked at Kai and mouthed her grandmother's question. Kai shook his head.

"No," said Amy sadly.

"I will say a prayer and burn some sage for them," her grandmother said solemnly. "Your father will be there to greet them."

Kai saw a look of deep sadness wash over Amy's face, but he didn't know why.

"Tell him to bring some of that Chinese food," her grandmother said loudly, followed by her deep laughter.

"You heard that right," said Amy as she hung up.

Kai laughed. "Your grandmother made sure I heard it, but not the part before. The part that made you sad."

Amy took a deep breath, then reached across the table, resting her hands on Kai's. She saw the disapproving look from the couple at the table across from them, but ignored them.

"My father was lost in a storm while fishing. Just after I was born."

Kai turned his hands. Taking hold of Amy's and holding them tight. He didn't say anything. He didn't need to. They were interrupted by the waitress setting their food down.

"You guys ignore the looks," the waitress said, loud enough to make sure those nearby heard her. "The two of you make a cute couple, and you," she said turning to Amy. "Are a bit of a hero today."

Amy smiled reluctantly.

"Hear that?" said Kai, as he spread some peanut butter on his toast. "I make us look like a cute couple. You wearing my hoodie probably helps."

Amy smiled as she shook her head. "That's what you heard, is it?

"Yup."

"Titan's Haul," said a man loudly as he burst into the café, holding up a couple of life jackets. "Already got stuff washing up on shore. They say Scatarie is a mess."

Scatarie Island's coastline was notorious for shipwrecks. Its unpredictable currents and hidden shoals had claimed countless vessels over the years. It was once home to a seasonal fishing community, but was now a protected wilderness area, its abandoned lighthouse standing as a silent sentinel. The location of the island and the currents around it often left its treacherous coastline scattered with debris.

"Boys at the port say she left fully loaded. That'll be thousands of sea cans of goods. Gonna make a killin' when it starts washing up on shore!"

"How many crew?" asked one of the men. Kai recognized him as one of the fishing boat captains.

"Ain't got no idea. All I care about is the loot coming ashore. Davy Jones can have the bodies."

"Christ! Time for you to shut-up Barry." The fishing boat captain turned in his chair, looking for the waitress. "Kathy, get him a coffee to go and get him out a here."

"Already on it," said Kathy as she came out of the back, a coffee in a to-go cup in hand. "Here you go, Barry. Nice and hot." She handed him the coffee and gently pushed him towards the door. "You find your spot to go watch your loot roll in. The coffee will keep you warm."

"Did you add the good stuff to it?" Barry asked.

"You always got a dram in your pocket, Barry. You can add your own."

With a last little shove, she got him out the door. The patrons clapped as she pulled the door shut. Kathy turned and took a deep bow. "Eat up and be gone, cause we all know he'll be back soon enough."

Kai asked for the bill when they finished breakfast, but Kathy told them it had already been paid by the same man who had Barry chased out of the Café. Amy and Kai stopped to thank him as they left.

"Your girl did a good thing this morning," the man said, though he talked right past her to Kai. "Saving that sailor. Two of you are the last people I expected to see together."

Kai was about to ask what he meant, but Amy tugged him away.

"Need to stop by my place first," said Kai as they drove out of the parking lot.

"Why?"

"You will see."

The roads in town seemed unusually busy. Kai suspected it had a lot to due with the sunken ship. Amy pulled her car into his driveway, and he asked her to wait there for a minute. He was back out in about five minutes with two bags in his hands. He closed the car door and handed Amy the first bag, and she looked into it.

"Oh my god! Really. I don't even fold them this neat." Kai's mother had washed, dried, and folded Amy's wet clothes from that morning. "What's in the other bag?"

Kai proudly held the bag up, holding it open. Amy looked in. "Chinese food!"

"Just leftovers," said Kai, "But enough for all of us."

"You know you don't have to kiss up to my grandmother, right? She already likes you."

"Oh, this isn't kissing up," said Kai. "I am going to hand this to her, then tell her I expect bannock and moose meat next time."

Amy shook her head as she put the car in gear and headed for her house. "You might regret that. Moose meat tastes like crap."

"Wait," said Kai. "She really cooks it and eats it?"

Amy just shook her head and smiled.

They all sat in the living room as Amy told her grandmother about the morning, her story punctuated by the sound of her grandmother's knitting needles clicking together. It was a familiar sound in this house. She always seemed to be knitting something when he was over visiting Amy, though he never saw her finish anything. Her grandmother never took her eyes off Amy as she talked, but Kai noticed she never dropped a stitch in her knitting either.

"That's a crazy morning," her grandmother commented. "Is it a nice piece of driftwood you got?"

It seemed like an odd response to Amy's story, but Kai was starting to understand the woman's laid-back ways. She never seemed to stress about anything, at least not outwardly.

"You know what was really odd," said Kai. "When we said thank you to that guy for buying us breakfast, he mentioned something about the two of us being the last people he expected to see together. What do you think he meant by that? Was it a racist thing?"

Amy shot her grandmother a look, but her grandmother ignored it.

"You should tell him."

"It's not important. Doesn't matter."

Amy's grandmother held up her knitting. "You two are like this. Your lives are woven together by somebody's hands. Secrets…" She grabbed a piece of wool, and the knitting started to unravel.

"Can you tell him, please. You were there."

Amy's grandmother nodded. Amy snuggled into Kai, weaving her fingers into his, and resting her head on his shoulder. Kai loved the feeling, but felt a little awkward with her grandmother right there. He was more nervous about what he was about to hear though.

"No judgement until you hear the whole story."

Kai nodded and Amy's grandmother started. There was more to the story of Amy's father being lost at sea than Kai ever expected. When Amy was born, it was hard times in the community. Fishing was bad. Lobster was bad. Prices were bad. It had been a difficult birth, and both Amy and her mother were not doing well. They needed medicine and more food, but there was no money for any of it. Amy's father was a proud man, but he was desperate to care for his family, so he approached Kai's father at the plant to ask for an advance on future catches. Kai's father said no.

"Understand Kai, your father's answer was the right one. The plant wasn't doing well either, and even if your father had the money, advancing for one of the fishermen would have led to everyone at his door. I respect his decision."

She continued with the story.

Amy's father stormed out of the office at the plant, yelling about how he needed the money now. Everybody heard him as he said he was going out to get a boatload of fish right then. Kai's father had tried to stop him. There was a storm that had kept boats off the water for two days, and it showed no signs of letting up. Amy's father was a stubborn man, and he went out anyway. His boat washed ashore the next day, but he was never seen again.

Kai started to say something, but the old woman held up her hand and continued. Amy's mother didn't take her husband's death well. She dropped Amy off with her grandmother and disappeared for almost 10 years. When she returned, she wanted nothing to do with her daughter, and it was only recently that they started talking.

Kai started again, but once again she held up her hand. "Here is the important part, Kai. The people think we hold your dad responsible for my son's death. We don't. My son was his own man and made his own choices, but that is probably why they never expected to see the two of you together. Your father, though...he blames himself. I don't know if your mother even knows this, but he bought this house and made sure we always had a little money and food. When Amy's mother returned, he gave her a job when no one else would. Your father...he is a good man and should never have carried that guilt.

Kai stared at Amy's grandmother, her words still settling like cold stones in his chest. His father, the man who had always seemed distant, hard, and impossible to impress, had been quietly carrying this guilt all along. The image of his dad checking his forehead that morning came back to him, and suddenly it made sense. That wasn't just a worried father. That was a man who had spent years convincing himself that one bad decision had cost a life. "Why didn't he tell me?" Kai wondered.

He looked over at Amy and found her asleep. Her grandmother laughed quietly, getting up to throw a blanket over her granddaughter.

"Bad news," she whispered. "Boyfriend rules say you can't move even an inch. You are stuck like that for a while."

Kai didn't mind. He enjoyed Amy close to him like that, and it gave him a reason not to talk. Amy's grandmother turned on the TV and picked up her knitting. "When she wakes up, you can warm up some of that food you brought."

Amy slept for a couple of hours, and probably would have slept longer, if it wasn't for the knock at the door. Her grandmother moved surprisingly fast, opening the door to find an RCMP officer there.

"Is Amy home, Sue?" the officer asked. "Wanted to check in on her, and I need to get a statement too."

This was the first time Kai had heard Amy's grandmother's name.

"Come on in," said Sue, pointing to Amy sleeping on the couch against Kai. Amy was just starting to stir."

"Sorry to wake you up, Amy. Things like this morning tire people out more than they think."

Amy sat up, getting her bearings, and looked sadly at Kai.

"Come sit at the kitchen table," said Sue. "You too, Amy. I will get you both a coffee."

Amy's grandmother quickly made some instant coffee and set a cup in front of each of them. She sat down at the table, too.

"You don't need to be here. It's just a statement."

Kai watched as Amy's grandmother looked at the police officer like he had three eyeballs.

"How long you been working in this community?" asked Sue. "You know by now I don't let any of my people sit and talk with you alone. I sure am not leaving my granddaughter alone."

The officer nodded. "Yeah, should have known that." He took a sip of his coffee. He made every effort to look as though he liked it, but his face gave it away.

Sue laughed loudly. "A bit of sugar? Maybe some cream?"

"Oh, please," said the officer. "You aren't going to drink yours like that, are you, Amy?"

Amy picked up the mug in front of her and took several large sips, smiling in between each one.

The officer laughed, knowing Sue would tell this story to everyone. He slid a form across the table. "Just need you to write in your own words what happened this morning. You know, how you were there early looking for driftwood from the storm and came across the container and the man, and kind of what you did to help him." He handed Amy a pen. "Doesn't need to be long. We pretty much know where he came from now and what happened."

"Is the man okay?" asked Sue.

"He is in the hospital in Halifax, recovering, but he is talking now. He was a crew member on the cargo ship Titan's Haul. Says he has no idea what happened. We can't figure out how that container washed ashore so quickly, but if it hadn't, it would have been a different story."

"No others?"

The police officer shook his head. "Coast guard is looking, but there is a lot of debris in the water, and still not the best flying conditions. Everyone around here says there is going to be a mess to clean up, and we should be organizing to get ready."

"They are probably right," said Sue. "They know these waters."

"Yeah, probably are. But my new sergeant, the one you met this morning, Amy, is taking a wait-and-see attitude."

"The prairie boy they posted to the fishing village," said Sue, a bit of sarcastic tone in her voice.

"That'd be the one," said the officer, sipping his coffee and still not liking it, but determined to finish it.

"I can help with that," said Kai. "I can help organize some shoreline cleanup, and my friends at the rescue center will be ready to help any animals stuck in the debris or soaked with oil."

The officer turned to look at Kai, who was still on the couch. "That'd be great. Then I have nothing to do with it, and it doesn't look like I went over the sergeant's head. And between you, your parents, your friends at the rescue, and Amy's grandmother, you probably get more people involved in an hour than I would in a week."

Amy slid the form and the pen back across the table. The officer quickly read it over.

"Perfect. That's all I needed." The officer stood up and quickly choked down the last of his coffee. "Sorry for waking you up Amy, but you look like you are in good hands here. I am going to leave my card in case you need to add anything. You can call too, Kai, if you need any help."

Sue started to stand, but the officer motioned for her to stay sitting, which she appreciated. "I know where the door is, Sue. I can let myself out. Good to see you again."

The officer left and Amy seemed to relax a little.

"Time for my nap," said Sue. "Heat her up some of that food, Kai. She is hungry. But leave enough for me."

Kai found the food in the fridge and heated a couple of plates up in the microwave. He set them down on the kitchen table and joined Amy. They both ate quietly for a while, then Amy set her fork down and looked at Kai, taking his hand. It was that same sad face she had when she woke up.

"I am sorry I fell asleep while my grandmother told you that. I am sorry I couldn't tell you myself. I wanted to tell you myself," Amy said quietly. "But every time I try, it's like…I don't know. Like I get stuck in the past." Amy took a deep breath. "Are we okay?"

Kai looked surprised, and that worried Amy even more.

"That was the story of our parents," said Kai. "It's not our story. We write our own story…with dragons."

Kai felt Amy relax.

"Besides, you are a part of this with me." Kai lifted his pendant over his head and held it in his palm, taking hold of Amy's hand with that same palm. Amy could feel the warmth and vibrations. It was the first time she had really felt warm since that morning.

"I learned a lot about my father today that I didn't know, though," said Kai as he returned the pendant to his neck. "You know what else I learned?"

Amy shook her head.

89

"Your grandmother's name. Sue! I have been coming over here for almost three weeks now, and I have never called your grandmother anything, because I didn't know what to call her. What do I call her?"

They heard the voice of Amy's grandmother through the wall. "Grandma! And what did I hear about dragons?" She followed this with her deep laughter.

Amy shook her head and rolled her eyes, before picking up her fork and eating some more.

"Grandma it is," said Kai.

Chapter 10

"Is Amy okay?"

Kai was surprised that was the first question from both his parents when he walked in the door, but not as surprised as he would have been before knowing the story about his father.

"She is. Slept most of the afternoon. Police stopped by and had her fill out a report. Oh, and grandma, I mean Sue, said to tell you the food was delicious."

"You call her grandma?" Mei exclaimed.

Kai shrugged. His father looked at him strangely for a moment. "Good. Respectful. She earned that respect."

Mei looked at her husband the same way he had looked at Kai, then shrugged. She turned back to her son.

"Your nightmare was real. How can that be?"

Kai shook his head. He didn't know how to answer his mother.

"I am really tired, Mom. Is it okay if I head to bed? We can talk tomorrow."

91

"Yeah, it was a long day for all of us I think. No nightmares tonight."

Kai bent over so his mother could give him a kiss on the cheek.

"But we talk tomorrow," she said as she walked away. "And your father is going to talk to you about the birds and bees."

"Oh my gawd, mom!"

Lu laughed so hard he snorted out the tea he was drinking. That was another first for Kai, hearing his father laugh like that.

Amy texted Kai as soon as she got home from dropping him off. While she waited for his response, she spread the papers in the plastic envelope across her bed. She quickly realized that she was looking at two lists of sea can numbers. One list showed the containers that contained regular items like lumber and parts, and equipment. The second list had the same sea can numbers, but   items listed in the container were written in by hand. She snapped some pictures of the handwritten list and sent it to Kai. "Do you know what this stuff is?"

Amy didn't have Kai's full attention. He was talking with Jacob and Hannah, wondering why he couldn't get through to Uranus. Jacob explained that there were times the dragons shut themselves off from their people. Neither Jacob nor Hannah knew why, but they guessed that it was to protect them. They all had felt how overwhelming the emotions of a dragon could be. Anne's presence was felt in the conversation, and her quiet hello was greeted cheerfully. At the same time, both Jacob's and Hannah's phones rang with a message from Anne's mother. It was another of Anne's pictures, this one not a rough sea, but a coastline strewn with litter, a stain floating on the surface of the water sticking to everything it washed over. Jacob sent the image to Kai, and told him to check his phone. That's when Kai noticed Amy had texted him, but Anne's drawing caught his attention.

"That's what we are about to see here," he told the others. "It will take some time for everything to find its way to our shores, but it will."

"How can we help?" asked Hannah.

"I don't know yet," said Kai. "I don't know what to do." There was a pause, then Kai said goodbye so he could look at Amy's messages.

Kai looked over the pictures of the pages Amy sent him. He had been wrong when he first guessed what was in the envelope, it wasn't the manifest. That would have been thousands of containers and hundreds of pages. That kind of information was on a computer somewhere, probably at the bottom of the ocean. This was something different. A very specific list that someone had made. There were several containers listed on one sheet as wood products like dimensional lumber, oriented strand boards, and rough lumber, but the sheet with the handwritten details listed the contents as non-recyclable plastics. Other lines listed agricultural products on the printed manifest, and on the handwritten manifest, they were recorded as 'stolen vehicles'.

Hauling illegal cargo was not something new. Newspapers and social media had stories about it, dock workers speculated, and there had even been a recent documentary that Kai had watched about how quickly a car could be stolen and loaded into a sea can. They could be on a ship and on their way to another country before various police forces could coordinate with port police quickly enough to stop the export of stolen vehicles, even when the owner had a tracker on the car showing where it was. The 'non-recyclable plastics' note didn't surprise Kai either. What did surprise Kai were the containers listed on the one manifest as "industrial byproducts for recycling," but on the handwritten manifest, there was a bracket grouping several containers with the note "rare earth mining byproducts-toxic slurries, arsenic residues, radioactive dust and materials. TO BE DUMPED IN OCEAN"

"This is the poison that Uranus screamed about," he whispered to himself. "This is death for the ocean."

Kai stared at the pictures again. Someone had written this by hand. Someone who knew exactly what they were trying to hide. He couldn't shake the feeling that whoever made this list wouldn't want it found. And if they knew Amy had it...

Kai quickly texted Amy. "Glad you are home safe. Put the papers away. Hide them."

"Why?" Amy texted back.

"Not over the phone." Kai wasn't sure if he was being paranoid, but he wasn't taking any chances. As he typed the message, he felt the call of Uranus.

"Uranus is calling. I have to go. Get some sleep, please. Goodnight."

Amy's reply came almost immediately. Her goodnight message was punctuated by a little heart emoji, which was new. Kai smiled as he found a comfortable position on his bed, closed his eyes, and answered Uranus' call. He felt Uranus' presence flicker, like a candle struggling to stay lit. For the first time since meeting the dragon, Kai felt afraid. The strongest of dragons, his dragon, was drowning in exhaustion.

Uranus had not stopped moving since the ships went down. The dragon had been swimming circles, creating his own current, trying to keep the poisons leaking into the water in one area. He was failing, and he knew it.

"How can I help?" asked Kai.

"I fear you cannot," said Uranus.

As the dragon spoke, Kai could see through Uranus' eyes as the dragon surveyed the oceans. There were only a few containers that remained floating. Others, battered against each other by the angry ocean, had broken open and spewed their contents into the water. Between the currents and the winds, everything that was left floating in the water was being scattered far and wide. On the ocean bottom, sea cans littered the area like Lego blocks scattered on a living room floor. In the midst of all those containers, the colossal corpse of Titan's Haul lie broken and battered. The ship's rusted steel hull that only a short time ago towered above the waves was now twisted and scattered across the ocean floor, split into three jagged sections. Each piece rested at an unnatural angle, half-buried in silt and shadow.

The bow section rested on its side, its nameplate barely visible beneath a thick layer of settling sand. The steel plating had buckled inward, leaving jagged ribs of metal protruding like broken bones. The anchor chain trailed out of the shattered hawse pipe, stretched taught and half-buried in the seafloor, its weight anchoring the wreck in place. The bridge, once the ship's command center, was a skeletal ruin. The windows were gone, shattered by the force of the sinking. There was something else in there, but Uranus turned his head. Kai knew the dragon was protecting him from the sight of the dead that the bridge still held.

The midsection was a chaotic wreck of twisted metal and strewn cargo. Rows of shipping containers remained strapped to the deck, the steel beams that once supported them now warped and sagging. Some of the containers had broken open, jagged gashes spilling their contents onto the ocean floor.

Pallets of electronics were strewn like wreckage from a looted warehouse, circuit boards and plastic casings tangled in the debris. Barrels, some cracked and leaking, bled chemicals that drifted in slow, oily clouds. The water above the ship was tinged with rainbow sheens of fuels, rising from ruptured tanks and spreading in greasy spirals toward the surface. The remains of cranes and cargo booms jutted upward at sharp angles, their twisted cables still holding remnants of lost cargo. A single fluorescent life jacket floated near the wreckage, snagged in the rigging.

The stern lie partially inverted, its heavy engines twisted and half-crushed by the fall. The ships massive propellers were barely visible beneath the sand, the curve of one blade poking skyward like a rusted fin. The Rybaka's tangled trawl nets drifted out from the steel they wrapped, snaring fish and crabs. Fuel leaked steadily from ruptured tanks, dark tendrils curling through the water like ink. The images Uranus showed him were so real that Kai thought he could even smell the stench of the diesel as it clung to the water.

Uranus followed the net from Titan's Haul's stern. It hung in the water like a ghost, trapping anything that came near. Fish, crabs, sea cans, and debris were all trapped by its near-invisible webbing. The netting turned into heavy cables, which led to the mangled wreckage of the Rybaka.

"There was a second ship," said Kai. "A fishing trawler."

"As deserving as the first," grumbled Uranus.

Kai ignored the words of the dragon.

The dragon circled back, finding a place to settle on the ocean floor, and watched from a distance as some of the containers leaked a murky, sludge-like substance, forming plumes of clouded water that drifted outward like smoke in the currents. Already, fish that swam through the tainted water twitched and jerked like broken puppets. Crabs scuttled sideways, their legs curling in on themselves.

"Heavy metals," said Kai. "From mining waste."

"It doesn't belong in the ocean, or water anywhere," said Uranus. "I have tried to stop its spread, but even dragons have their limits." The sadness in Uranus' voice, usually strong and gruff, was obvious.

"I will find a way to clean it up," said Kai. "Whatever it takes."

"There is only one way," said Uranus. His voice was quieter now, almost distant. "But there is a cost…a terrible cost. One that I am not sure is worth paying."

Kai felt a chill run down his spine, questioning just what Uranus meant.

Uranus didn't answer right away. Instead, Kai saw through the dragon's eyes, the poison spreading in dark tendrils across the ocean floor, the lifeless bodies of fish drifting in the current, and the sluggish, weakened movements of crabs crawling aimlessly through the contaminated water. Even the kelp swayed as though sick, its leaves curling at the edges.

"I have seen how your kind kills waters," said Uranus. "Time and time again. Greed and ignorance. The oceans are paying the price."

Kai swallowed hard, feeling the bitterness in the dragon's voice.

"I don't know if our world deserves what I must do," Uranus said. "But the ocean deserves better." His voice cracked, and for the first time since they had bonded, Kai felt something new from Uranus…fear.

"I know what Nessie would do. What Nessie would want me to do…" The dragon's voice trailed off for a moment.

97

"I need you to focus on the other problems," the dragon continued, his voice heavier now. "You know what they are. That is in your hands now, Kai."

"I am just one person. Still a kid…"

"You are my person. Dragon-bound, to me. The strongest of the dragons. There is a reason for that," replied Uranus. "And you are not just one. You are two, and you are many. You will realize that soon. I must rest."

Then Uranus was gone, his presence retreating so far that Kai could barely feel it. The emptiness left behind was like cold water closing over his head.

As he lay down on his bed, he wondered what Uranus meant when he said Kai was two people, and many. He took a last look at his phone before closing his eyes, and saw Amy's goodnight text with the heart emoji. Could that have been what Uranus meant by two? Or was it something else, something bigger? He didn't know, but one thing was certain, whatever came next, he couldn't face alone.

As Kai fell asleep, Uranus bolted North through the oceans, bursting out near Greenland, and heading high into the sky. The northern lights were bright, and the dragon was grateful for that. He would need the energy to do what must be done.

Chapter 11

Kai woke up to a knock on his bedroom door, his father letting himself in.

"I am going down to the pier. I would like you to come with me."

This was odd. There were times when his father would wake him up to take him to work at the fish plant, but he wasn't working this part of the season. Taking him down to the pier was something that had never happened.

"Maybe ask Amy and her grandmother to meet us there. We can all have breakfast after."

Now Kai was very confused, but his father didn't give him a chance to ask questions. Kai got out of bed, thinking he would be tired, but he felt surprisingly refreshed, and Uranus' presence was strong with him. He quickly texted Amy and was surprised to find out that she and her grandmother were up. Kai was happy to get the chance to see Amy, but this whole arrangement had him asking many questions.

99

At the pier, most of the fishermen were gathered around talking. It wasn't the usual hub of activity it was in the mornings because the Coast Guard was still warning everyone about the dangers of all the debris in the water, as well as the large area that was closed off for clean-up and containment. A few were readying their boats to head out, but Lu had them called over as soon as he got there.

"The plant is closed again today, and will probably be for a couple of days," his father announced. "That means I cannot buy any fish you bring in until it re-opens."

There was cursing and grumbling among the men around him.

"I know money is tight, for all of us, and that means some of you will head out despite warnings to fish and travel further to sell your catch. I would rather see all of you safe with your families so, for those that need it, the plant will advance you the price of a catch or two. All I ask is that you stay off the water until the Coast Guard says it is safe, and that you promise to sell your catches to me when you are back to fishing."

The cursing quickly stopped, and the grumbles became murmurs. Kai looked up to see Amy and Sue watching off to the side.

"It's not an infinite pot," said Lu. "If you don't need it, please hold off so there is money there for those that do. You have all been good to my family and the plant, and that is why I can do this, this time…" Lu's voice dropped a little. A heavy slap on his shoulder got his attention.

"You're a good man."

Lu held up his phone. "You can email me or text me. We all know each other. It's just between us."

Kai had a new respect for his father. He was proud of him.

The group of men quickly dispersed several of them helping off-load the boats that were preparing to go out. Lu looked at his son. "It will be tough, but we can help this time. Not like it was the last time."

"You know I know about that," said Kai quietly.

Lu nodded as he looked up and saw Amy and Sue approaching. "Grandma," said Kai's father, with a bit of a sarcastic tone. "Wouldn't let a secret like that stand between you and Amy. She knows the town talks, and you would have found out anyway."

Kai looked at his father seriously. "You're a good man, Dad. It wasn't your fault, but you always do the right thing, even if nobody knows."

"You are a good man," said Sue as she hugged Lu. Kai watched the uncomfortable look on his father's face. "Now I heard the word breakfast. I don't leave the house this early in the morning for nothing, you know."

Breakfast in the café had a different feel for Kai and Amy, compared to the last time they had breakfast there. It just felt like a friendlier place. People stopped to say good morning to his father and Amy's grandmother. When Sue broke out in one of her unfettered fits of laughter, others in the restaurant joined in. His father and Sue had a lot to talk about as they caught up on each other's lives. Kai guessed from this conversation that aside from the help his father had provided for Sue and Amy, he had kept his distance. He was a little stunned when Lu turned to talk to Amy, though.

"Amy," Lu said suddenly, "what are your intentions for my son?"

Amy nearly choked on her toast. Sue broke out in uproarious laughter, holding up her fist across the table. Lu understood the gesture and returned her fist bump.

"Oh, we all want to know," chimed in a voice from the next table, the man peeking over a large mug of steaming coffee.

Amy looked at Kai for some help. He didn't offer any. "Turnabout is fair play. Grandma grilled me when she met me, and now it's your turn."

Flushed with embarrassment, Amy began to stammer, but Lu let her off the hook.

"Kai will be going away to school next year. Marine biology and engineering, he tells us." Lu looked proudly at his son as he spoke. "I like seeing you two together. Kai seems...more involved in life. I just ask that you not keep him from leaving to go to school."

"I wouldn't do that," said Amy. "He has told me how important it is."

"Thank you," said Kai's father kindly. Lowering his voice he added, "There was a fund set aside for you to go to university too. You don't have to go where Kai goes. It is totally up to you. If you want to go to university, don't let that part worry you."

Amy was stunned. Sue was shocked. Kai thought he saw her hide a tear.

"Now," said Lu, returning to his normal voice. "Since Kai can call her grandma," he said, pointing across the table to Sue. "It is fair, I think, for you to call me Lu and Kai's mother, Mei."

"Oh, hell no," said Sue. "Mr. and Mrs. Chen it will be," she said, looking sternly at her granddaughter. She turned and looked at Lu and gave him a quick wink. "Until you tie the knot, then you can call them ma and pa."

Kai and Amy both blushed this time. It was Lu that held up his fist for a fist bump from Sue this time. Kai was seeing more of his father this morning than he had ever seen, but at the moment he wasn't thrilled with it.

Sue stacked the plates on the table to make the clean-up easier. When Lu asked for the bill Kathy refused. "Your money is no good here today. Kind of our thing around here. You take care of us, we take care of you."

Lu bowed his head. "Thank you."

"You want to come back with us. We can help plan that clean-up," said Amy as she stood up from the table, reaching out her hand to help her grandmother.

Kai looked at his father who just shrugged his shoulders.

"I'll meet you at the car in a couple minutes. Just want to finish my coffee."

Kai watched as Lu slipped a generous tip under his plate. "Does mom know, about the house and help, and money for school?" Kai asked. "I just need to know what I need to keep a secret."

"No secrets," his father said. "Your mother knows. The school money was her idea."

"I really don't know you two," said Kai, almost apologetically.

"There is a Chinese proverb," said Lu. "The child is like the father, but the father does not know the child. I think it is accurate, but it goes both ways. The parents are like the child, but the child does not know the parents."

Kai had always thought of his father as cold and distant, someone who kept his feelings buried under work. But this morning he saw it clearly. His father didn't just feel responsibility, he carried it like a stone strapped to his back, never asking for help. His father interrupted his thoughts.

"You go think somewhere else. Amy and Sue are waiting for you."

103

Kai gulped down the last of his coffee and left.

At the house, the first thing they did was go directly to the manifests Amy had hidden behind some books on her shelf. She spread them out on the kitchen table, and Kai picked them up one at a time as she did. He looked over to Amy's grandmother who was sitting in her chair knitting.

"The walls are thin, Kai," Sue said, as though she heard his thoughts. "Even if I was in the other room, I would hear you two talking. The reason there are no secrets in this house is that every word can be heard everywhere."

Kai raised his eyebrows as he looked at Amy.

"This isn't the full manifest. I think it was someone specifically keeping track of illegal cargo," said Kai. "Did the police say who the guy was you saved?"

Amy shook her head.

"You see this," he said, pointing at the handwritten sheets. "Stolen cars. Plastics that can't be recycled. I didn't think we could ship that stuff to other countries anymore."

"Don't they recycle it there?" asked Amy.

"No. If I remember right, they just put it in their dumps."

Kai did a quick search on his phone and opened a couple of links. He handed his phone to Amy. The first link was a news story about shipping containers sent to the Philippines. The containers were held for several years when it was discovered they didn't contain recyclable plastics, but materials that couldn't be recycled. The second story was about Malaysia returning hundreds of containers of plastic waste, no longer accepting being "the world's garbage dump."

"I don't get it. Why do they say it's recyclable and collect it, if they just put it in dumps?"

"It makes people feel good about themselves," said Sue, her knitting needles clicking away. "Money twists us that way.

104

People pay money for plastic, then pay more to get rid of it. They think they're doing good, but they're just lining someone else's pocket — paying twice for their own mess. The guys with the most money…well, they just get paid to recycle it and pay pennies to dump it in someone else's yard."

"Tell us what you really think," joked Amy, trying to lighten the moment.

"Idiots," said Sue. "People are idiots."

Kai continued to run his finger down the pages. He stopped at the mining by-products note.

Kai stared at the paper, his stomach twisting. This was what Uranus had screamed about, the poison seeping through the water, spreading like rot. No dragon could stop this. No one could. He swallowed hard, gripping the paper tightly as if he could crush the truth in his fist.

Kai felt a moment of panic, but then he felt Uranus. The dragon was stronger than when they last spoke. "You aren't just one, Kai. We are one. You, I, Amy, and the others."

Kai understood.

"This is the one Ur…," he caught himself saying the dragon's name. "This is the one that is the most dangerous. Arsenic and mining waste. Look how many containers there are. It will put poisons in the water forever."

"Show me," said Sue. She was standing at the side of the kitchen table. Neither of them had noticed her get up from her chair. Kai slid the pages across the table.

Sue looked at the papers carefully. "Where did you get these?"

"I think the guy I found on the beach slipped them into my jacket," said Amy. "I used it as a pillow for him."

"This arsenic and mining waste. That is the same stuff that poisoned the waters and food in N'dilo. The water has never been safe since the mines were there. Their people are always sick."

Sue sat down heavily, sliding the papers back to Kai. "You think this is in our waters? We won't be able to eat the fish anymore. We won't be able to sell the fish or lobsters or crab."

"I know it is," said Kai.

Sue looked deep into Kai, then at her granddaughter, and back into Kai. "You do, don't you…the pendant."

Kai nodded.

"So, what do we do?" asked Sue. "The oceans have obviously put their trust in you, so I do too."

Kai shifted the paper back and forth across the table as he thought.

"We need to let people know," said Kai. "As soon as they can, the fishing boats will return to that area. But we have to do it in a way that no one knows where the papers came from. This wasn't supposed to be found. I…we need to keep Amy safe."

"Hand me the phone, Kai."

Kai handed her his cell phone.

"Not that thing. Mine."

Kai got up and took the handset off the phone on the wall. He untangled the cord so it would reach Sue.

"Now dial this number," said Amy, then rambled off a bunch of numbers. Kai could see the numbers on the phone dial, but he had no idea how to use it. Amy rescued him, dialing the number for him.

Not long after Sue got off the phone, a young indigenous man showed up at her door. Sue let him in and sat him at the table.

"This is John. I used to babysit his mother, and then I babysat him. Now he works for the Department of Fisheries."

Amy set a cup of good coffee down in front of John, along with some cookies, while her grandmother continued. "John, you know my granddaughter, and this is Kai, her boyfriend."

Amy's face flushed a little. Kai felt a sense of pride in being called her boyfriend.

"These papers you see here on the table. They were found on the beach in that plastic envelope, by…some…children," Sue emphasized. "Lots of stuff washing up. The CHILDREN gave that to me cause they thought it was important. We looked through it, then called you."

Sue shifted the papers across the table in front of John.

"Good thing those KIDS brought it to you. They always bring things like that to the elders."

Sue smiled. John understood.

"You want to look at the handwritten one," said Kai. "Page five, I think."

John's eyes scanned the pages as he sipped at his coffee. They knew when he got to the part about the mining waste. His eyes went wide and his hand trembled slightly as he set his coffee down on top of his cookies. Amy stopped the mug from tipping over.

"This is from the ship that went down."

"Must be," said Sue.

"This…" he whispered, his voice unsteady. "If this leaks in to fisheries…" He didn't finish the sentence. He was already halfway out of his chair.

"Gotta go. My boss needs to see this, but I think I might run into one of the Coast Guard guys first." John hadn't been in the Department of Fisheries long, but he knew how governments liked to hide information sometimes. If his boss did nothing with it, the Coast Guard would, he hoped.

"Take your cookies," said Sue as she got up and handed the untouched cookies to him. "Thanks. I didn't know who else to call."

"I got your back. We protect our own."

Chapter 12.

Kai's phone buzzed as it vibrated across the kitchen table.

"That's my signal to go back to my knitting," said Sue.

"What are you knitting?" asked Kai. "It seems like you have been working on the same thing for weeks.

Sue laughed. "Never know until I am done."

Amy slid Kai's phone over to him, noticing the name on the screen. "Is that your friend in Ontario you were telling me about?"

Kai nodded as he opened the message so both of them could see it. It was a link to a website. Amy motioned for Kai to follow her to the couch, where her laptop was on the end table. She carefully retyped the link from Kai's text message, and it brought them to a website called "Young Dragons."

"This started when we first took on the air pollution problem to help Jupiter," Kai heard Jacob say. "There are groups of young people everywhere who want to see a future for the Earth just like the dragons. If you use this site, you will

109

be able to find help recruiting people to help with the clean-up that is coming."

Kai watched as Amy scrolled through the website. "Jacob says we can find help here to recruit people for the clean-up."

Amy looked at Kai's phone. She hadn't heard it vibrate. Then she realized and put her hand over the spot where Kai's turtle pendant hung under his shirt. "Dope! I wish I were a part of that."

"You are," said Kai, taking her hand.

"There is more," said Jacob.

Kai listened as Jacob explained that the young people that were part of the Young Dragons weren't just good for helping clean things up. There was a reason it wasn't an official organization, and they didn't have a membership or track people on the site. There were those that could help behind the scenes too, and to encourage change and spread the message.

"They can find information on companies causing the problems, and do things like get that manifest you have out in public," said Jacob.

"No," Kai said firmly. His internal voice, that he used to speak with Uranus and the other dragon-bound, was not the voice he used. He surprised Amy and her grandmother with his tone. Amy stopped what she was doing on the computer.

"Sorry," Kai said when he realized he had spoken out loud. "I just realized I forgot to send an email. Remind me when I get home, okay, Amy?"

Jacob's suggestion was flashing through his mind. If they exposed too much, or pushed too hard, Amy could be in real danger. The memory of Uranus' warning came back to him. "There is only one way," the dragon had said. "But there is a cost I'm not sure is worth it." Was this how it started? The beginning of that cost?

Amy stared at Kai. His voice had been sharp, too sharp. That wasn't like him at all.

"Can't you use your cell phone and do it?"

Kai gave a bit of a surprised look at Sue.

"What? I may be old and I hate those things, but it doesn't mean I don't know how they work."

"The email address I use only goes to my computer."

Sue shook her head and continued knitting. The rhythmic clacking of the needles was relaxing.

"There is someone taking care of the manifest," Kai said to Jacob. "If it gets out, I am afraid Amy will be in danger. That wasn't information they wanted anyone to have."

"Okay. Check out the message board on the site."

Kai pointed out the message board icon on Amy's laptop. She clicked on it, and there was a new post at the top of the board.

A CARGO SHIP WENT DOWN OFF CAPE BRETON. THERE IS PLASTICS AND ALL KINDS OF DEBRIS WASHING UP ON THE SHORES AND FRIENDS ARE ORGANIZING A CLEAN-UP. CAN SOMEONE HELP DESIGN SOME INFORMATION AND RECRUITING POSTERS? – GANYMEDE

There were already responses.

TELL ME WHAT YOU WANT IT TO SAY AND I CAN DESIGN IT FOR YOU. – K

I CAN PUT SOME UP. I LIVE IN LOUISBURG – SHEILA

I CAN PUT UP A WEBSITE SO PEOPLE CAN FIND INFORMATION – TERRY

Kai looked at the messages and felt a surge of hope. Uranus was right, he was not alone. "I don't know what to tell them," he said quietly.

"I got this," said Amy.

I AM AMY. WE ARE NEW AT THIS SO ANY ADVICE WOULD HELP. THE SHIP THAT SANK IS TITAN'S HAUL. IT WAS OFF CAPE BRETON. EAST OF LOUISBURG I THINK.-AMY

Replies came in quick.

I HAVE CREATED A WEBSITE. CLICK HERE FOR THE LINK. I AM ADDING A EMAIL SIGNUP FOR PEOPLE THAT WANT TO GET NEWS ABOUT THE CLEAN-UP AS IT HAPPENS. - TERRY

I WILL CREATE A PDF POSTER THAT ANYBODY CAN PRINT AND HAND OUT. CALLING OUT TO EVERYONE IN CAPE BRETON.-K

HERE ARE LINKS TO NEWS STORIES... -D.K.

DO YOU HAVE HELP ORGANISING? - TAYLOR

FIRST THING YOU SHOULD DO IS TALK TO THE FISHERMEN. THEY KNOW THE COASTLINE AND WHERE YOU CAN GET PEOPLE IN TO CLEAN. IT ISN'T ALL SAFE. THOSE TIDES AND STORMS COME IN QUICK. - VICTOR

GOOD PLAN! THEN WE CAN MAKE A MAP WITH SAFE AREAS. - K

I AM IN IRELAND, BUT HAVE A LOT OF FOLLOWERS. I CAN SPREAD THE WORD. -C

Sue watched as Kai and Amy read the messages. They looked happy and excited.

"I should say something," said Kai.

112

"Or maybe not," said Amy. "Let me be your voice. See the first message." Amy scrolled up the screen. "They use the name Ganymede. This is a moon of Jupiter. Everyone else uses their real name or initials. I think Ganymede is your friend, and there might be a reason he doesn't use his name."

Kai was impressed that Amy had caught that. He had completely missed it. He was happy to let Amy take the lead. Being in front of people and the center of attention wasn't his thing. He thought for a moment, then quickly searched up the moons of Uranus on his phone. There were twenty-seven of them. He liked the imagery of Miranda with its extreme geological features like cliffs and valleys, and Ariel, Uranus' brightest moon evoked the ocean, but that was mostly because of a children's movie. Titania had a nice ring to it, but as he thought about it, it seemed awfully close to Titan's and Titanic. He paused at Oberon. The name hung in Kai's mind. The second-largest moon of Uranus. A leader and protector in Greek mythology, according to the website. If he was going to take this on, he couldn't just hide behind Amy's voice. He'd have to be more than just the kid with a dragon. He'd have to take responsibility. Kai held his phone up for Amy to see.

"Perfect," she said.

"Yes, it is," Kai heard Uranus rumble.

Kai took the laptop and added a post to the message board.

THERE IS GOING TO BE A LOT OF PLASTICS AND OTHER STUFF IN THE OCEAN. STUFF THAT CAN TRAP AND KILL MARINE LIFE. PLASTICS THAT WILL BREAK DOWN AND BECOME MICRO-PLASTICS THAT THE ANIMALS WILL EAT, AND THEN PEOPLE WILL EAT. WE NEED TO CLEAN UP WHAT WE CAN, BUT MAYBE THIS IS A CHANCE TO SPREAD THE WORD ABOUT POLLUTION IN THE OCEANS. – OBERON

He showed Amy the message. She read it, then hit enter, not giving Kai a chance to change his mind.

"You catch on quick, Kai" said Jacob "Or should I say Oberon?"

We will see if we can get the ship's manifest.

This message had no name attached to it. Kai thought about the portion of the manifest they had, and he could tell Amy was thinking about it too. Kai shook his head, and Amy understood.

We will put out a media release from the Young Dragons about ocean pollution and micro-plastics. We have connections to influencers who will spread the word.- Isabella

Kai's phone vibrated. He looked at the message, and held it for Amy to see as well. It was from Kai's father. The Coast Guard submersible had discovered the second ship on the bottom of the ocean. They had also recovered a few bodies that were now rising to the surface.

Kai thought about the image of the second ship and the cables that led from it to the net.

"Is there a net attached to it?" asked Kai.

"How did you know? They were mapping out a dive plan to cut it free, but something changed. They won't put divers in the water anymore."

"John," said Amy quietly. "He must have gotten the information to the Coast Guard."

"That's the fourth time that car drove by here," said Sue, setting down her knitting and walking to the picture window. She pulled back the sheer curtains to get a better look. "I know every car around here, and only a few come down to this end of the road. No one needs to come down four times unless they are up to no good."

Amy closed her laptop and joined her grandmother at the window. It was a brand-new car with a rental company sticker on its bumper. The driver made a U-turn at the intersection and was coming back. Amy thought she recognized the person driving.

"Kai..."

Kai recognized the sense of urgency in Amy's voice. He started to go to the window, but quickly changed his mind, heading for the front door instead, and stepping out onto the porch where he could be seen. The driver saw Kai and immediately hit the gas, speeding off, not bothering to stop at the intersection as he turned onto the main road. Kai watched for a minute before returning to the house. Amy was waiting for him inside the door and gave him a hug. Kai could feel her body shaking, and felt her breath, quick and fast as she pulled herself into him.

"What do you mean, you don't know if he is still in the hospital, and you can't tell me anyway?" Sue was on the phone, and her tone was one Kai had never heard before. "I am telling you that Amy just saw him drive in front of the house, Sergeant."

They couldn't hear what the police officer was saying on the other end of the phone, but they could see that Sue wasn't happy about it. She tapped her cane forcefully into the floor over and over as she listened.

"Sergeant, I know you are busy. I know the sinking has everybody busy. But my granddaughter is not seeing things. She's not a child with a vivid imagination, as you called her. She is a young woman. A young woman who saved a man's life. People remember the faces of people they save, but maybe you wouldn't know that. This isn't just a phone call. It's an official report that I will back up with an email to you and your superiors. I expect your constable to be coming by to get more information."

Sue didn't wait for a response, hanging up the phone, then picking up the phone from its cradle and forcefully slamming it back into the cradle a few more times.

"Bring me the computer," said Sue as she sat down. "I have an email to send. That damned prairie boy talking to me like that. He is about to find out who he is dealing with."

This wasn't an idle threat coming from Amy's grandmother. She was one of the elders of the local Mi'kmaq community, not just well-known, but well-respected. She had dealt with police harassing members of the community for years, advocating for them, and fighting discrimination. She already had the contact information of those higher up in the RCMP above the Sergeant, and many of them already knew her name. Sue typed her email slowly, using one finger on each hand, the hard tap of each key vibrating through the old kitchen table.

"Prairie boy's about to regret ignoring me," Sue muttered as she hit send. "I'll be hearing from them before the night is out."

"I should stay here tonight," said Kai.

"I don't think your parents would approve, or grandma."

Kai knew she was right. He tried to think of what else he could do.

116

"It's a bonfire type of night," said Sue. "Send out the message, Amy."

Amy quickly understood. It was the perfect solution. It was a practice her grandmother had started many years ago to protect a woman who was a victim of family violence. The police wouldn't do anything then either, so Sue had brought together community members in the woman's front yard, where they had a bonfire, music, and food. When the person the woman was afraid of approached the house, everyone in attendance stopped what they were doing and stood up in a line to let them know he wasn't welcome. It became a regular practice when members of the community needed some support and couldn't get it from the authorities.

Kai was amazed as Amy told him about the practice. It gave him a new sense of respect for Sue, and a better understanding of Amy.

"I will get my Dad to pick me up," said Kai. "That way you can stay where all the people are."

Amy leaned in and gave Kai a quick kiss. "Thank you for going outside. It was brave. Stupid, but brave."

She quickly started texting people, and Kai messaged his parents. While he waited for a response, he got a message from the rescue center. The center had heard about the net in the water, and they were concerned because a pod of right whales had been seen in the area recently. They were sure there were other animals trapped in the net already, so they were gathering a team to go out in the morning, trying to find as many divers as they could.

"Those people can't go in the water," said Uranus. "Those poisons will kill them."

Kai wandered over to the kitchen table and sat down, staring at the message, his heart pounding. He knew the people at the rescue center, not just names, but faces. Bill, who had been at every cleanup since Kai was a kid. Morgan, who had once spent three hours in the freezing water to save a tangled humpback calf. These weren't just volunteers, they were friends. And if they went into that water...

The sound of a vehicle racing down the road and stopping in front of the house got his attention, though, and he quickly made his way to the picture window.

An old pickup truck parked in the driveway, and a few people stepped out of it and started unloading a barbecue and chairs, and firewood onto the front lawn. As he watched them, Sue hobbled out to talk to them, giving each of them a hug.

"When is your Dad coming?" asked Amy.

Kai had forgotten about messaging his father. He quickly looked at his phone, but there was no response. "Haven't heard back from him yet, but I got this," he said as he handed Amy his phone. "I need to find a way to tell them they can't go in the water."

"We can think about it," said Amy. "If I have to, I still have pictures of that manifest on my phone. We can show them that."

Kai sucked in a deep breath, but Amy stopped him before he could say anything.

"In the meantime, since you are going to be here a while, you will have to meet my friends and family. If you think grandma gave you a hard time, you haven't seen anything yet, and there is nothing I can do to protect you."

"I can just hang out in here. Work on coordinating the clean-up."

"Not a chance," said Amy. "Remember what you said to me this morning. Turnabout is fair play."

Kai sighed, and his shoulders dropped. Sue broke out in one of her joyous fits of laughter.

"Oh, and my mother will be here too," said Amy much less confidently. "Can you stay close when I am with her?"

"Of course," said Kai.

Lawrence Nault

Chapter 13

This was new to Kai. His extended family lived across the country and in China. He rarely saw them, and he couldn't remember a family gathering. Everyone Amy introduced Kai to at the gathering on her front lawn was introduced as an Auntie or Uncle. Kai quickly realized they weren't all relatives, and the terms were more a sense of community, but they all seemed like one big family gathered there. It was a happy gathering, and Amy's warning about the ribbing Kai would be the subject of, was more than accurate. Embarrassment was a permanent state of mind for him as he was introduced to everyone. Apart from that, the food was fantastic and plentiful, and there was good music as well. He worried when Sue's neighbours came home and started over that they were coming to complain, but they just helped themselves to some food and joined in the party. If this had been his house, the police would have been called by everyone in the neighbourhood.

Amy brought a plate of food to her grandmother, who sat in a rocking chair by the fire. Kai watched her as she interacted with everyone around her so easily. He was a little jealous. Blending in like that, being so at ease, was something he never managed. He smiled when she approached him, noticing her smile was not quite as enthusiastic as it had been. She took his hand and whispered in his ear. "Come meet my mother."

Kai followed Amy and knew who her mother was immediately. She looked just like her daughter. Amy's fingers tightened around Kai's hand, and for a moment, he thought she might turn back.

"Hi Mom," said Amy. Her voice was calm when she spoke, but Kai could feel the tension behind her smile, like someone bracing for a slap that might never come. "I thought you should meet Kai, my boyfriend."

Kai expected to get another hug, which everyone seemed to have for him that night, but what he got was a cold handshake.

"You are Lu's boy."

Kai nodded, noticing Amy staring her mother down.

"Nice to meet you. I don't imagine your father has told you much about us," her mother said.

"Mom…"

Kai interrupted. "He has told me everything, I think. Like grandma says, no secrets."

"Grandma?" Amy's mother sounded surprised.

"He is family now, Mom."

Amy and her mother had a short conversation, and Kai stayed close as he promised her he would. The conversation warmed a little, but not much. It wasn't what Kai expected between a mother and daughter.

The celebration went silent when a car turned down the road. Everyone looked at Amy.

"I think that is the car," she stammered.

"Not yet," said one of the men, watching the car get closer. "Now," he signalled when the car was close enough that the driver could be seen.

As a group, everyone lined up along the front of the lawn, many of them holding up their cell phones, the flashes going off. Others stood, arms crossed, an unpleasant look on their faces. The car quickly turned around, driving across a lawn as it did, and raced off down the road. It was chased by a couple of people on dirt bikes until it turned into the intersection, tires squealing as another vehicle narrowly avoided it. A cheer went up from the group, and the party quickly started back up. Within minutes, phones were dinging away with notification tones.

Amy held her phone for Kai to see. Seemed everyone who had gotten a picture of the car and driver had posted it to their social media with a message asking if anyone knew the man. Most of the pictures weren't very good, but there were a couple of clear images of the man's face, and one of the license plate.

"Does anyone get away with anything around here?" Kai asked.

"Not under Sue's watch," said a man nearby.

"You would know, wouldn't you?" said Sue loudly. Her laughter rose over the noise of the party, then things went quiet again as another car came down the road.

"I think that is my ride," said Kai.

Everyone relaxed as the car pulled up beside the others, and Lu got out.

"Mr. Chen! Long time, no see," someone called out.

Kai started to say goodbye to Amy, but was surprised to see his father coming over. Several of the people stopped to shake his hand and talk to him. Out of the corner of his eye, Kai noticed Amy's mother leave.

"This looks like fun," said Lu as he approached his son. "Hope you haven't been drinking."

"We gave him a few beer," said one of the men. "But they have all been the root kind."

Lu laughed. "We should go. Mother was worried I was picking you up because there was a problem."

Amy gave Kai a gentle kiss. "I will come over in the morning if that's okay."

Kai looked at his father, barely hearing Amy's words. Lu just rolled his eyes and walked back to the car.

"I'll text you when I get home," Kai said, moving quickly to catch up with his father.

"Is that one of Sue's safety-parties?" asked Lu.

"You know about those," said Kai.

"People talk at work. Why is it at her place, though?"

Kai considered making up a story, but his father would find out anyway. People talked in a small town.

"You know that man Amy saved? She is pretty sure she saw him driving around the house today. The police wouldn't tell Grandma anything about him, so she figured it was better to be safe."

Lu was quiet the rest of the way home. Kai looked back at the messages on the phone. There were more messages from the rescue center about going out in the morning. He still had to find a way to tell them they shouldn't put people in the water.

Kai took a few minutes to sit with his parents and tell them about the plans they were making to clean up debris that washed up on the beach. He told them about the rescue center's plans for the morning, too.

"I am proud of you, taking the lead and planning a clean-up," said Mei. "But I am going to say no to going out there with the rescue center. I know you do a lot there, but it is not safe yet, I don't think."

"Probably better that way," said Kai, trying not to sound too relieved. "I think they have a full crew anyway."

His mother and father both looked relieved.

"They say they may open the water for fishing in a couple of days," said Lu. "All the big stuff has gone to the bottom, and most of the floating stuff is small and spread out."

"That's good," said Kai, even though he knew it was not. "Should make everyone happy."

"Ugh," said Mother. "We are going to be tossing product for months because of plastic in their guts."

"I know," said Kai. "It's one of the reasons I want to go to school for marine biology and engineering. Not soon enough to help with this."

"You will make a difference. You care," said Mei. "And your father tells me he talked with you and Amy about going to school."

"He did."

"Did he talk to you about that other thing, too? The birds and bees thing?"

Kai saw his father give him a quick wink.

"Yes, Mom. He did," said Kai, sounding embarrassed because he was a little. "But I have a question for you. When the guy …."

Mei bolted up and started walking away. "Nope, nope, nope. You talk to your Dad. He's the doctor."

Kai smiled at his father, who had a face that was trying to look stern while holding back laughter.

"I am off to bed. Amy is coming here in the morning. Probably early."

"That will be nice, but no closed doors. Your mother will be at the hardware store looking for a chainsaw to cut it down."

Kai texted Amy as soon as he was in his room. "Home. Dad says they are opening up the fishery in a few days. And I still don't know how to stop the rescue center."

"I am inside," replied Amy. "Lot of the guys are hanging out for the night."

"That's good," said Kai. "I don't have to worry about you being safe."

"John stopped by. He said he didn't think anyone was going to do anything with that manifest. Not right away, anyway."

"I have an idea, but I don't know if you are going to like it," replied Kai. "Call me."

It felt odd answering a phone call from Amy. Kai couldn't remember the last time he used his phone as a phone. He spoke quietly, so his parents didn't hear him, and Amy listened carefully on the other end. Kai explained how all that public attention from the guy's picture on social media was probably a good deterrent that would keep him from returning. He speculated that if the manifest they had was made public, there would be no more reason to come looking for it, and probably more reason for them to run and hide.

"What do you think?" asked Kai.

"I think I trust you and whatever you decide, I will support."

Kai took a deep breath. He suddenly felt the weight of the world on his shoulders.

126

"The pictures are on my phone, and yours. Did you save them anywhere else?"

"My phone backs up my pictures to my computer," said Amy.

Kai scrolled back through Amy's text. His gut twisted. Exposing the manifest might stop people from coming after her, or it might make her even more of a target. Either way, it was on him now.

"Okay, let me think about this. I will see you in the morning. Don't leave the house unless you know you are safe."

"Look at you all big and protective," said Amy. "Only I know you are a big ole cuddly dragon. See you soon."

"Can you see Amy?" Kai asked Uranus.

"I can feel her presence, through you," the dragon answered.

"So, you can't protect her…"

"Kai, you will feel if Amy is in danger before I do. I can't explain. I don't understand the bond between the two of you."

"Are there whales near the net?" Kai asked. "Can you keep them away?"

"I am doing that. They have a mind of their own, though."

"Jacob, I need your help."

"Jacob is working," Hannah replied. Maybe I can help.

Jacob explained the situation to her. She said she knew just what to do. "Tell Amy not to be worried if she sees someone on her computer," said Hannah. "It will be someone helping us."

Kai was stressed. He got up and went to the washroom, then changed. When he heard his phone vibrating, he realized that he had taken longer than he intended.

"I was watching videos, and someone else is on my computer," texted Amy.

"They got there before I could warn you. That is a friend. They just want to find the manifest. That way, there will be no record of you sending it to anyone but me."

"Jerk. Warn me next time."

Kai wasn't sure if Amy was mad or joking.

"Sorry," he texted.

The kiss emoji he got back let him know she wasn't angry.

Kai had a restless sleep. In that space between awake and sleep, a myriad of thoughts and scenarios raced through his mind. As sleep took over, visions filled his head. Some were from Uranus, but others he wasn't so sure about. Dead bodies floating in the ocean, not clear enough to tell if they were those of the sailors that had gone down with their ships or his friends that planned on diving the next morning. Fishing boats in boat cradles, paint peeling, tarps rotting from the sun, clearly not having felt the waters of the ocean support their hull in a long time. Streets empty and houses falling into disrepair, like a scene from a dystopian movie. His father's fish plant boarded up, leaning heavily to one side, succumbing to the constant winds from the ocean battering against it.

He found himself walking along the ocean bottom, walking the six-hundred-foot length of the Rybaka's net. The corpses of already rotting fish hung in the net, and other fish came to feed on it, finding themselves trapped. In the distance, he could see the brown cloud of death like a sandstorm on the desert. At the base of the cloud lay Uranus, his strong, massive body lying weak and deflated in the sand, his head bobbing in their current, and his eyes clouded over. He wanted to run to his dragon, but he couldn't. Instead, he found himself walking the length of the net. Containers were caught in the net, some empty, some still full, the scars along the ocean floor the only evidence that it was Mother Nature herself who had moved the containers to the net. He watched as something floated out of one of the containers, another piece of plastic, that raced to the surface free from the metal container that had held it down. He continued walking the net, until he came to the Rybaka. It had moved since Uranus had last shown it to him, rolled, the window of its cabin open, and a body half-hanging out.

Kai woke with a start. He could feel the sheets of the bed soaked with sweat and hear his heart pounding in his chest. His body tried to drag him back into sleep, but his mind was having a tug-of-war with his body, pulling him the other direction, and winning. Kai got up and shuffled to the washroom. He filled the sink with water, wanting to wash some of the salty sweat from his face and body. He stood leaning against the vanity, watching the water plunge from the tap into the sink, hypnotized by it. The image of Uranus' limp body refused to leave Kai's mind. Even as he stood at the sink, washing cold water over his face, his dragon's lifeless eyes seemed burned into his memory.

As he reached to turn the tap off, he knocked a bottle of hand soap into the sink. It bobbed in the water. That was the moment something clicked in his mind.

"Uranus, are you there? Tell me that wasn't you in my dreams."

Kai was relieved to hear the familiar rumble of the dragon's voice. "I tried calling to you, but I could not break through your dreams."

"You can see what I see, right?"

"Yes," said the dragon.

"So, you see this bottle floating in my sink."

"I do," replied Uranus.

Kai fished the soap bottle out of the sink and pulled the plug. He found his way back to his bed, his movements more intent now than the shuffling that had taken him to the washroom.

"Did you see my dreams?" Kai asked.

Kai almost felt the breath the dragon took in. "I did. You call them dreams. We call them visions. Glimpses of things that are and things that could be. A draft of a story that the authors can still change."

"Can you lift the Rybaka to the surface? Break open one of the containers and fill the net near the ship enough so it looks like that is what caused the wreck to return to the surface."

Kai watched as Uranus swam to the Rybaka and circled it, the dragon careful never to show him what was in the cabin.

"I can do that, but for what reason? The dead will remain dead," said Uranus gruffly.

Kai explained to Uranus that they wouldn't send divers down to free the net from the Rybaka, but if the ship floated to the surface, other ships could hook onto the cable and pull the net from the ocean bottom. Uranus would have to free the net from the Titan's haul as well, but there was more to his plan.

"Are all of the containers of that mining waste broken open?" asked Kai. "I think there were eight of them."

"Only three are open and leaking," replied the dragon, the anger in his voice clear. "Three too many."

"Can you put the others into the net?" asked Kai. "Can you do that and be safe?"

Uranus understood Kai's plan now. The dragon ignored the question about his safety. "I can do that. I will move the ship now."

"No," said Kai. "Wait until daylight so it doesn't sink again before they find it."

"Understood," said Uranus. "This is a good plan. The plan of a dragon-bound."

Kai felt a brief sense of pride, but then he remembered seeing Uranus in his dream.

"In my dream, Uranus, you were…"

"Visions of things that could be," Uranus interrupted. The dragon seemed to pause in his thoughts for a moment. "The pen of my dragon-bound is rewriting that story."

Lawrence Nault

Chapter 14.

Kai never fell back asleep. He found himself sitting at his computer, searching for information about the Cape Breton coastline, hoping he could find a map or satellite images that he could use to help plan the clean-up. His searches brought him to news stories about the sunken ships, and a headline caught his attention.

"Titan's Haul Hauls Radioactive Waste to Ocean Bottom."

Kai clicked on the link that led to the news article that had just been released.

Unconfirmed documents indicate that the Titan's Haul, the cargo ship that sank off the coast of Nova Scotia, was hauling illegally heavy metal mining waste along with stolen cars, plastics to be disposed of in other countries, and other illegal cargo. Port authorities have been unable to verify the portion of the manifest we showed them (see attached image), but we have been able to confirm the container numbers match containers loaded onto the ship at the Halifax Port. We have had no response from the Coast Guard or Fisheries and Oceans Canada.

Kai clicked on the link to the manifest, and sure enough, it was the pictures Amy had taken, though they had been edited and cleaned up.

"Delete all the pictures of the manifest from your phone and computer as soon as you see this. Make sure to delete them from your trash, too." Kai looked at this text message, pausing before sending it. He wondered if they might need those pictures again if they disappeared from online like documents sometimes did. He decided deleting the pictures was the right action.

Kai started to delete the pictures from his own phone, but stopped to send Amy another message.

"Oh, and good morning. See you soon."

It was barely four-thirty in the morning. Kai was pretty sure it would be at least a couple of hours before Amy woke up. He finished deleting the pictures from his phone, then returned to his search on his computer. More news stories were coming out, and they were finding their way to social media as well. Kai heard his father, who had always been an early riser, wander past his bedroom.

"Dad, you should come see this."

Lu opened the door to Kai's bedroom. "Did you sleep?"

"Not much," Kai replied honestly. "You should see these news stories."

Kai got up from his chair, letting his father sit down to read the stories. Lu clicked through the tabs, reading all of the news articles.

"That explains a lot. This is why DFO told me I should be looking for other sources of fish to keep the plant open," said Lu. "They wouldn't give me a reason."

"You never told me that," said Kai.

"No," said Lu. "You seem to have a lot going on, and there wasn't really anything to tell yet."

Kai heard the words, but he knew his father was just trying to protect him in his own way.

"I see your maps. I have a big one. There will be a lot of people at the café this morning, probably all talking about this news, but if you ask, they will tell you where is safe and where isn't."

Lu got up from the chair and pushed it back under the desk.

"Good people about to face hard times," Lu mumbled. "You try and get some more sleep."

Kai knew his father was thinking about more than just the fish plant. The whole town depended on the ocean, and now it was poisoned. He managed to get some more sleep, much more restful this time. He woke up to the sound of Amy's text message saying good morning and that she was on her way. "One of the guys is following me into town," she added. He had a quick shower and was waiting at the front door for her car to pull up. His mother popped out of the kitchen and handed Kai a map.

"Your father said you need this. Also, if anyone asks what we said about the news, you tell them that I said it just seems like a little contamination in the water, and that it will disperse in the ocean currents quickly."

"Is that what you think?" asked Kai.

"No," his mother said. "There isn't enough information to know, but people will be scared. They need some hope."

Kai gave his mother a quick hug, then raced out the door, hearing Amy's car pull up. A truck pulled up behind her and

Kai recognized the man behind the wheel. He walked up to the truck as the window rolled down.

"I got her," said Kai, feeling confident and proud. "Thanks for watching out for her."

"I think you do, bro," said the man. "Any problems, just send up the smoke signal."

Kai's head tipped at that phrase. "Is that still okay to say?"

The man laughed. "Probably not, bro. Politically correct and all that. But you know what I mean. By the way, you got all our approval. You took the jokes better than half of us would have. Even Amy's mom likes you."

Kai knew why he recognized the man now. He was the one Amy's mother had left with.

The first stop for Kai and Amy was the rescue center. There was a group of people loading equipment into the van when they pulled up. "You guys aren't planning on going in the water, are you?"

"We do what we gotta do," said one woman. "You know that Kai."

"Did you see the news this morning, about the stuff in the water?" asked Kai.

The woman looked at the others. They just shook their heads. Kai thought he would have to show them the news stories, but the center's director came along.

"Change of plans. No one in the water today. They think there is radioactive waste and other stuff being released in the area."

"Whoa!" exclaimed one of the volunteers.

"Yeah," said the director. "We can still head out and assess the situation, but that's about all. Kai, you coming out?"

Kai noticed Amy stiffen at the director's question.

"Not today, sir. We are working on planning a shore clean-up."

Saying no to the director was a difficult choice. He had promised his mother, but he wanted to be out there when Uranus lifted the Rybaka. He thought briefly about changing his mind, and if Amy wasn't with him, he probably would have, but he needed to stay with her and protect her.

"Good for you. Send me the info."

Amy relaxed as soon as Kai said he wasn't going out. Kai asked her about it when they got back in the car.

"I love the ocean, but it scares me," said Amy. "Probably cause of my dad."

Kai understood now. He would have said something, but he heard Uranus. His mind shifted from Amy to the wreckage on the ocean floor.

"There are other ships here now," the dragon said. "The net is free from the cargo ship. The unopened containers of that stuff are in the net."

Kai watched as Uranus showed him what he had done, including filling the net just behind the Rybaka with a bunch of plastics that were already working to lift the remains of the ship.

"Take it to the surface. Make sure it floats long enough for them to get hold of it, but stay out of sight."

Kai felt the energy of the dragon as it bolted for the sunken ship, lifting it from the ocean floor like it was a toy. When he opened his eyes, he noticed they were already in the café parking lot.

"Uranus?" asked Amy.

"Yeah, sorry," Kai said, unable to hide the smile on his face. "I think we have a way to get that net and some of those containers out of the water. Uranus is going to lift the fishing trawler to the surface."

Kai sounded excited, and Amy got excited with him. "You were busy," she said. "Did you sleep at all?"

"Little," said Kai, holding up the map. "Dad gave me this. Said some of the guys in here can tell us where the coastline is safe."

"Well, let's go," said Amy. "But first…"

Amy pulled Kai close to her and kissed him deeply, before wrapping her arms around him and holding him tight. "I never introduced any other boyfriends to my friends and family," she said quietly. "You're the first, and they all liked you."

"I never had a girlfriend before, so it is a first for both of us," said Kai.

Amy let Kai go, leaning back to look at him. "Really?"

Kai shrugged.

"Let's go eat," said Amy.

Kathy looked up as the bell rang when they entered the café. "Your corner booth is empty," she called out.

"I think we are going to sit here today," said Kai, "If that's okay. I need to get some help with this map."

"You do you," said Kathy. "I'll bring out coffee as soon as the new pot is ready."

"What do you need to know about your map?" There was a group of men sitting at the next table. Kai wasn't sure who had asked the question.

"Amy is organizing a shore clean-up, for all the stuff about to come in from that ship. We need to know which areas are safe to send people to."

"Going to have to be careful. They say there is stuff there that'll kill you."

"My mother said it seemed like it was only a small amount that will get spread out in the currents and won't even be measurable."

The men at the table sat up straighter, the sunken shoulders lifting. A murmur went through the café. Kai recognized the look of hope.

"Hand us the map. Eat your breakfast. By the time you're done, we will have it marked up like a park's trail map," offered one of them.

Kai enjoyed a fairly quiet breakfast with Amy. They watched as the map was passed from table to table, Kathy bringing some crayons out that she kept to occupy children, so they could mark the map up. As Kai ate, he watched the shadows of the ships overhead as Uranus lifted the Rybaka through his dragon's eyes. He could feel what felt like joy from the dragon. Amy could tell when Kai's mind wandered to his dragon. She used those moments to watch the map circulate the room, old fishermen that had been working the water for years, methodically marking spots with confidence. They looked like big children as they used the crayons, and from the smiles on their faces, Amy wondered if they felt like it. She knew using crayons triggered that feeling for her.

The battered hull of the Volya Rybaka breached the surface like a wounded beast as the crews aboard the Coast Guard vessels watched. The ghost ship, rust-streaked and trailing debris, groaned as it rocked in the churning water. Its bow rose jagged and skeletal, half-submerged and barely afloat. The collapsed wheelhouse tilted dangerously to one side, windows shattered and lifeless. Tangles of netting and cable clung to the hull like rotting vines. Some noticed the massive shadow of something pass under them, but the sudden rising of a sunken ship had their attention.

139

"Lieutenant," called one of the Coast Guard crew. "Looks like she's ready to sink again if we don't act fast."

Lieutenant Morgan planted her boots against the deck railing, binoculars tight to her face. The Rybaka had surfaced barely fifty meters off their starboard bow, and from this distance, she could see the ghost net, a tangled mess filled with plastic containers, still snaking off the ship's stern, dragging through the water. She assumed it was that mass of plastic in the net that lifted the ship's carcass to the surface.

"We can't send anyone in," Morgan said, turning to her crew. "We know what's in the water, and we aren't equipped to dive in that." She looked back at the wreck. "We'll have to get floats under her from here."

"I've got the air bladders ready, ma'am," Petty Officer Grant called from the equipment locker. "We can launch them by line gun."

"Do it. And Fast."

Grant hauled the launcher to the railing, a heavy, squat tool with a wide barrel. He loaded one of the orange flotation bags into the chamber, tied to a weighted line. Aiming carefully, Grant squeezed the trigger. The line hissed through the air, arcing over the Rybaka's exposed rail. It splashed down on the far side, and a deckhand aboard the other Coast Guard vessel snagged it with a boathook. Working quickly, they began pulling the float beneath the hull, inflating it with compressed air as they went.

The Rybaka groaned and shifted, settling slightly higher in the water as the bladder expanded.

"Good! Keep them coming!" Morgan barked. Grant fired a second, then a third.

With three of the large flotation bags secured beneath the hull, the Rybaka stabilized, still half-sunken, but no longer at immediate risk of disappearing beneath the waves.

"Now that cable," Morgan said grimly.

The cable connected to the massive trawl net trailed out behind the Rybaka, snaking down into the dark water. If they could get hold of it, they could winch it aboard a second ship and haul it clear.

"Ma'am, we can get the cable, but we can't pull all that net in. I suggest we call into shore and get one of the fishing trawlers at dock to help."

Lieutenant Morgan considered the suggestion. There was a risk to bringing civilians in to help, but they had the equipment and definitely had the experience. "Make that call. Get me an ETA," ordered the Lieutenant, checking the skies. "And get an ROV in the water. I want to know what's caught up in that net."

The door to the café burst open, the bell ringing loudly.

"They got the bastard Rybaka off the bottom. Cable to the net still attached. Coast Guard called for my trawler to haul it in, but I need a crew. Mine left on r and r while we were down."

Almost every man and several women got up without being asked a second time.

"I can use you all. We gotta clear the deck first. I don't imagine they'll complain if a couple others want to head out to help either."

Several of them looked back to Kathy.

"Just go," said Kathy. "I know where to find ya'll"

Lawrence Nault

Chapter 15.

A few of the women who remained behind in the Café helped Kathy clear the tables. One of them picked up the map and brought it back to Kai and Amy. "You're doing good work. My son saw something about your clean-up yesterday online. If you can get that boy out pickin' up garbage, you'll have performed a miracle, let me tell ya."

Kai folded up the map and went up to the counter to pay the bill. Kathy pulled a paper from under the counter and showed it to him. "This you?"

It was one of the posters for the clean-up website. "Amy," said Kai.

"One of the kids dropped it off. Asked if I put it up. Wanted to make sure it was legit first."

"It is. It would be great if you could put it in the window or something."

"Consider it done. And if she gives me a few more, I can get others to put it up."

Kai and Amy speculated about who it was that dropped the poster off at the café during the drive home. They took turns tossing out names until Amy didn't reply when it was her turn, her eyes focused on her rear view mirror. Kai turned to look and saw the RCMP cruiser behind them. He quietly watched the cruiser in his side mirror, not wanting to distract Amy. The cruiser followed them turn for turn. Thankfully, they weren't far from his house. Kai texted his mother to let her know they were almost there, but they were driving slowly because the police were following them. He added a laughing emoji to this text, but he knew she would be waiting and watching for them at the door.

The cruiser followed them right to Kai's house, pulling into the driveway behind them. Kai could see the stress in Amy. "Just get out," he said. "My mother will be out in a minute."

"Can I talk to you, Amy?" said the officer, getting out of his car as they did. Kai recognized the Sergeant the others had complained about.

Amy walked towards the officer, and Kai followed. The officer held up his hand. "You don't need to be here, son. You can go inside."

Kai reached for the newfound confidence that being bound to Uranus had given him. "You can't question a teenager alone," Kai said, holding up his phone. "Maybe I should ask her grandma."

"There is no need to be a problem," the Sergeant said, voice low and tight, like he was daring Kai to push him further.

"It's okay, I already did," Kai heard his mother say behind him. "Her grandmother asked me to stay with her while you talked to her. Was she speeding or something?"

The anger in the officer was obvious. Kai thought he was going to lose it, but then noticed the officer's eyes travel to the front porch. Kai looked behind him and saw his father standing there, casually drinking a cup of coffee. A second police cruiser pulled up, the officer who had taken Amy's statement stepping out.

"We were going to come out to talk to you about the pictures on social media from last night," said the Sergeant, the frustration in his voice obvious. "Saw you driving and thought I would catch you in town instead of driving all the way out to your grandmother's house. I'll let the constable update you."

Amy heard the Sergeant's explanation, but she didn't believe it. He wouldn't have been the first officer who tried to get back at her grandmother for going over their head, through her.

The Sergeant took a few moments to talk with the constable before turning and giving a quick wave to Lu, and no one else. He got in his cruiser and pulled quickly out of the driveway. The tires kicked up some gravel as he sped off. Kai was sure he saw the constable shaking his head. "Should we step into the house?" asked the constable, looking around to see faces in the windows of the neighbors.

"That would be good," said Mei. "Should I call Amy's grandmother?"

"Sergeant said you had already done that."

"Oh, he must have misunderstood. I meant I knew her grandmother would want me there until Amy could call her."

Kai smiled, and he noticed the constable crack a little smile as well. "My Sergeant can be a little challenging, it seems. You should know you aren't in any trouble, Amy. Just some news about the man you found on the beach."

Kai reached for Amy's hand. She wasn't relaxing at all.

The four of them sat at the table in the dining room, Mei putting a cup of freshly brewed coffee in front of each of them. Lu remained off to the side, listening intently.

"I hate to say it," said the constable. "This coffee is a whole lot better than what your grandmother served the other day.'

This actually got a smile out of Amy. "You passed her test and finished it though," said Amy.

"Well, how about all future meetings we hold here?" said the officer, holding his cup of coffee towards Mei to show his appreciation.

"Or maybe there aren't future meetings," said Lu.

The officer looked over at Lu and nodded. "That would be good too."

The officer explained that they had seen the pictures of the car and driver on social media. He commented at how effective the community was at protecting each other and apologized that they didn't respond sooner to her grandmother's concern. "Sarge might have been a little intense because of some reminders from his superiors that it probably needed quicker action." He slid one of his cards across the table. "I know I left one of these with you, but if it's not a 911 call, maybe your grandmother might want to call me directly."

"I will pass that along," said Amy. She was relaxing a little, but she still had a death grip on Kai's hand under the table.

The officer continued, explaining that the man driving the car appeared to be the same man taken from the beach to the hospital in Halifax. When they checked, they were surprised to find out that despite his poor condition, he had left the hospital on his own, and the RCMP were unable to find him. They were able to use the license plate number from the social media pictures to trace the car to a rental agency, and using the tracker attached to the car, we found it parked at the Port of Belledune

146

in New Brunswick. They had people checking the Port, but suspected he was already on a ship.

"I am guessing all those cameras put a scare into him and he is running," said the constable.

Amy's hand finally relaxed in his. Kai didn't realize how tightly she'd been gripping him until his fingers tingled with returning blood flow. He gave her hand a squeeze back, silently promising he'd always be there if she needed him.

"I don't understand," said Mei. "Why would he run if he is still sick, and why would he be looking for Amy?"

"I can't tell you everything," said the officer. "But a lot of the story has found its way to the media somehow, so here is what I can tell you. The ship was carrying illegal cargo. According to documents that reportedly washed up on the beach, some of that cargo was very dangerous. We think the man, who worked on Titan's Haul was the person who made those papers, and he was looking for them."

Amy and Kai were waiting for a question about the manifest that had made its way to the media, but the officer never asked it. The officer's eyes said he knew, though.

"Lots of people are involved now. It's far over my head, but long story short, I don't think you need to worry about that guy anymore. With the pictures your friends took, and everything in the news, there is nothing left for him to hide or protect."

"Well that is good news," said Mei, reaching a hand for Amy. She could tell Amy was on the verge of tears as the stress lifted from her.

"By the way, I have seen some of the posters for the clean-up. You guys are on top of that! It's great. Keep me in the loop. Me, because Sarge is getting some flak about that too."

The constable got up from the table, thanking Mei for the coffee. Lu followed him out the front door and walked with him to his cruiser.

"Thanks for coming," said Lu quietly. "I don't think.. what is it the locals call him?"

"Prairie boy," said the constable.

"I don't think Prairie Boy had the best intentions in dealing with Amy," said Lu.

"He is still trying to figure out the dynamics here," the constable said, but his tone suggested he didn't believe his own excuse. "Every small town is different."

Lu shook the constable's hand. "You going to join everyone for coffee at the usual time?"

"Probably won't make it this week. Things are a little crazy right now."

"Yeah, they are."

Back in the house, Lu pretended not to see the tears on Amy's face. He knew he should stop to offer help, but watching Kai sit there, lost and unsure, made him hesitate. Lu knew he didn't know what to do with a woman's tears. He was still learning that he couldn't just fix things, but a woman's tears shook his foundation in ways he couldn't explain. Emotions in general were not something he had ever learned or been encouraged to understand.

Chapter 16

The fishing trawler, Marlene K, bobbed just beyond the wreck, her hastily assembled deck crew already stationed at the stern. The crew was prepared to haul the net, but there was a problem, they didn't have the capacity to handle the containers the ROV had found tangled in the net. Worse still, the Coast Guard had identified several of those containers as the ones holding the toxic mining byproducts.

"We need to get that cable off the Rybaka and secured to the Marlene," Lieutenant Morgan said. "If those cans break loose mid-haul, they'll scatter, and we probably won't be able to get them again."

"Can't send anyone in," Grant reminded her. "Too dangerous."

Morgan scanned the wreck, then the ROB's monitor. The cable connecting the net to the Rybaka was visible, partially tangled around the stern railing.

"We'll cut it from her," Morgan said. "Get the line gun. We'll attach the lead to the trawler."

While they had waited for the Marlene K to arrive, the Coast Guard had used the ROV to secure one end of a line to the net. It took some skilled maneuvering to secure two carabiners in the knotted cable that still held the net to the Rybaka. It would never be secure enough to haul the net in, but they were confident it would hold enough to pull that cable to another ship.

Grant loaded the line gun with a reinforced rope and positioned himself at the rail. He aimed carefully, sighting the tangle of net and cable just beneath the surface. With a sharp thwip, the line shot out, arcing perfectly over the Rybaka's stern rail. The crew of the Marlene K retrieved the line, splicing it into their cable and feeding it into the winch.

"Cable secure!" one of the trawler's crew called over the radio.

Lieutenant Morgan scanned the area, a last-minute check for any hazards. The entire situation was hazardous with the Coast Guard ships, the Marlene K, the barge they had brought in, and a few other small vessels, all within the same small area. The only thing that gave her confidence was the calmness of the ocean, like it knew they were trying to help it. Morgan knew that could change at a moment's notice, though.

"Cut the cable," Morgan ordered.

The ROV repositioned and clamped its hydraulic cutter over the section of cable still attached to the Rybaka. With a sharp snap, the cutter severed the line. The net sagged free from the Rybaka, shifting dangerously in the current before the trawler's cable snapped taut and steadied it. The Rybaka, free from its tether, immediately started drifting on the waves towards one of the ships, the airbags holding it buoyant.

"Tell the tow ship to get that out of here now. Straight to harbor," ordered Morgan.

The message was quickly delivered over the radio, and the tow rope that had already been secured to the battered hull went taught as Rybaka had its last ride on the ocean to its final resting place.

Morgan keyed her radio. "Get the salvage vessel into position," she ordered. The second vessel, a barge equipped with a crane, maneuvered closer to the Marlene K, positioning itself down current to intercept the containers.

"We'll have to rig slings on the surface," Morgan explained. "As those containers come up, we'll need crews in boats to secure them before they drift."

"We can guide the slings in with the ROV," Grant offered. "Let's do it."

As the Marlene K's winch slowly hauled the net upward, the first of the battered containers broke the surface, a rusted, mud-slick mass draped in mesh and dragging debris behind it. The ROV maneuvered carefully, guiding a rope sling around the container's corners. A crew in a small launch moved in, grappling the sling and tightening it in place. The crane aboard the salvage vessel took the weight and lifted the container free from the net, lowering it onto the barge's deck.

"One down," Morgan muttered. "Let's keep it moving."

The next container rose from the depths, and they repeated the process, this time having to carefully cut away some of the net to free the container. The net dragged more than containers with it, though.

Dead fish, cod, halibut, crabs, and even sharks, dangled lifeless in the tangled mesh, their scales dull and coated with a murky sludge. Strands of torn kelp and shredded seaweed clung to the net's edges, and clusters of coral, broken and dislodged, were tangled in the webbing. A battered lobster trap, twisted and barely recognizable, emerged alongside a splintered section of wooden plank, likely remnants from a long-lost wreck.

On the deck of the Marlene K, the crew moved fast. Deckhands in heavy gloves leaned over the rail, wielding boathooks to snag fish, crabs, and debris before they could spill back into the water. Some of the dead fish were tossed overboard, their bloated bodies too far gone to salvage, but crabs and lobsters still clinging to life were placed in buckets of seawater.

"Clear that plank!" a deckhand barked, hooking the splintered timber and dragging it away. Another man reached with a hook and snagged a tangle of seaweed, pulling it free before it fouled the net's line.

"Watch those sharp edges!" Grant warned as a jagged length of coral tangled in wire mesh swung dangerously close to one of the crew. The experienced deckhand had already seen the hazard coming. He ducked low, twisting the boathook to drag the tangled mess away.

"This whole net's a mess," hollered the man on the winch. "Stay sharp, people. We don't want that net to tear."

From the decks of the Coast Guard ships and the barge, they watched the crew of the Marlene K with respect. Life at sea was always tough. The way the Marlene K's crew survived off the sea was one of the toughest.

"Coming up on another container!" the ROV operator called. The next battered can broke the surface, dragging more debris. Clumps of rope, plastic waste, and a twisted fishing buoy crusted with barnacles hung from it.

"Next one is mining waste, Lieutenant."

"Sound the horn," Morgan ordered.

At the sound of the horn, everyone stopped. The winch ground to a halt, and engines were slowed on the Marlene K. The speakers on the deck transmitted Lieutenant Morgan's voice, and everyone paid attention on all of the vessels.

"The next container contains highly toxic materials. The ROV shows it is still sealed tightly. We can't risk it opening. Do not handle the container, the net, or any material from that area of the net without full gear on. We move slow on this and the other containers like it. Slow and cautious. Proceed."

"You all volunteered to be out here," the Captain of the Marlene K said over the speakers of his ship. "No disrespect if you stand back for this one. We all got families waiting for us."

Nobody moved from the deck. The Captain didn't expect anyone would. He signalled and the winch started.

Kai had been watching the net get hauled in from Uranus' perspective. The men above didn't realize it, but they had help. The dragon was monitoring every tug and every movement of the net, at times helping so the net didn't catch, and making sure containers did not fall free from the net. He took special care to make sure the containers of mining waste didn't break open. Kai laughed when the ROV approached close to the dragon as Uranus swatted it away with a wave of his wing. There wasn't a chance the dragon was going to let it see him.

In between, Kai worked with Amy to coordinate shore clean-ups. They spread the map out on the living room floor, and realized just what a big task it was they had taken on. It wasn't just one or two beaches they needed to worry about, but potentially 100 kilometers of coastline. Amy had Kai's tablet and was chatting with people on the Young Dragons site as she tried to piece together a plan.

"Is that crayon?" asked Lu as he walked past them.

"That's what we had to work with said Amy."

153

"Tell me you got pictures of those weathered old men coloring with crayons."

Amy looked up from her spot on the floor. She was disappointed in herself. "I wish. Somebody must have."

"We should ask Kathy," said Kai, as his father wandered off. Kai wasn't used to seeing his father wandering around the house. With the plant closed, he seemed out of his element. "It would make for some great social media to promote this."

Kai pointed to Scatarie Island on the map. It had been marked as a no-go zone by the fishermen. "We'll have to work with Parks to get that done."

As he pulled his finger away, Amy stopped him, pushing his hand back down. She shuffled his hand down the coastline a bit at a time, and Kai watched her eyes brighten.

"That's it. One hundred kilometers is too big, but five kilometers is bite-sized. We need to find one person every five kilometers to check the shoreline, because it isn't all going to come in at the same place and same time. We have a team attached to each 5k area. When stuff washes in, the spotter sends out the message, the team rolls in. Others can help if they want."

"I knew my son wasn't the smart one of you two," called out Mei, who was in the kitchen cooking up more food than Kai had seen her cook in a long time. She was bored without the fish plant, too.

"Thanks, Mom," said Kai sarcastically. He closed his eyes for a moment, then held up the same finger Amy had used to measure the map and smiled as he watched the first container of mining sludge hit the deck of the barge. The crew on the barge rushed to wrap the container in several tight layers of plastic and secured the doors with cargo straps.

"What does that mean?" asked Amy.

"They got one of the containers of the mining waste out of the water," Kai whispered.

"Perfect!" said Amy.

"So is your 5 K plan," said Kai. "Let's mark them off on the map. We'll work outwards from our beach."

"Our beach?" said Amy. Kai blushed.

"Well, dragon beach."

"Okay," said Amy. "We will call our beach Dragon Beach."

Kai laughed. he found a ruler and marker, and they went to work dividing up the coastline.

Amy took over the process as Kai's mind wandered to the deeper ocean occasionally.

"Three Kai whispered. All out of the water safe."

Amy gave Kai a fist bump.

"Can you take a picture of this map. The camera on my phone isn't great."

Kai got up and stood over the map. His mother called Amy into the kitchen while Kai took a few pictures, trying to catch all the details. He sat down and used the photo editor on his phone to make the pen and crayon details of the map clearer. He sent them off to Amy, hearing the notification tone of her phone as she returned from the kitchen with a tray of cookies.

"Why do we get cookies when Amy is here, but not any other time?" Kai said loudly.

His mother popped her head through the kitchen doorway. "Amy, did I just hear Kai say he wanted to start cooking his own food?"

"Pretty sure," said Amy.

"That was Dad," said Kai, grabbing a cookie off the plate.

Amy posted the picture of the map on the Young Dragons site.

CAN ANYONE MAKE THIS DIGITAL, AND CAN WE LINK IT TO THE WEBSITE? I NEED A SPOTTER FOR EACH AREA AND A TEAM FOR EACH AREA.- AMY

I CAN CLEAN IT UP AND MAKE IT A DIGITAL IMAGE. - RANDY

THE WEBSITE GUY WILL BE ONLINE LATER. HE CAN GET IT ON THE WEBSITE. - DREW

WHAT SHOULD WE CALL EACH ZONE? - RANDY

MAYBE JUST NUMBER THEM. – AMY

GIVE THEM A NAME. PEOPLE WILL ATTACH TO THAT BETTER. I WILL DO THAT FOR YOU. – EMILY

THANK YOU EVERYONE – AMY

"You really got this under control, don't you?" said Kai as he watched the message exchange over her shoulder. "I wouldn't have been able to do it."

Amy sat up and gave Kai a hug. She appreciated his support. She also felt like she had a purpose, which, before all of this started, she hadn't. Taking care of her grandmother seemed to be her life. She started to fold the map up, but Lu came along and took it from her. "Follow me. Both of you."

The two of them followed Kai's father down the hallway into a spare room. Kai knew this room as a storage space, though it had a desk and chair, and a small table in there, somewhere under all the boxes. He was surprised to see all of the boxes neatly stacked in the closet, and the desk and table cleaned off. Lu fished through one of the desk drawers, finding the pushpins he was looking for, and he hung the map over the desk.

"Operations central," he said. "What do you think?"

Amy wasn't sure what Lu meant. Kai was still confused by how clean the room was.

"The clean-up is a big operation," said Lu. "You need a better spot than the living room floor, so this space is for you to work out of. Amy gets the desk. Kai, the table. I will find another chair."

"Really!" said Amy. "You didn't have to do that."

"What you and Kai are doing is very important," said Mei, letting herself in the door and finding a spot next to her husband. "It's important to our business, and the fishermen, and the communities. It's a big job. This way you can keep everything in one place and work together undisturbed by things like fresh cookies."

"Wow," said Kai.

"Kai will give you the front door code," said Lu. "In case nobody is here."

"And I talked to your grandma. If you are too tired to drive home safely, cause there will be some long days, you can sleep in Kai's room. We will lock Kai in the guestroom in the basement for the night."

"Really, Mom."

"Kai," said Lu. Kai recognized the tone, telling him he was about to get a fatherly speaking to. "You and Amy are a couple, and we support that. More than you know. But the two of you are still kids. We are putting an immense amount of trust in you to behave responsibly. Don't disappoint us."

"Yes, sir," replied Kai. "We won't"

"If your father's warning isn't enough, Amy's grandmother told me to tell you something," said Mei. "You know all those people you met last night?" Kai nodded. "Well, grandma said if anything happens to her granddaughter, she will send them after you."

Kai laughed nervously. He wanted to laugh more, but something told him grandma meant what she said.

157

"You guys need help with anything, ask," said Lu. "Do we have an understanding?"

"Yes, Sir," said Kai.

"Amy?"

Amy threw her arms around Kai's father and hugged him. Lu stiffened like a board, the shocked look on his face not surprising Mei. "Thank you, sir. You won't have any problems." She moved directly from Lu to Mei, and it was Kai's mother with the shocked look on her face now. "Thank you, Mrs. Chen."

Kai's parents left the two of them in the office space without another word.

"You scared them with a public display of affection," said Kai quietly.

Amy giggled. "I think so."

She sat down at the desk, looking up at the map. "I can bring my laptop from home."

Kai found a spot to sit against the wall. Amy recognized the look on his face. He wasn't with her at the moment.

Kai watched as the last of the containers was loaded on the barge, and the net stowed safely on the Marlene K. It had all gone smoothly, and the ships were heading back into the harbor. Uranus settled on the ocean floor. The water around him was cloudy with silt stirred up from the net. The dragon tucked his head under his wing to rest. Kai noticed something wasn't quite right.

"Uranus, are you okay?"

"Just tired, Kai. Your plan worked. It made a difference."

"No, it's not just tired," said Kai, concerned. "It's something else."

"It made a difference," said Uranus, repeating himself. "It was the best we could do."

"I can do more," said Kai.

There was no response. Uranus was there, but he wasn't listening anymore. Kai could feel the dragon close himself off.

Lawrence Nault

Chapter 17.

If there was anybody watching the skies over the Antarctic that night, it would have been a sight to see. There wasn't, though. It was, after all, the depths of the winter season, and temperatures in some regions dropped as low as -60 degrees Celsius. The few people in the region were enclosed in their research stations, bundled up in layers of insulated clothing. Even if they happened to step out and glance up at that vast, frozen sky, no one would have believed what they saw.

The Southern lights shone nowhere near as bright as their northern counterpart. Yet, on this particular night, they were putting on a spectacle, dancing across the heavens in ribbons of green, purple, and gold. It was as if the very sky was alive with color, rippling in patterns that flickered and flowed like the breath of the earth itself.

Among those beams of light in the aurora australis, there were shapes. Huge shifting silhouettes blended seamlessly with the lights, their massive wings beating the cold air with an almost hypnotic rhythm. The dragons had come.

Uranus led the way, his ocean green scales shimmering faintly under the aurora's glow. He had travelled from the ocean bottom off the coast of Cape Breton, answering a call that had come from Pluto herself. Pluto was waiting for Uranus, ready to fly out and meet him if necessary, not confident that Uranus could make the distance without help. Uranus was the reason that Pluto had called the dragons together. True to form, though, Uranus soared through the icy skies, his wings spread wide, carving through the darkness with effortless grace, refusing to show any sign of the darkness that was consuming him.

Mars and Jupiter followed, their massive forms cutting through the night like living mountains. Mars was the first to break the silence, his roar echoing across the icy expanse far below. His red scales gleamed in the aurora's glow, a fitting reflection of the fierce fire that burned within him. Jupiter, with her majestic blue scales, was quieter, more reserved, but her presence was equally commanding. Together, the four of them danced in the lights of the aurora, or the aurora danced around them, recognizing a force that could not be ignored.

Neptune and Saturn were late, their arrival marked by the rumble of distant thunder. They appeared from the edge of the world, the shadows of their wings casting long, stretching silhouettes against the glowing lights. Neptune's scales, a spectacular gradient that transitioned from pink-orange to orange-peach, reflected the hues of the aurora, while Saturn's dark, almost black scales absorbed the light, making her look like a shadow in the sky. Their entrance was graceful, despite their late arrival, and their heavy, powerful wings sent gusts of wind spiraling downward toward the frozen earth. Mercury arrived like a falling star, weaving in and out between his kin, childlike and playful.

As they gathered in the sky above the ice shelf, absorbing the energy of the aurora, their wings beat in unison, sending shockwaves through the atmosphere. The aurora responded to their presence, flashing brighter, swirling with more intensity. It was as though the very air itself was alive with their energy.

The dragon-bound, all in the embrace of sleep, saw the dragon's aurora dance and felt as though they were there, dancing among the great beasts. Kyle felt an overwhelming joy, seeing Mars out of his shelter, recovered from his battle with the fires. Jacob was reserved, like his dragon Jupiter, walking through the lights, recording every image in his head so he could draw them later. Hannah did not show Jupiter's reserve, though. She found Anne and took her by the hands, swinging her through the air. Kai felt the worry he had earlier that night lift from him, and he joined Jacob and Kyle in watching the dragons, and Hannah and Anne.

Amy dreamed of dragons as well. It wasn't the dreams that the dragon-bound were having, but the dragons dancing among the lights played like a movie in her dreams. There were others that night who had that same dream. It was strange and unusual to them, but beautiful.

The dragons had not gathered like this in a thousand years, and not been together in one spot since making the return trip to the Earth and stopping briefly on the moon. That was almost two years ago. The world had changed since then. The dragons could feel it, deep within them. There was energy among the young humans, fighting for a future. Their future. Ready to make sacrifices if necessary. That hope battled against their fear, as one man, who led one country, assumed he could rule the world, and was willing to sacrifice anyone who got in his way. The humans called him a President, but that man was not the first of his kind, and he was not for the dragons to deal with. That was a human problem, but his irresponsible actions affected the planet they were trying to protect.

But tonight, they were not here to observe the human world. They were here to recharge, to reconnect with the ancient forces that bound them to the earth. The aurora, that shimmering ribbon of light, was their source. It was here that they could feel the pulse of Mother Earth, and where their strength could be renewed.

There were two missing, though. Nessie, her lifeforce confined in a single tear, and Venus, who stood guard over that Tear and sang it the song of the dragons.

There was a change in Uranus as he basked in the lights. The others could see it and feel it. They left him bask until the time came to talk.

"Have you made a choice, Uranus?" asked Pluto.

"I have not," Uranus replied, the lights of the aurora dancing like the sound wave of his voice.

"There is hope," said Jupiter. "I feel it. My dragon-bound feel it."

"I agree," said Mars. "My dragon-bound has found roots that bind him to Mother Earth, and his voice is heard among others."

"The girl, bound to me, but who hears all of us. She sees things we do not. She sees them before we do," said Mercury. "She draws images of love and beauty and family. She speaks little, but when she does, it is a song of a bright future. There is hope."

Uranus flapped his wings, moving all the dragons, and sending a ripple through the southern lights like a tidal wave through the sky.

"My bound is wise," said Uranus. "But time is slipping away. There are oceans on this world that are already dead, their waters stagnant tombs where only the lost stumble through the world of the dead and scavengers feast on the remnants of what once thrived."

"It is you alone that can give him that time, Uranus," said Jupiter.

"I have a second to my dragon-bound that I don't understand. She is bound to mine, and through him to me, but I cannot speak with her," said Uranus. "How do you have two, Jupiter?"

Venus wasn't there in the lights, but the dragons felt her gentle laughter. "Do you not see it, my friend?"

"I admit, I do not," said Uranus, sounding slightly defeated.

"She is bound not to you, Uranus, but to what will be, the life that Nessie's tear will become," said Venus. "As you and Nessie were once one, so too will be the boy and girl. All that remains is for that circle to complete. Will you once again be bound to what will become?"

A sense of wonder and surprise enveloped the dragons. None of them had seen it, but none was more surprised than Uranus. "Thank you for that wisdom, Venus," grumbled the dragon. "I could not see it. I could feel it, but I was too close to see the entire picture."

Uranus waved a mighty wing. The air moving at his command, shifting the others so he could see into all of their eyes. "A decision has been made. I will be the one to remain behind when the dragons return to their homes. I will be the one to finish the song of the dragons to the Tear. I will be here for what will become, and we will see if the circle will be complete."

The dragons nodded as one. Jupiter moved forward, shifting in the sky as though bowing to Uranus. "Our strength is yours."

"I will need it," said Uranus quietly. "Finish what we have started."

Uranus remained with the others, basking in the lights, all of them playfully swinging their wings, forcing the lights to dance around them like the water around the hand of a child, making shapes in the water. What had started as a celebration had become far more sombre. As they left to return to their resting places on Earth, they broke into song. The planet heard them, the creatures above the ground and below, in the water and in the skies, asleep and awake, moved to the dragon's song. It was a song of hope.

Chapter 18.

Kai slept in. He woke up to what sounded like a very busy household, which was unusual. He wandered out of his bedroom to the kitchen where all the noise was coming from. His mother was in there working away, along with Amy, her grandmother, and two other women that Kai recognized but he didn't know who they were. They all seemed to be hard at work. Mei was the first to notice him and she elbowed Amy.

Amy smiled when she lifted her head and saw Kai. She gave him a quick kiss and whispered in his ear, "I dreamed of dragons last night."

Amy grabbed Kai by the elbow, leading him back down the hall towards his room. "They said the boats can go back out," she explained as they walked down the hall. "We are making food for everyone that comes into the fish plant today to help wipe it all down and get it ready to start back up."

They stopped in front of the door to Kai's bedroom.

167

"Now go put some clothes on before you traumatize the kitchen again."

Kai realized that he had wandered out of his room wearing just the pair of shorts he slept in, and then he realized he had stood in front of all the women in the kitchen like that. "Oh my god!" he exclaimed as he bolted into his room, slamming the door behind him.

Amy looked up to see Kai's father at the end of the hall, shaking his head. "Pretty sure you are the brains of the pair of you," he said, lifting his phone to his ear to answer a call.

Amy laughed and returned to the kitchen. Mei handed her two dishes. "Breakfast for the both of you. You can eat in the office. You guys got your own work to do."

Amy took the plates to the office, and Mei followed her with two mugs and a pot of coffee. As Kai's mother came out of the office, Kai exited his room. "She's in there, with your breakfast," she said as she quickly walked by. Kai was relieved he didn't have to go back to the kitchen.

"Tell me about your dragons," said Kai as he sat down.

Kai cleaned his plate while Amy talked, her food getting cold. There was a sparkle in her eyes that he hadn't seen for a while, and it made him happy to see it return. He pointed at her plate, waiting for her to stop talking about the dragons and start eating.

"Your dream," said Kai. "Not just a dream. I saw it too. All of them. It was mind-blowing."

"They were beautiful. Did you know about all of them?"

"I knew they were all here, but I hadn't seen them all."

"What were they saying?" Asked Amy.

"I could feel them, but they were not talking to me last night. I don't think they wanted to be heard." Amy could hear the disappointment in Kai's voice. She would have been

168

overjoyed to feel them, but she had to remain content with her own joy of just watching them. "Uranus looked good, though. I was worried about him."

"Look at this," said Amy, opening up her laptop.

The website for the shoreline cleanup looked fantastic. There were details of the area, links to news stories, a place to sign up for updates, and the map that the community had helped with was front and center, each five-kilometer section named.

Amy's fingers danced over the keyboard as she spoke. "The Young Dragons are incredible! People our age, from halfway across the world, are already helping. Look at this…"

Amy opened another page of the website. There was a poster there looking for boat crews to adopt each zone. "The person who volunteered to name the different zones improved her idea. We are going to let a boat crew adopt each zone. They will see stuff before the watchers do on shore."

"The person who made the poster made it so anyone with a color printer could print it. I have messages saying it's already been put up at the piers. But even better…" Amy clicked open her email. "We have four zones already adopted by boat crews, and a watcher for all of the zones on land. They will email me if they see anything."

Amy was excited. She was almost bouncing in her chair as she showed everything to Kai. He was excited with her. Another email came in as they were looking at the screen, and Amy was on top of it. Kai picked up the plates from breakfast and returned them to the kitchen. He passed by his father, who was sitting in the living room, calling in workers to let them know what was happening at the plant. A thought clicked as he placed the dishes in the dishwasher. The women were just packing up all the food they had made, about to head out the door. He stopped to talk to his father on the way back to the office.

"Can I get a burner phone?" he asked his father. "People are going to have to call and text Amy, and I don't think she should have her own phone number out there for everyone."

He felt a pat on his back, and he turned to see Amy's grandmother heading out the door with the others.

"Good job," she whispered, giving Kai a wink. Kai puffed up a little with pride.

"We have that emergency cell phone in the kitchen drawer," said Lu. "It's nothing fancy, but its active. Use that, and when this is all done, we can just change the number on it.

Kai popped back into the kitchen and grabbed the phone out of the drawer. "Let me know how much the bill is. This is my idea," said Kai.

"Okay," his father replied. Lu knew he wasn't going to let his son pay for the phone bill, but he was proud of him for stepping up. "I am heading to the plant. You two need anything before I go?"

"You mean like a reminder of the rules?" said Kai, smiling. "You have a good day, Dad."

Lu nodded.

Kai made one more stop before going to the office. He grabbed his laptop and the large monitor from his gaming computer. "This is for you," said Kai, setting it on the desk in the office. "It will plug straight into your laptop so you can work off two screens, and the big screen will make it easier to see things."

Amy moved to the desk and plugged the monitor cable into her computer, and immediately went to work placing things where she wanted on the two screens.

"One more thing," said Kai, setting down the cell phone. "You can use the number on this phone for the clean-up. You will want to be able to get phone calls and text messages."

"My phone is good," said Amy.

"Not the safest to have your personal number out there online for everyone to see. That stuff stays out there forever."

"Thank you," she said sincerely. It hadn't occurred to her, but Kai was right.

"I am going to sit at my table and do some research. You got your stuff under control."

"Perfect," said Amy.

They worked quietly through what was left of the morning. Amy put together teams and contact information for each zone. Many of the people volunteering were willing to travel well out of their five-kilometre zone as well, so she created a spreadsheet that would help her know who to get hold of in all situations. Kai was focused on researching ocean pollution and specifically micro-plastics, chatting with some of the dragon-bound as he did, and occasionally checking in on Uranus. The thrum of the engines of the coast guard ships cruising around and over the dragon was stressful to Kai and Uranus.

"I think they are just patrolling to make sure other boats stay out of the areas."

"Not just that," grumbled the dragon.

Kai watched as an ROV maneuvered through the waters. He recognized the niskin bottles used for collecting water samples.

"The three containers. Are they still leaking?"

Uranus turned his head, and Kai could see the hazy cloud of death in the water.

"I am trying to come up with a plan," said Kai.

"You came up with the first plan," said Uranus. "I have a plan for this. You have to look at the bigger picture now. Your world needs to know this can't continue."

"So, what is the plan?"

"You will have to trust me," said the Dragon. "It involves all the dragons, which is why we met last night."

Kai didn't like the sound of that, but he didn't have time to object. He could hear Amy calling his name.

"Sorry," said Kai. "Talking to friends."

"I figured," said Amy. "You get a look on your face. Do you know who provides all the garbage bags and gloves when we do the annual shore clean-up? Your mother organizes that, right?"

Kai shot off a quick text to his mother, and she responded right away. "Talk to the rescue center director. He has the connections."

Amy was looking over his shoulder when the reply came in. "Want to take a drive. We need to check our beach anyway, and I want to stop by the Café."

"Sounds like a plan," said Kai, closing his laptop.

The sky was filled with clouds, but the sun managed to peak through. They made their first stop at the beach where they met Uranus. They didn't go down to the shore, choosing to walk along the cliff tops instead. Amy used her phone to take a video of the shore. There were a few items among the rocks, but not enough to call in the local clean-up team.

At the rescue center, Kai introduced Amy to some of the animals they were caring for. They stopped to watch some volunteers cleaning oil and diesel fuel out of the feathers of some eider ducks and a puffin. "Came in from near the wreck site this morning," the girl explained. "Bound to see some more soon."

They found the director sitting in his office, clearly busy, but he stopped what he was doing to talk to them. "I was just about to call you, Kai."

"Really? We were stopping by to see if you might know who Amy should contact to get cleaning supplies for the shore clean-ups."

"That's you organizing all of that," replied the director. "Impressive." He fumbled with the keys on his computer for a few minutes, then got up a retrieved a sheet of paper from the printer.

"Email these people and tell them what you are looking for. Copy me and I will give them a call to follow up. Now Kai, we have reports of a young right whale caught up in ghost gear. We need one more spotter on the rescue team. You up for it?"

Kai looked at Amy, a look that asked for permission and forgiveness at the same time. Amy understood. She gave him a kiss on the cheek. "Be safe. Call me as soon as you are back."

The director looked relieved. Amy left, thanking the director again for his help, trying to hide her worry.

"Can you let Mom and Dad know where I am?"

Amy turned, smiling a little. "Mom and Dad, eh?" she joked, liking the familiarity. "Grandma would flip if she heard me call them that."

The crew from the Marine Animal Response Society (MARS) had been on alert since the news of Titan's Haul going down, knowing that drifting gear and refuse posed a major risk to wildlife. Now, some of that debris had found its victim, a young North Atlantic right whale. Thankfully, it had been spotted outside of the zone the Coast Guard had closed off.

Kai stood on the deck of the response boat, squinting against the glare when the sun broke through the clouds and hit the ocean. The air was cold, salt spray biting at his face as

173

the boat cut through the choppy water. The crew moved with swift precision, donning gear and prepping equipment. They were well equipped with sharp blades designed to cut thick trawl cables, grappling hooks, long poles, and a large orange float with the word RELEASE stenciled across it.

"Eyes open, Kai," called Lisa, the team lead. She adjusted her life vest as she spoke. "We'll need you spotting before we're in range. The whale will be moving."

Kai nodded and climbed the ladder to the observation platform. From there, he had a better view of the rolling swells. He gripped the railing tightly as the boat surged forward, the engine growling beneath him. Much further beneath him, he could feel Uranus watching his every move.

"Whale at two o'clock!" Kai shouted, pointing ahead. A dark shape broke the surface, its sleek, black back marked with pale callosities. The whale arched gracefully, but Kai's heart sank as he saw the tangled mass trailing behind it, a web of netting dragging heavy cables. Each time the whale surfaced to breathe, the gear jerked painfully against its tail fluke.

"Got it," Lisa confirmed. "Alright, people, no sudden moves. We're going to approach slowly."

The crew eased the throttle back, steering toward the young whale in a wide arc to avoid spooking it. The whale thrashed once, its broad tail slapping the water. The net tightened, and the animal flinched.

"It's panicking," Kai said from above. "It's dragging more net with every move."

"We'll need the float," Lisa called. "Kai, keep your eyes on it. We need to know if it dives."

The team moved quickly. One crew member readied the long pole with a blade attachment while another prepared the float. The goal was simple. Cut one section of the net and

174

attach the float to ease tension and slow the whale's movement.

"We're going in," Lisa announced.

The response boat drew closer. The young whale's blow shot high into the air, followed by a deep rumble in its throat, a sound somewhere between frustration and fear. The crew worked fast. The pole extended over the side, the hooked blade angled toward the knotted net.

"Steady…Steady…" Lisa murmured.

The pole struck the netting, snagged, then slipped loose. The whale thrashed hard, the spray drenching Kai's face like ice. For a heart-stopping second, the net tightened again."

They gave the whale a moment to settle down, then tried again. This time, the blade snagged the netting, slicing through a thick strand of rope. The crew immediately tossed the float into the water, and it bobbed up, catching tension in the drifting net. The whale lurched forward, startled, but this time the net slackened slightly.

"Good! We need to cut more," Lisa said. "Kai, is it diving?"

"Not yet," Kai answered, watching the whale carefully. "It's circling. Looks like it's tiring."

The team moved to the starboard side, repeating the process. The hooked blade struck again, and this time a long section of the net peeled away, rising toward the surface like a shroud. The whale gave one powerful thrust of its tail, pushing itself clear of the final tangle.

"It's free!" Kai shouted, pretty sure he heard Uranus say the same thing.

The whale surfaced once more, its blow strong and steady. It lingered a moment, almost as if it knew the crew had helped, before diving beneath the waves and disappearing.

"Nice work, everyone!" Lisa called, grinning at her team. "Let's gather that net before it claims anything else."

Kai exhaled slowly, still watching the water. Uranus circled, unseen but vigilant, ensuring the whale was safely on its way.

The sun was setting as the rescue team headed for home. The crew members were scattered about the ship. Movies and stories always pictured rescue crews celebrating long after a rescue, but the reality was far less entertaining. The rush of endorphins and stress as they rescued an animal was followed by a crash. Energy drained, stimulation gone, crew members often found a quiet place of their own to manage their emotions in their own way. Some wrote. Some read. Some sang quiet songs. Kai, was talking to Uranus.

"I can feel Amy. Can you feel her?"

"I can feel her presence, but only because I feel her through you."

"She isn't happy. She is worried. Scared even," said Kai. "I don't understand. She saw you in the lights with the other dragons last night. She told me how beautiful it was. Jupiter speaks with both Hannah and Jacob."

Uranus was surprised to hear that Amy had seen the dragons in her dreams. "Amy is not bonded to me, Kai."

"I don't understand."

"She is bonded to you. She is to you what Nessie was to me."

Kai's thoughts filled with images of Uranus and Nessie, flying, playing, talking, and just being with each other. He watched quietly, understanding more each moment just how important Nessie had been to Uranus, even when they were planets apart.

Back at Kai's house, Mei entered the office quietly. It took several moments for Amy to realize she was there.

176

"You are still here," said Mei.

"Sorry, Mrs. Chen. I was waiting for Kai to get home."

Mei sat down. "My mother was like you. She lost family to the water as well. Every time my father would head out, she would worry. Didn't matter what the weather was like, or what he was going out on the water to do, she always worried."

"How did she deal with that?" asked Amy.

Mei held a hand out. "Come with me."

They didn't go far. Just to the bedroom of Kai's parents, which was next to the office. Mei pointed at a painting over the bed. Two dragons, one golden and one emerald green, coiled and weaved through the clouds. The golden dragon spiraled upward, its sinuous body gleaming like sunlight. Its scales were meticulously detailed, each reflecting hints of amber and copper. Flowing whiskers streamed back from its fierce, bearded face, while flame-like tendrils trailed from its limbs, giving the impression of motion even in stillness.

The emerald dragon mirrored the golden dragon's movements. Its scales shimmered in shades of jade and turquoise, with delicate silver highlights along its spine. Its serpentine body coiled gracefully, weaving through the clouds like a ribbon of living energy.

Billowing clouds, rendered in soft whites, greys, and faint blues, framed the dragons, curling in spirals that mimicked the dragons' twisting forms. Touches of gold ink outlined the cloud edges, giving them a radiant glow that enhanced the celestial feel, and delicate brushstrokes added pine trees and mountain peaks to the mist below.

"She found a place in herself that let her do this. Her chores would wait. My father would go out the door, and she would pick up her brushes and paint. I sat at her feet for hours and watched her."

"It is beautiful," said Amy, mesmerized by the scene.

"You know, Kai's father and I were your age when we fell in love in our fishing village. There are many similarities to our stories. I think you and Kai will be looking at this painting in your home one day, and your beautiful art will hang beside it for your children."

Amy always got compliments on her art, but to her, it was people just being kind. When she carved, though, she often lost track of time, getting lost in the tiniest of details. She doubted she could ever create anything as beautiful as the painting she was looking at, but she understood the peace Mei's mother found in creating her art.

Amy's phone rang, interrupting them.

"Thank you," said Amy, giving Mei a heartfelt hug, which Mei returned.

"Answer your phone and go pick up my boy."

Chapter 19

As Amy climbed into her car, she noticed the piece of driftwood in the back seat. She had forgotten about that being there, but in the dim glow of the car's interior light, the grain of the driftwood seemed to shift. Amy blinked and tilted her head. From this angle, she saw it—a curve like a wing, a jagged shape that might be scales. The wood wanted to be something more. She smiled and made a mental note to start carrying her carving knives with her.

Kai was waiting in the parking lot of the rescue center when she pulled up. He went to climb into the car, but Amy climbed out of her side first. "Don't you even think about getting in there without giving me a hug."

Kai walked around the car and wrapped his arms around her. She pulled himself tight to her, her head against his chest. Holding him quietly.

"Did you save the whale?"

"We did," said Kai.

"Proud of you. The thought of losing you to the ocean will always worry me. It took my father. It can take you. But I will never stop you," Amy whispered.

Kai hugged Amy a little tighter.

"You stink like the ocean," she said. "I'll get you home. Your mother said she would have hot food ready."

"How did your afternoon go?" Kai asked as they got in the car.

"I got some stuff done. Emailed those people about the supplies. Honestly though. I wasn't totally focused."

Kai wasn't sure how to respond to that. He knew his being out on the ocean was the reason she wasn't totally focused.

"Your Mom and I had a good talk, though, and I think I have that figured out," added Amy.

"Oh…" said Kai.

Amy laughed. It was good to hear the stress out of her voice.

"Yeah, she showed me that painting in her bedroom."

"That old thing!" said Kai. "I think they brought that with them when they came to Canada. It's nice, but I am not sure why my mother thinks it's so special."

Amy smiled softly. For Kai, it was just an old painting, but to his mother, it was something far more profound. In sharing that story with her, Mei had trusted Amy with a piece of her heart. Amy felt warm inside, the lingering weight of the day's worry replaced by something calmer, something that felt like family.

"What else did you two talk about?"

"Just things," said Amy. "Women's stuff."

"Oh my god…" Kai mumbled. "Sorry."

Amy laughed. Kai wasn't sure why.

Food was waiting on the table, and they all sat down to eat, including his father, who had come home stressed and exhausted. It had been a long and stressful day, much of it dealing with government officials. They would start processing fish early the next morning, but there were going to be several government people watching over the operation and taking samples. They wouldn't be able to ship any of what they processed until it had been cleared by those people. Lu didn't like it. He knew they would be slow with their results, and that would mean product loss, but it was better than the alternative, which was not operating at all.

"There was a pallet of boxes dropped off at the plant late in the afternoon with your name on it, Amy," he added. "Garbage bags and rubber gloves. I think."

Amy's eyes brightened. She hadn't realized anyone had responded to her requests yet.

"Sorry," said Amy. "Not sure how they ended up there."

"Not a problem," said Lu. "It's a good spot to get stuff like that. We are set up to unload it and have room to store it."

Amy helped clean up after supper. Kai sent his mother off and helped with the cleaning. Amy left shortly after supper, despite Mei's suggestion that she stay. She was concerned about leaving her grandmother alone overnight. As tired as she was from the stressful day, Amy knew her grandmother would be more tired than usual from helping with the food for the plant workers. That meant she wouldn't be getting around all that well, so Amy needed to be home.

Amy found her grandmother sitting in her chair, knitting needles in her hands, snoring quietly. She woke her up gently, then helped her to the bedroom. As she cleaned up a little and put the knitting in the bin, she recognized what her grandmother had been knitting. It was an Aran sweater, with a bold and intricate design of a turtle carrying the world on its back at the center and a dragon on either side of the turtle. As she admired her grandmother's work, the way she used the braided cables to define the spines of the dragon and segment the shell of the turtle, all blended in with the traditional designs used in fishermen's sweaters, she wondered how her grandmother put the dragons together with the turtle. Either Kai and her talked more about the dragons around her grandmother than they realized, or her grandmother knew something. She remembered what Kai had told her about Kyle and his dragon. One of his ancestors had spoke of dragons. Could her grandmother know about the dragons too?

Amy carefully tucked the unfinished sweater into the knitting bin, along with all the many partial skeins of brightly colored wool. She took some time to put her carving chisels together, unrolling the leather pouch she had made to hold her tools, and checking that each one was in its place. Her first carving tool of her own was a small jackknife given to her as a gift when she turned eight years old. She remembered that because her grandmother sat her down and handed a piece of hide to her that night.

"Before you use that, you must learn to respect it. We will use this to make a roll to keep that, and the others you will collect in the future, clean and dry and sharp."

Amy remembered it taking forever to make that roll, always wanting to just use the knife to carve. That was the same roll that she held in her hands today with her wood carving tools in it. She never used that first knife anymore, but it still held its place in the first spot in the roll. Well used, but in as good condition as it was the day she received it. She set the pouch by the door so she would remember to take it with her in the morning.

A message was waiting for her when she climbed in bed and went to text Kai goodnight.

"You won't believe it! Jacob and Hannah and Anne are all coming out here with their families next week for a short vacation. They want to help with the clean-up!"

"Night. See you in the morning."

That last text message had a heart and a kiss emoji added to it. Amy smiled as she said goodnight. That was the first time Kai had sent her a heart or a kiss. She fell asleep thing about the conversation she had with Mei, feeling a sense of security and family, knowing Kai's mother had chosen to share the story with her that not even her own son knew.

Kai slept well that night, the fatigue of the rescue pulling him quickly into the realm of dreams. They were only dreams this time but behind them he could feel Uranus, resting, but steeling himself as though he had a great challenge to face. There was something the dragon wasn't telling him. Kai knew it, and it scared him. Kyle had told him the story of Mars and the fire tornado the dragon had created. Seeing the dragons together in the southern lights was the first time Mars had moved from his place of rest since that event.

Uranus had already told Kai that the leaking mining waste was something he would deal with. Knowing the stories of Mars and Jupiter, it wasn't a reach to know that Uranus was going to face similar challenges as those dragons after this trial. Kai couldn't help but think there was more to it. It wasn't going to be just a matter of rest and recovery for the mighty dragon. There was a deeper sacrifice on the line.

The house was quiet when Kai got up, his parents back to their normal schedule with the fish plant back in operation. He grabbed a couple of protein bars and poured a cup of orange juice, then padded down the hall to the office where he had left his laptop. A quick thought hit him, and he eased the door open to his parents' room. The morning sun was filtering through the trees in the yard, highlighting the painting that hung over the bed. Kai looked at it, curious about why his mother had shown it to Amy.

He couldn't see anything special about it, though he appreciated the dragon theme more now than he had before. It just seemed like so many paintings he had seen in Chinese restaurants. Kai looked closer at the painting, frowning. Why did his mother show it to Amy? He still didn't see anything special, but then again, maybe that's why his mother had shared it with her instead of him. He made sure to close the bedroom door tightly. He wouldn't hear the end of it if his mother knew he went into her bedroom without permission.

A quick touch of the spacebar brought the laptop to life, all of the windows he had left open the day before still waiting for him. He popped in his earbuds, turned up the music, and got down to work. The research he was doing was important to the task Uranus had told him was his, but it was more than that. His father had reminded him that if he was going to apply for scholarships, he would have to write essays to go with his applications, and having an article or story about his work with marine life and the oceans wouldn't hurt.

"We have put money aside for your school, so you don't need to worry," his father had informed him. "We fully support your choice to pursue biology and engineering, but I think we are going into some troubled times for the fisheries in this area. It will make things tight, so scholarships might help."

Kai understood how difficult that conversation was for his father to have with him. He was a proud man and always worked hard to provide everything they needed. Admitting that he might have some trouble paying for Kai's education was probably one of the most difficult things his father ever had to do.

Kai was surprised by the feel of Amy's arms around him and a kiss on the top of his head. He popped out his earbuds, turning to give her a real kiss.

"I rang the doorbell," said Amy. "Not surprised you didn't hear me with your music turned up that loud."

Kai laughed.

"Take a break. Make a pot of coffee while I get settled. Then I have something to show you."

"Yes, ma'am," replied Kai sarcastically.

Amy paused a moment. "Oh my god! I sounded as bossy as my grandma. I am grandma!"

They both laughed. Kai got the coffee pot started while Amy connected her computer and set up some things on the desk she brought from home. It made the desk look less stark and gave it a bit of personality. When the coffee was ready, Kai poured them each a cup and sat down with her.

"What's the plan for today?"

Amy took a big sip of the coffee. "So much better than grandma's," she said quietly as she savored it. "I stopped by the café when you were out on the rescue yesterday. Did you know they have security cameras in there? Kathy let me have some of the recording, and she texted the women she knew were in for breakfast when we brought the map. You wouldn't believe how many of them took pictures and video of their husbands and others coloring in our map."

Amy opened a window in her browser. "See this?" Kai could see it was the website for a local news station. Amy clicked on a story about the clean-up being planned along the Cape Breton shores. A video filled the screen, a montage of weathered old fishermen coloring the map with crayons, while the newscaster talked about the website and the amount of organization that had already happened in preparation for the inevitable flood of debris that would wash up on the coast.

"Holy crap! How did you get that on the news?"

"More young dragons. Someone took the video and images and made the video. It went up on the website. Then a ton of them sent it to media everywhere," said Amy. "I even have phone calls from news people for interviews."

"You don't sound so sure about that interview stuff," Kai said, noticing the change in her tone.

"I am a sixteen-year old Mi'kmaw girl," said Amy. "Pretty sure they expect something else. Someone older, and more white."

Kai reached for Amy's laptop and pulled it closer to him. He opened up the website for the cleanup and scrolled through it as Amy watched. "You did this. You had help from young people around the world, but this is happening because of you. Look…" Kai pointed to one of the team lists, recognizing some of the names on it. "There are adults joining in. Adults that know you. This isn't me just being a good boyfriend."

"But you are…"

"I am what?" asked Kai as he looked at all of the new pictures that were added to the website, some of them being uploaded as he watched. Every watcher took pictures and video each day as they checked on their section of the coast, uploading them to the website so any changes could be seen by everyone.

"A good boyfriend."

Kai stopped scrolling. He looked at Amy. "I try, but this really is all you. You are kind of amazing at it."

The phone rang and Amy answered it, holding up her finger to her lips signalling for Kai to be quiet. Kai listened long enough to realize that it was someone from a newspaper wanting to interview her. He quietly stepped out of the office, pausing for a moment to take a picture of Amy. When he returned Amy was hard at work responding to emails.

"They wanted a picture of me. I don't have any good pictures."

Kai sent her the photo he took a short-time ago. Amy looked busy, sitting at her desk, phone to her ear, the clean-up website on the screen of the computer in the background, and the map on the wall.

"Sneaky," said Amy. "You think that will work?"

"I think it will be perfect," said Kai, sitting down at his own computer.

Amy emailed the picture off, before she had second thoughts, then returned to answering her other messages. She chewed her lip as she scrolled through the messages. What did these reporters expect her to say? That a sixteen-year-old Mi'kmaw girl had all the answers? What if they only wanted her because it made a better story, the 'feel good' headline to go with the wreckage washing ashore?

As she scrolled, a message came up that was marked as important. Amy opened it to see a picture that made her immediately realize the easy part of what she had been doing was over. She showed it to Kai, feeling her stomach twist as she stared at the picture.

It would have been a beautiful picture of a Cape Breton beach, the rocky cliffs softening into a narrow strip of beach, the dark sand flecked with shells and seaweed, were it not for everything else in that picture. The tide, on its way out, had left a litter of wreckage up the shore, plastic shards, tangled rope, and twisted strips of metal rusting to orange, strewn across the dark sand. A battered shipping crate lay wedged between two rocks, its metal door buckled inward. Fragments of shredded plastic drifted like ribbons in the water, snared in clumps of kelp washed ashore. Closer to the water's edge, a half-submerged drum rolled gently in the surf, its surface scuffed and marked with faded hazard symbols. Further down the beach, broken foam insulation clung to the rock in stubborn clumps and splintered wood lay scattered like driftwood, but jagged and sharp-edged, the unmistakable remnants of shattered cargo.

"What do you need me to do to help, boss?" asked Kai, seriously.

Chapter 20

Amy and Kai got there early. They walked the beach, both of them taking video as they did. The tide was rolling out as they walked along the shore, leaving behind much more debris than the picture from the morning had shown, They had called for every on the team in that area to be there for five, but as they made their way back to the car, they noticed other vehicles arriving. Amy took a deep breath, preparing to meet everyone, hoping this came together as well as she planned. She wasn't so sure it would when the first car she saw was an RCMP cruiser. Thankfully, the officer standing beside it was the constable, not the sergeant.

"We saw all the social media about this. The sergeant was concerned you might not have a permit to gather all these people here."

Amy's shoulders slumped. The thought of needing permits to clean garbage off the beaches had never even crossed her mind.

"So here is a letter from the County, and from Parks Canada and DFO."

Amy's stomach twisted. Her fingers tightened on the letters. She couldn't believe it. After all the planning, all the work, they were shutting her down before she even started.

"As long as you avoid any private property, you are good for the next thirty days anywhere in the zones on your map, and beaches aren't private property."

It took a moment or two for the constable's words to register. As they did, a smile spread across her face.

"You make sure your grandmother knows I helped," said the constable. "I am your official contact at the RCMP now, so add me to your contact list. I will make sure there is an officer who at least stops by to check in, but they will probably hang out for a while."

"Thank you. I never even thought of this."

"I just picked up the letters. They already knew you had it under control. Apparently, you have been harassing them a bit. Takes some persistence to get the county to send trucks and people out to bring garbage to the dump on short notice. So, how can I help?"

A van pulled up next to them. The passenger rolled down the window. "Got the pallet of supplies for you. Where do you want us?"

"Can you drop it off at the top of the trail?"

"Can I park the van there. We can just hand the stuff out from the back of the van?"

Amy leaned in to see inside the van. She thought she recognized the second voice. It was her mother.

"Ummm, yeah. That would be perfect."

The dust from other vehicles could be seen coming down the road as the van moved to the top of the trail.

"How about I take care of traffic control. Looks like you may have more people showing up than expected."

"That would be perfect," said Amy, a little relieved. There was still two hours before people were supposed to be there.

Amy looked around. Kai was helping set up a folding table to set the boxes of garbage bags and other supplies on. He was chatting with her mother as they lifted boxes out of the van, and Amy was surprised to see them having such a casual conversation. As she got closer, she heard Kai telling them about all the work she had done to plan this and get supplies and people out. She heard the pride in his voice, about her, and it surprised her. It was genuine. She hadn't expected that. Kai didn't know she was there, yet he spoke about her like she was someone important and capable. The warmth in his voice settled something inside her that she hadn't realized was still unsure. She was about to join them when she saw the familiar volunteer fireman barbeque being towed in. Everybody recognized this barbeque, a trailer shaped like a fish trawler, that was at all the community events.

Amy made a point of greeting everyone as they arrived. By the time five o'clock hit, what was supposed to be twenty was close to a hundred. The television station was there as well with their cameras, and other journalists, all of whom wanted some of her time. That was probably why she never noticed her grandmother arrive with someone. She was walking with the crew from one of the television stations when she realized it was her grandmother sitting at one of the tables Kai had set up. Sue had a book she was getting everyone to sign. The book was a wedding guest book, but nobody noticed or seemed to care. They all signed to say they were part of this. Amy paused at the book, flipping a few pages. Names filled the lines—old fishermen, teens from town, even kids leaving scribbles beside their parents' notes. She was keenly aware of the camera on her as she read a couple of the notes.

On the beach, people were everywhere., Volunteers in bright yellow vests fanned out along the shore, some clustered near the rocks, others combing the sand. Pockets of conversation drifted in the wind, tired voices trading instructions, the occasional burst of strained laughter. The sounds of shovels scraping against stone and the crinkle of garbage bags being filled punctuated the air.

Near the rocky outcrop, a man wrestled with a tangled mass of netting half-buried in the sand. He grunted, pulling hard until a wave surged in, loosening the net enough for him to drag it clear. A young woman stepped forward with a hooked pole, helping pull the heavy mesh away from the rocks. Together, they bundled the net into a large plastic sheet, wrapping it tightly before hauling it up the beach.

Further down, a teenager knelt beside a pool of salty water trapped between the stones. Carefully, she scooped up bits of plastic, bottle caps, cigarette butts, and the shredded remains of a plastic bag, dropping them into her garbage bag. The pool's surface rippled faintly with a thin sheen of oil, the rainbow film shimmering in the light.

Off the shore, a fishing boat passed, blasting its fog horn in encouragement. Almost every person on the beach raised a hand to wave back at them. At the top of the beach, a group of volunteers worked steadily, hauling bags to the bins the county had hauled out. Some of the volunteers lugged the bulging bags themselves, trudging uphill through the loose sand, while others formed a relay chain, passing the heavier bundles from hand to hand.

"How did you get all these people out on such short notice?" the television interviewer asked Amy. Amy moved some hair from in front of her face and held it back, the wind insisting it knew where her hair should be better than her. "Young people, like me, from around the world," said Amy. "They care about our environment, just like theirs. They helped me get the word out." Amy looked around her. "And then there is community. I don't think there is any sense of community greater than a Cape Breton fishing community."

The interviewer made a sign, and the cameraman lowered his camera.

"Thank you. It really is amazing how everyone has come together. My daughter watches that Young Dragons site. I might call you again to find out more about that."

Amy shook the interviewer's hand and said goodbye, then headed straight towards an older woman who was wiping her brow with her sleeve. Amy didn't notice the camera was back on her as she helped the woman lift a battered drum out of the sand. A volunteer in gloves taped a bright red HAZARD marker to the side of the drum, and they all stepped back to let a containment crew, sent out by the Coast Guard to help with the clean-up, take over.

As the tide had begun to rise, and fresh waves crept steadily closer to the debris line, an air horn sounded. Volunteers hurried to gather what they could before the ocean reclaimed it. A boy, no older than ten, darted forward to grab a plastic crate just before the water caught it. His father called after him, and the boy hurried back up the sand, dragging the crate behind him.

Some of the volunteers complained as they were asked to head up to the gathering area, but one of the hard rules Amy had set and insisted the volunteers follow was that they not take any chances trying to beat rising tides. The complaints didn't last long when they found food and music waiting for them at the top.

Amy finally took a moment to sit down. This was her first real chance to just stop and take everything in. As she sat there, she made mental notes about what worked and what didn't. She didn't expect all of the clean-ups to be like this, but she had to be prepared.

"Your father would have been proud of his girl."

Amy turned to see her mother standing beside her. She was holding a plate of food.

"We never saw you pop by the barbecue. Thought you might be hungry. Can I sit with you?"

Amy nodded.

"Hope you don't mind me coming. Mei thought I should be here, which is why she asked me to drive the van. I think maybe she had other reasons to see me here."

"Did you get some food?" asked Amy.

"Yeah, I actually helped with the barbecue. I had to get away from that boy…man of yours. He wouldn't shut up about you."

"Ugh," Amy groaned, but she couldn't help smiling.

"Thanks for helping…and being here."

Amy's mother just nodded her head.

"Do you really think he would be proud of me?"

"Not a doubt in my mind. You see what you did here. He would have done something like this. He was a good leader. You, are going to be a great leader."

Amy's mother leaned in a little closer. "Better than your grandma," she whispered.

That got a smile out of Amy.

"I am going," said her mother as she stood up. "Going to drive your grandmother home."

"I didn't even say hi to her," said Amy. "I should go say thanks and goodbye."

Amy's mother shook her head. "No need. She knows. Besides," she said, pointing with her chin. "Somebody wants to check in on ya."

Amy turned to see Kai standing quietly off to the side in the shadows. When she turned back her mother was gone.

"All good?" asked Kai.

Amy stood up and gave him a hug. That was the only answer he needed.

Lawrence Nault

Chapter 21.

Dark had set in. It took longer to clear people out and pack things up than they had expected. With the car loaded up, they headed home, both quiet, exhausted from the day.

"Just so you know, grandma instructed me to take your keys when we get to my place and make sure you sleep in my bed."

"I am okay to drive home," insisted Amy.

"Nope. Grandma insisted. She was also very specific about me staying locked in the basement until my parents released me."

"I'll bet she was," said Amy, laughing.

"We need to make a stop before we go home?"

"Where? Everything is closed?"

"Dragon beach."

Amy looked at Kai.

"Trust me," he said.

Amy reluctantly pulled into the parking lot at the top of their beach. The car's tires crunched softly over gravel as they pulled into the empty lot. The air smelled cold and briny, the scent of salt carried on the night wind. Amy rubbed her eyes, exhausted, but something in Kai's expression told her this wasn't just a detour, this mattered.

They worked their way carefully down the trail to the beach, and as the sandy portion of the beach became visible, Amy stumbled, tired, but Kai caught her arm. "Kai, if this is just…"

Then she saw him. Uranus stood at the water's edge, looking out to the ocean. All her fatigue vanished. The stars of the sky and the moon in the background framed the dragon like the cover of a fantasy novel. He turned his head to face them, and any fatigue Amy felt was gone. She stepped forward quickly, reaching a hand for the dragon's chest.

"It is so good to see you again."

"What was it with this girl?" Uranus thought. "Nobody reached to touch a dragon, especially one they barely knew." As he spoke to himself, he found understanding. "Amy was bonded to the life force in the tear. To Nessie. And he was as familiar to Nessie as the scales of her own tale.

"Come, both of you," the dragon grumbled. "I have much to share with you."

They moved to the top of the beach, where Uranus wrapped his wings around them, and with a very controlled breath, heated the rock and sand in the center of them. They could hear the mist of the ocean fall against the wings of the dragon like raindrops, but sheltered from waves and the wind, they felt like they were in a warm living room watching the glowing embers of a fire cast off the last of its energy.

"Before I start, Amy, that spot on my chest you always reach to touch."

"I am sorry," said Amy. "I won't do it again. I can see it makes you uncomfortable."

"It does," Uranus grumbled. "But not for the reasons you think. Find that spot once more."

Amy looked at Kai, then carefully stepped around the heated sands and reached for the dragon's chest.

"That is it," said Uranus. "Now, carefully slide your hand under that scale and take what is there."

Amy slid her hand beneath the scale. She wasn't sure what she expected to feel, but what she found was much more pleasant than that expectation. The warmth surprised her. Not hot, but like placing her palm against sunlit stone. Her fingertips brushed something impossibly soft, like the down feathers of a bird. Then her fingers closed around something hard. It felt cool, smooth, and metallic. She hesitated. What if she was reaching too far? What if she was touching something she wasn't meant to touch?

"Go on," Uranus rumbled softly. "It's yours to take."

Amy grabbed hold of the hard piece her hand had brushed against and gently pulled it out. She cupped the scale in her hand, feeling its weight. It was lighter than it looked, the bright silver color reflecting the wings of the dragon wrapped around her, and Uranus looking down at her, a gentle look that was unexpected to see on the face of a dragon.

"In Nessie's youth, Earth's dragon had scales of shimmering silver. She looked like a sun flying across the sky. Like the polished roof of an ancient temple, when she lay on the ground. Like the brightest star in heaven…" Uranus drifted off for a moment, lost in memories. "That is a piece of one of her scales that broke off in play. I have carried it with me since that day. It belongs to you now."

"It holds a special place in your heart, Uranus. I can hear it in your voice," said Amy softly. "I can not take it from you."

"But you must, for you are dragon-bound, and that binds you to the dragon that was, and will be."

Amy held the piece carefully in her hand, looking at it as a million colors seemed to reflect off its surface. Then she held it out.

"I can not take this from you. I am not worthy of it."

"It is not about being worthy," said Uranus. "There was a time not long ago, when I would say no human is worthy of that bond, but human children, like Hannah and Jacob, Anne and Kyle, Kai, and you, have shown me otherwise. But it was never my choice anyway."

"Who chooses?"

Uranus looked down at Amy. She was bold, a strength and confidence in her, wrapped in love and empathy that the girl herself had not fully discovered. He could see Nessie in her.

"Something greater than the dragons themselves. Like the song of the dragons that keeps our memories eternal, there is a song in some families that carries a bond through generations. Some were never destined to find the words to that song, because the dragons weren't here, but others …"

"Grandma," said Amy quietly. "She knows the song."

"The song, but not the words. You will know the words."

Amy looked at Kai. "The painting. Your grandmother."

Kai looked confused. He wasn't quite understanding. Amy looked up at Uranus, and together they shook their heads. There was no time now to explain to Kai what the painting his mother cherished meant. Their heads filled with an image of the beach they cleaned up, scattered with garbage. It shifted to an image of the beach as it was now.

"You did that, Amy. Kai, you have your tasks ahead of you. Continue to seek the knowledge you chase. It will be your weapon and your shield in the battles yet to come. My task lies before me as well. It will tether me to this world, but that is not a bad thing. It means that I will be here to finish the dragons' song for the Tear, and to greet what is to be…your dragon Amy."

Uranus closed his wings closer together until Kai and Amy found themselves standing next to each other. A massive claw reached down, and as if it was a tool wielded by a skilled surgeon, placed Kai's hand into Amy's and the silver scale in those hands. They each felt a gentle poke, and the warmth of their blood running from their hands over Nessie's scale, not tarnishing it, but causing it to shine even brighter.

"This is something that has never happened on your world. There have always been dragon-bonded, each to their own dragons. At times, there has been more than one person bonded to a dragon, as chosen by those powers beyond the dragons. Here, now, I, Uranus, the mightiest of all the dragons, have chosen willingly to bond the four of us. The dragon of Uranus, of the oceans, and the dragon to be, and the two of you. The four are now one. We will do great things and return life to the oceans of Earth."

Uranus began singing, a voice deep and melodic that rumbled through the ground beneath his feet. The other dragons joined in, creating a harmony that vibrated the depths of the planet. Creatures of the world joined in the song. And then there was a silence. Not an empty silence. A silence filled with the sound of peace and calmness.

There was no good-bye as Uranus took to the sky and headed out over the ocean. There didn't need to be. They stood listening to the rhythm of the waves, feeling the mist, and then they both felt something brush against their feet. Amy's heart raced as she looked down. At their feet was a massive leatherback turtle, almost unreal in its size. It moved in a deliberate, slow crawl toward the ocean. The creature's shell, covered in smooth, leather ridges, gleamed faintly in the dim light.

"Thank you for letting me bear witness." Amy and Kai felt the words more than heard them.

The turtle's flippers moved with slow, powerful strokes, each one dragging it closer to the water, its massive body pushing against the sand. It was a graceful and ancient dance, as though it had been coming to this very beach for centuries, long before humans had ever set foot on it.

Kai and Amy remained silent, watching the turtle's struggle. It was clear that the journey was hard. Each movement seemed to take effort, the sand soft and resistant beneath its weight. But there was something mesmerizing about the way it persisted, driven by instinct and an ancient pull toward the ocean. Watching the turtle crawl forward, Amy felt something shift inside her. It was slow, deliberate. A reminder that strength wasn't always fast or loud. Sometimes it was quiet. Unshakeable.

Kai saw something in the movement of the turtle as well. It wasn't courage, at least not the kind that roared or demanded attention. It was quieter than that. A kind of strength that came from simply keeping on. He was like that turtle, learning to move forward, slow but certain.

The turtle reached the water's edge, its flippers now skimming across the wet sand as the waves crept forward, eager to embrace it. The moonlight shimmered on the surface of the sea, casting a silver path that seemed to invite the creature home.

For a moment, the turtle paused, as if considering its next move, then, with one final push, it slid into the ocean. The water closed over its body, and for a moment, there was nothing but the sound of the waves crashing softly against the shore.

Then, a ripple passed through the water, and the creature vanished into the depths, leaving only the quiet remnants of its passage behind.

Amy and Kai stood there for a long time, the night stretching out around them, feeling as though the world had shifted ever so slightly. Not a word was said as they found their way back to the car and got in. Kai looked at the clock on the dashboard. He thought they had been there for hours, but it had only been minutes.

Amy set her piece of Nessie down gently on the seat beside her, wrapping it in a sweater first. She turned the key, the engine coming to life, then rested her hands on the steering wheel, staring off over the ocean.

"I have a dragon. Dragons," she said quietly, whispering to herself as though trying to convince herself it wasn't all a dream. "

They probably would have stayed longer if it weren't for the lights of a passing truck that stirred them from their reverie.

"No human hand can alter the form of a dragon's scale," Amy heard Uranus whisper as she drove towards town. "But your hands can. You will know how to shape it. Make it as beautiful as the dragon I love."

As they drove through the quiet streets, Amy kept her hand over the scale, feeling its warmth through the sweater. For the first time, she didn't feel like she was chasing something uncertain. She felt chosen, not because she demanded it, or because she was with Kai, but because she'd earned it. Now she belonged to something ancient, powerful... and waiting. A found family.

"It takes some getting used to," said Kai. "The feeling of that presence. The absence of it against your skin."

Amy realized Kai had not heard Uranus just now.

"So cool…" she said.

Kai's parents were waiting for them when they got home. Mei made sure they were both fed, insisting they all sit at the table and share in some snacks. Both Lu and Mei went on and on about everything they heard about the clean-up. They had nothing but praise for the two of them, but Amy and Kai were fairly quiet. "You two are exhausted," said Mei. "I can see it in your eyes. I changed the sheets on Kai's bed. There are some clothes on the bed you can change into to sleep in, Amy."

Lu pointed at the basement door, not saying a word. Kai understood the message. Amy got up from the table and said goodnight, finding her way to Kai's bedroom. She quickly changed into the sleeping clothes Mei had set out, and crawled under the covers. She wanted to nose around the room a little, but she was too tired. There was a gentle knock at the door, and Mei poked her head in.

"Do you need anything?"

"I don't think so."

"There is a new toothbrush, still in the package, in the right-hand drawer in the washroom."

"Thank you," said Amy. "Mrs. Chen…Thank you for sending my mother out."

Mei came further into the room, sitting on the foot of the bed. "Your mother talks about you and your art all the time at work. You know how Kai and his father are? Quiet. Hardly talk to each other. Stubborn as goats with each other."

Amy nodded.

"I think Mothers and daughters are like that. You two just have a loss that…created a space between you two. Building a bridge over that, is important."

"Can I ask you something?" asked Amy.

"Of course."

"Do you dream of dragons?"

Mei looked surprised at the question, but she thought about her answer. "I dream that a dragon stands over my son, protecting him. I think that is from the stories of my childhood. Dragons are very symbolic in my culture."

Mei looked at Amy, ready to ask a question of her own, but Amy had nodded off. Mei tucked the blankets around her and left the room quietly. She paused at the door. "You know," she said softly, "sometimes those old stories hold more truth than we realize." She smiled faintly, as though remembering something. "Sleep well, Amy."

Lawrence Nault

Chapter 22

Evening was setting in on the shores of the Bra d'Or lake, and the sky over Cape Breton had begun its slow exhale into dusk. The water shimmered with the fading light, reflecting streaks of molten orange and soft lavender that bled into the distant hills. A breeze skimmed across the surface, rippling the mirrored sky, and carried with it the faint scent of woodsmoke and salt.

As Amy drove slowly through the winding gravel path of the campground, the tires crunched softly beneath them. Kai leaned his head against the window, his breath momentarily fogging the glass as he took in the scene. The place was alive with the gentle hum of summer. There were kids chasing each other barefoot between tents, the soft clink of cutlery on enamel plates, and murmurs of conversation broken occasionally by bursts of laughter. Some families sat in collapsible lawn chairs, cold drinks in hand, watching the sky dim. Others gathered around fire pits, flames crackling as they poked at logs with long sticks. A few worked over well-used barbeques, smoke curling up into the air alongside the sizzle of sausages and burgers.

It was crowded, yes, but not chaotic. There was something easy about the way everyone settled into the rhythm of the evening. It was as though there was an unspoken agreement to slow down, to exhale, and to let time pass more gently here.

Kai had never been camping. Not like this. Not on land. He supposed the overnight field missions with the marine rescue center, sleeping on cots inside a converted trawler with shared gear and rotating watch shifts, might count, but there had never been lawn chairs and hot dogs and bare feet on sun-warmed grass. There had never been this kind of warmth.

Amy turned the wheel and pulled around a bend flanked by tall spruce and birch trees, their branches swaying gently. As the campsite came into view, Kai sat up straighter. Three figures stood at the edge of a clearing, Hannah, Anne, and Jacob, all waving excitedly as the car approached. A crooked, hand-painted sign stuck in the ground beside that read 'Ontario Crew', decorated with a cartoon moose wearing sunglasses.

Amy laughed under her breath. "We found them."

They pulled in slowly, tires dipping slightly into the uneven ground of the site. Before the car had fully stopped, the doors were opening. Hannah was the first to wrap Kai in a hug, grinning widely. Anne followed, throwing her arms around Amy, while Jacob clapped Kai on the shoulder with an easy familiarity. They had never met each other in person, but being dragon-bound they all felt like they knew each other a lifetime.

Behind them, the campsite buzzed with life. Three long picnic tables had been pushed together under a string of solar-powered lights, already aglow like fireflies. The tables were crowded with food. There were covered dishes steaming with grilled vegetables, bowls of salad, plates stacked with buns and condiments, pitchers of lemonade, and coolers overflowing with ice. The scent of cedar smoke and charred meat hung in the air, grounding the scene in comfort.

The lake itself was only a stone's throw away, visible through a gap in the trees. It stretched out like glass, broken only by the occasional ripple from a fish or a drifting kayak. The far shore was bathed in the deep blue of shadowed hills, and above them, the first stars were beginning to pierce the sky.

Kai stood for a moment, drinking it all in, reaching for Amy's hand and intertwining his fingers with hers. They could both feel it, the welcome, the warmth, the stillness of the water, and the quiet joy in being there, in that moment. For the first time in a while, the world didn't feel like it needed saving. It just felt...enough.

Kai and Amy were directed to the picnic tables and were introduced to everyone else there. Jacob's parents took the lead and dished up plates of food for everyone. "I have been camping all my life, but I am pretty sure I am bringing Anne and her mother with me from now on. The food has never been this good."

Anne's parents sat across from them, Anne's little brother, Murray, chatting away between them.

"I heard you were a chef," said Amy. "And you have a restaurant near Algonquin Park. How did you get away at this time of year?"

"I have good staff, and Hannah and Anne have a way of convincing people of things."

"Oh my god, I know," said Hannah's father. "Eighteen years with her and you think we would be immune to it, but nope."

The laughter and conversation was fun and friendly around the tables. They talked about the drive to Cape Breton and other trips they had been on. A lot of time was spent trying to figure out the best places to visit while they were there.

"After we help you guys," added Jacob's father. "We have set aside a couple of days for shore cleaning, though the news says you have it well in hand."

"It has gone well. This has been such a crazy couple of weeks, this last one especially," said Amy. "This is my first real break from it all."

"Well then, enough of that talk," said Hannah's mother. "That's a tomorrow thing."

Amy smiled and nodded, letting the weight of it all slip away, if only for tonight.

"Why don't you guys take a stroll down to the shore. We will clean up here, and I am sure you all want to talk away from the boring adults." Jacob's mother got up as she was talking, picking up some plates from the table and handing them to her husband, before she grabbed more. He got the hint and got to work helping her.

"Thank you for the food," said Kai. "It was amazing."

Hannah got up, and Anne quickly followed, looking to her mother for permission. Her mother just winked. Anne was much younger than the others, but she knew she needed to be with them, and Hannah and Jacob would make sure she was safe. The five of them followed the narrow path down to the lake, finding a spot to sit in the sand. Voices filtered through the trees down to shore and out over the lake. A pair of fiddles and a guitar created the background music as though they were in a scene from a movie.

"All we are missing is Kyle," said Amy.

"I am here," they all heard him say. "I just wish I were really there in person because all that food made me hungry."

"Any of you expecting to see a dragon show up?" asked Jacob.

"That would be awesome," said Kai. "Can you imagine Uranus walking up onto this beach? That poor guy over there fishing would run for the hills. Everyone would think they were feeling an earthquake as he walked along the shore."

"Just how big is Uranus?" asked Hannah.

"This big," said Anne, spreading her arms wide, pushing Hannah and Jacob over.

"That's pretty accurate," said Kai. "Thanks for coming out here. It is good to meet with the people leading us. I would have been lost without your help in the beginning."

Hannah and Jacob exchanged a quick glance.

"I don't think we are the leaders," said Hannah. "We were just the first, and Jupiter was very good about teaching us the ways of the dragons."

"Mars was a little less open," said Kyle. "I feel like I had to pry some stuff out of him."

"Mercury is fun," said Anne softly. "But I think I teach the dragons."

"I think you teach all of us," Hannah added.

"Jupiter is wonderful," said Jacob. "Hannah is right, though. Being first doesn't make us the leaders. It has been two years since we discovered we were dragon-bound. I head off to university this year. Hannah too, along with training for the Olympics. I think we are the support team now.

"There is a leader though," said Anne.

211

The others looked at her. Anne didn't speak a lot, so when she did, they knew it was something important.

"This was Nessie's planet," Anne said, using a stick to draw the Tear of the Dragon in the sand. They all recognized it. "This is your dragon."

Anne looked at Amy as she said those words. Each of them felt a familiar warmth and vibration from their draconalia, and they knew that was the dragons agreeing with Anne.

Amy sat quietly. She didn't know how to respond, but she knew Anne was right, and more than that, she accepted it. She feared it. There was a weight to that responsibility, but she had Kai, and Uranus, and the dragons, and more than that, the dragon-bound that were here, and those to come.

"You have the full support of Mars and myself," said Kyle.

"Jacob, Jupiter, and I as well," said Hannah, Jacob nodding in agreement.

Anne didn't say anything. She just winked as she had seen her mother do so often.

Kai took hold of Amy's hand. "I don't think I have a choice. I am as bound to you as I am to Uranus, and the dragon to be." He was trying to inject a moment of levity, but as the words came out, he realized the truth of them ran deeper than he'd meant. The tether between them wasn't just loyalty or circumstance, but something forged in fire, in fear, and choices that couldn't be undone. A silent pact stronger than any oath and heavier than any promise, and just as unshakeable.

"Tell me about that," said Jacob, his interest showing in his voice.

"You and Hannah must understand," said Kai.

Anne laughed loudly, and they heard Kyle laughing too. "Hannah and Jacob are more brother and sister than brothers and sisters are," he said.

"Oh, sorry," said Kai. "I thought since you were both bound to Jupiter, you were like Amy and I."

"Kyle, who I would give a good poke to if he were here," said Hannah, "is right. We are best friends, brother and sister and family, even if not by birth. When the time is right, which won't be for a while because school and training for the Olympic Kayak team will take all my time, I will find a boyfriend, and Jacob will still be my brother."

"As long as I approve of him," said Jacob. "You haven't made very good choices yet."

"Really," said Hannah. "At least I have tried. When are you going to find a boyfriend?"

"Can I find a boyfriend too?" asked Anne, surprising everyone.

"Am I the only one not looking for a boyfriend?" added Kyle.

They all laughed, like friends who had spent a lifetime together.

When the music stopped wafting out of the campground, they realized just how long they had all been sitting on the beach, talking about everything and nothing, but not about dragons or the challenges they knew they faced. Anyone listening to them would have assumed they were just a group of friends relaxing and catching up.

Anne had nodded off, her head resting on Jacob's leg. Jacob stood up, careful not to wake her, lifting her gently into his arms. Hannah helped him get her into her sleeping bag, since Anne had insisted on staying in her tent. They made plans for everyone to meet at the café in the morning as they walked to the car. When Amy opened the car door and the interior lights came on, Jacob noticed the driftwood in the back seat.

"What is that?"

He didn't wait for a response, opening the back door and pulling out the wood which Amy had already started carving. He carried it over to the fire pit so he could get a better look at it.

At the base of the carving, where two branches forked off, rising like a "V," there was a turtle. It was still rough around the flippers, but you could make out the shape as the shadows of the carved lines danced to the flames of the fire. The shell was nearly done, the faint lines of the continents showing.

"Turtle Island?" said Jacob as he ran his hand over the carving.

Amy nodded.

Above the turtle, on each arm of the V, dragons were roughed in. The heads of the dragons curled inward, both looking down toward the turtle.

"Their horns are just blocked out," said Amy. The lines around the eyes will come alive once I get in there with finer tools."

Jacob turned the wood around as he held it up. On the base, he could make out a whale breaching, its tail just beginning to lift. There was also a school of fish and an octopus arm curling toward the edge.

"Nothing's finished yet," said Amy, feeling a little uncomfortable about her unfinished work being scrutinized. "It's all still in the bones. You can see my scoring lines and the guide marks I scratched in."

Jacob held the wood so Hannah could get a better look. "Look at how they move under the firelight," he said excitedly. "Like they are breathing."

"It's not done. Not yet. But it's becoming," said Amy, needing to explain the unfinished piece. "The dragons, the

214

turtle, the ocean—they're all in there. I just have to carve away everything that isn't them."

Jacob handed the carving to Amy, only now realizing he had made her uncomfortable. "It is already beautiful. You can feel the power you are releasing from it. When you think about it, you use your hands to do what the dragons have done with each of us, carve away things that isn't us and releasing the life within."

Lawrence Nault

Chapter 23.

Kathy pulled a couple of tables together for the adults to sit at. Kai, Amy, Hannah, and Jacob found a large booth, and Anne and her brother squeezed in with them. The café was fairly quiet, a sign that life had returned to normal in the community. Several people took a moment to greet Amy. The amount of publicity surrounding the shore clean-ups had raised her profile from just another one of the kids at the high school to a bit of a local celebrity. She wasn't sure how she felt about that. As they settled into the booth, Kai broke out in laughter. He picked up a box of brightly colored crayons from the rack at the end of the table that held all the condiments, showing it to Amy. As they looked around, they realized there was a box of crayons on all of the tables.

"That goes with our new placemats," said Kathy, as she set a placemat in front of each of them. The paper placemats had a map of Cape Breton with one distinction from the usual maps, this one had the cleanup zones, their names in bold letters featured. There was a challenge printed on the bottom of the placemats. "Color the Cape Breton shoreline based on how safe it is. Compare your results with our official fisherman-approved map."

"Hope you don't mind," said Kathy. "The video of that map being colored in went viral, and I thought visitors and locals would all have some fun with this."

"I think it is wonderful," said Amy.

Everyone eagerly made plans. There was a shore clean-up planned for the end of the day. They always tried to time them with the tide going out so they could not only be safe, but also collect as much debris as possible. The amount of material washing up on the shores was slowing down, but it would never stop completely. She had read about debris from a Tsunami in Japan washing up across the ocean on the west coast of Canada. Ten years had passed, and there were still bits of debris trickling in. With an entire cargo ship of containers on the ocean bottom not far off the coast of Cape Breton, Amy wondered if her own children might still be cleaning stuff the containers of Titan's Haul were releasing into the waters.

Amy caught herself, internally cringing at the thoughts of her own children. That was not something she had ever thought of before, and at sixteen, not something she wanted to be thinking about now. This wasn't the first time her mind had wandered into thoughts of the future, which was unusual for her. She had always lived very much in the moment, but since she had received the scale from Nessie, she found her thoughts wandering far into the future.

Amy felt Kai's hand on her thigh and was brought back to the moment. Kathy was standing there with a carafe of coffee in her hand, waiting for Amy to say if she wanted a top-up.

"I will just top it up," said Kathy. "You look like you need it. You have been putting in some long days lately, I imagine."

"That would be great," said Amy.

"I think it is an artist thing," said Hannah, one finger pointing at Jacob and another at Anne. "Their minds go off to another dimension, and the walls could fall down around them and they wouldn't notice."

"Sorry," Amy said quietly. "My mind has been wandering the past couple of days."

"What will be," said Anne.

Amy looked at Hannah and Jacob, not understanding what Anne meant. They both shrugged.

"The Tear of the Dragon is what will be. That is the song that you are hearing."

Amy's hand went to the scale she carried with her in her backpack, which never left her. She could feel the warmth and vibrations. Now she understood exactly what Anne meant. The others wouldn't, but that was only because their dragon's songs were different. Anne pushed her placemat into the center of the table. She had flipped it over and drew a detailed picture of the Tear of the Dragon sitting on a green flecked rock.

Amy smiled a big smile. "I am going to hug you so hard when we get up," she said to Anne, as she looked up something on her phone.

"I know we are going to stop by the rescue center, and you two want to get out on the ocean in your Kayaks for a while," said Amy, excitement in her voice. "How would you feel about a bit of a mission before the cleanup? A hike with a seek and find mission."

Amy placed her phone in the middle of the table so the others could see the glowing screen. On it was a close-up image of a chlorite stone, not polished, just as it might look if found near the shore of Bras d'Or Lake. The stone filled the frame, a natural green-grey hue with subtle striations running across it like fine brushstrokes. The surface looked soft and layered, almost as if it could flake with a fingernail, but solid beneath. In certain spots, the light on the stone caught a faint, silky sheen, giving it a quiet, earthy shimmer.

"I know how I am going to keep Nessie close to me. That stone, the colors of Uranus, can be carved. I want to make it the background for a carving of the Tear, which I will make with the scale. Kind of like a traditional cameo."

"That will look incredible," said Jacob. "I am up for a hike. We can get out in the kayaks another day."

"Hiking it is," said Hannah.

Anne's mother approached their booth. She noticed the drawing on the table and smiled. "Even with crayons, eh?"

Anne smiled, a sparkle in her eyes. Jacob watched the interaction. He remembered when Anne's drawings worried her parents. Now they embraced them and encouraged them, no matter what the content was. Drawing had brought out Anne's voice, and that had changed all their lives.

"We are scheduled for a boat tour to see puffins and hopefully some whales. You two are coming with us," she said, pointing at her children. "That leaves the four of you on your own today. We will all meet at the clean-up this evening."

Hannah shifted out of the booth to let Anne out. Murray crawled under the table.

"Have a safe trip," said Amy.

The adults left, and the four of them quickly finished their coffee before heading over to the rescue center. At the rescue centre, Amy stopped to talk with the director, while Hannah found herself helping one of the volunteers with a bald eagle

220

that had been injured by a car. Jacob and Kai took a walk down to the shore.

"Seventy percent," said Jacob as he watched a cormorant fly over the ocean in front of him.

"The amount of Earth covered by water," responded Kai, even though it wasn't a question.

Jacob looked at Kai with respect. That was him two years ago when he met Jupiter. "Been doing your research, have you?"

"Nothing but," said Kai. "Seventy percent of the Earth's surface, and ninety-six percent of that is ocean. In those oceans are garbage patches the size of continents, and so much microplastics that we have no idea just how much there is."

"I know it seems overwhelming," said Jacob. "I went through that. Kyle did too. I had Hannah for support. Kyle had both of us. You have a huge task, but you have Amy as well."

Kai nodded his head.

"You okay with that?" asked Jacob, sensing some reservation or reluctance from Kai. "It would scare the hell out of me being bonded to another person so young. It scares the heck out of me now."

"My parents were a little younger than me when they started dating," said Kai, surprised by Jacob's question. So much had been happening that he hadn't stopped to think about how quickly things had developed with Amy, or about the fact that he was bonded to her through no real choice of his own, and what exactly that meant. He found himself breathing a little heavier than normal, each breath feeling a little weightier, but not delivering air to his lungs. He felt panic setting in, then he felt the vibrations from the turtle pendant against his skin, and his breaths slowed. They felt less heavy as

Uranus lifted the weight. They felt energizing, as the Tear shared its own vibrations, and then he felt peace as he felt Amy's vibrations. Alone, it would all have been overwhelming, but he was not alone, he was part of a whole.

Kai turned to Jacob. "I am just fine with that."

"I think you are, Kai," said Jacob.

"We are heading to the lake. You two coming?"

They turned to Amy's voice and saw her and Hannah up in the parking lot. Jacob laughed and slapped Kai on the back. "You are going to need strength, my friend."

It took a little over an hour to get to the East Bay Hills on the southeastern side of the Bras d'Or. It was a good chance to talk about the Young Dragons. Kai had thought he knew a lot about them, but he didn't realize just what type of dynamic resource the young dragons were. Jacob compared the young dragons to a network of mycelium. Like the underground threads of fungi, the Young Dragons thrived beneath the surface, impossible to uproot, each action feeding the whole. Hannah saw them a little differently. She thought they were like seeds scattered in the winds, some taking root in soil, others in concrete cracks, but all pushing green through the grit. It was an informative drive, but they were happy to arrive at the trailhead. Amy's car was a tight fit for people in the back seat.

The trail wound gently upward through a canopy of birch and beech, the dappled light shifting through a canopy thick with July leaves. The sun was already warm on their backs as they started up the trail just after ten. Birds trilled overhead, and the scent of pine and sweetgrass rose from the trail, baked gently by the summer heat.

Amy led the way with a quiet intensity, her shoes thudding softly on the dry path. Kai walked just behind her, and Hannah and Jacob followed. Jacob carried a light pack with his sketchpad and water bottles. Hannah packed her camera along.

"We've got until three," Amy said without turning. "I have to be at the clean-up site early. I would love to find the stone, and you two need to see what it looks like from the lookout."

They moved in a relaxed rhythm, climbing the gentle switchbacks, stopping here and there to photograph lichens or read the interpretive signs. Around noon, they veered off the trail onto a narrow deer path Amy knew about from taking the trail when she was younger, with her grandmother when she was more mobile. The shortcut led to a creek that fed into the lake.

The air was cooler by the brook, and the sound of flowing water dulled the hum of insects. Amy crouched first, scanning the stones with practiced eyes. The others joined her, rifling through the smooth riverbed pebbles in silence.

"Anything green?" Hannah asked, holding up a lichen-covered piece of granite.

"Close," Amy murmured, "but not it."

Kai moved a few feet downstream and paused. Nestled near a cluster of roots was a stone the size of a sand dollar, a deep green with a hint of silver veining. He noticed it because the color reminded him of Uranus. He continued moving downstream when he realized what he had just done. he stepped backward, taking a few moments to find the rock again, which he picked up gently.

"Amy."

She was at his side in seconds. The stone, even wet, caught the sunlight with a soft, waxy glow. Chlorite, unmistakably. Worn smooth by time and water, it sat perfectly in her palm, cool and silent, as if waiting for her to find it.

"This is the one," she said, slipping it into her backpack, beside the dragon scale.

Jacob glanced at the time. "If we want to hit the lookout and still get back by three, we should move."

By 1:30, they reached the summit. The Bras d'Or Lake stretched below like a living map, rippling, blue, and edged by forest and sky. Amy sat on a sun-warmed rock and pulled the stone from her backpack, letting it rest in her hand. Jacob sat next to her, opening his sketchbook.

While Kai found a place in the grass to lie down and watch the clouds overhead, Hannah took pictures of the lake and her friends. She captured Amy rolling around the rock in her hand, looking for the shape that wanted to be released from it. Jacob, slightly blurred in the foreground as he sketched, the lake and trees past him in sharp focus, was another picture she was sure would end up in her portfolio. The pictures of Kai, sprawled out on the grass, snoring, were ones they would all laugh at later.

By 2:10, they were packing up, making their descent with the easy confidence of a group that had found what they didn't even know they were looking for.

They were off the trail by 2:55, stepping back onto the gravel lot, bug-bitten, and quietly triumphant.

When they arrived at the clean-up site, Amy was pleased to see that the garbage bins had already been dropped off, and there were a couple of people from the fish plant there with the van and supplies, already set up to hand them out. Kai's parents had been very supportive of all the cleanups, always sending out a couple of their workers to help, and paying those workers while they were there. The RCMP already had their person there as well, and Amy wasn't so pleased to see it was the sergeant.

"I can go deal with him," said Kai.

"No, that's okay," said Amy. "I got it. Can you take Hannah and Jacob out to the shore and get some before pictures and video?"

"We got that."

Amy thought about waiting for the Sergeant to come to her, but she decided it would be best to face it head-on.

"Sir," said Amy, walking boldly up to him. "We didn't expect you here."

"I know," said the sergeant. "I get the impression that my landlubber status might have given me some misconceptions about things out here, so here I am. An old dog trying to learn new tricks."

"That's great," said Amy. "I don't think I have heard anyone use landlubber except in old movies, though."

The sergeant laughed, his smile not something she had seen before.

"So not just a landlubber, but an old landlubber."

Amy shrugged.

"I don't know that there will be a lot to do," said Amy. We are only expecting twenty or thirty people."

"I thought I might get behind the barbecue with the firefighters."

"Oh, that would be good."

"Amy, you have done some great work organizing all of this. Pretty impressive. Don't know what your long-term plans are, but the RCMP is always recruiting."

Amy couldn't help the surprised look on her face. It wasn't something she had ever considered, or that she would consider, but the offer changed her perception of the sergeant.

"Thanks," she said as she watched a couple of cars pull in. "I gotta go and greet people."

One of the cars that had pulled in was Anne and her family. Hannah's and Jacob's parents were close behind. When they got out of their vehicles, Amy had to try and keep a straight face. They were practically glowing, a combination of sunburn from the rays reflecting off the water, and windburn from the almost constant ocean breeze and salt water.

"We saw three whales," proclaimed Murray loudly. "And dolphins!"

"Cool," said Amy.

"All the time we spend out hiking and camping, and we ignored the warnings about being out on the ocean," said Jacob's father. "But it was worth it. Got some great pictures."

Hannah and Jacob came along, and they didn't hold back their laughter at their parents.

The shore clean-up went smoothly. In a couple of hours, they were able to get the job done, and everyone who showed up went home with bellies full of burgers and hot dogs that the sergeant had cheerfully served up. With the work done, their friends returned to their campsite, and Amy drove Kai home. It was an early night for them, compared to what they had been lately, but Amy wanted to get home.

"I have something I want to get done," said Amy. "If grandma helps, I will show you tomorrow."

Kai entered his house, finding his parents in deep conversation. Their faces were filled with worry. "What's up?"

His father just got up from the table and tried to look like he had something to do in the kitchen. His mother held up a piece of paper. "DFO might be closing the fisheries in this area. That mining waste that is still out there isn't diluting in the current. Radioactivity and toxins seem to be concentrating in fish and shellfish in the region."

Kai didn't have to ask what that meant. Not just to his family, but to the entire community. Closing fisheries had already left many East Coast communities near ghost towns. If Uranus was going to do anything, it had to be now.

Lawrence Nault

Chapter 24

Amy sat down at the kitchen table. She had let Kai know she was home safe, which was much easier now that she didn't have to text everything. She could sense that Kai had something heavy on his mind, and she would have probed deeper, but there was something she had to get done.

"Grandma, I need your help."

Her grandmother was already putting her knitting away when Amy asked for her help. She found her usual chair at the kitchen table, and as she sat down. Amy placed her chlorite stone in front of her. Sue picked up the stone between her thumb and forefinger, moving it under the light, watching the lines and grains and how the light melded with the colors.

"What do you see in that?"

Sue looked around, and Amy got up to retrieve the leather pad they used to protect the table when they worked on carvings and crafts there. It wasn't just years of meals and company that had left the scars of age on the kitchen table, but years of being a work surface for everything in the small home. Amy spread the leather pad out and set some pencils down with it. Sue set the stone on the pad, flipping it over, moving it around, and occasionally picking it back up and holding it tight between her hands, her eyes closed, feeling what was in that rock.

At the best of times, her grandmother's hands were shaky, but as she picked up a pencil and sketched lines on the stone, her hand moved confidently and deliberately. When she set the stone down, she was done. There was no need for a second thought. Amy pulled the leather pad, moving the stone closer to her. She turned the stone, careful not to remove the pencil lines her grandmother had made.

"You do know…" said Amy quietly, seeing the lines of a dragon wing, the veins and natural curves of the stone following the lines of the wing perfectly.

"No," said Sue. "I feel. I hear. I have seen flashes in my dreams. But I don't know. Not like you and Kai.

"Is it tradition, or family? What is the connection?" asked Amy.

"Not our tradition. Not our cultural tradition, as I know it. But every family has its stories. Stories that others think are more myth than memory. Creatures like what you and Kai call dragons are the myth of my family, told in quiet moments, in confidence and secrecy. My part of the myth, I think I see them in my dreams as my mind goes feeble, and I think my daughter talks to them."

"It is a song they heard," said Amy. "Our family's myth is the pictures of music, sung by creatures that protect our worlds."

"Songs carry the voices of our ancestors," said Amy's grandmother. "Now, grab my tools. We have work to do."

As her grandmother started the rough shaping of the chlorite using a rotary tool with a diamond burr, Amy pulled out the scale from her backpack. Her grandmother paused her work to look at the dragon scale, but she didn't ask any questions.

Amy ran her hand over the dragon scale. Uranus said she would be able to cut it, but Amy wasn't so sure. She knew what she wanted. Just a small piece to inset on the stone as a cameo. A piece that would look just like the Tear of the Dragon. To others, that tear would look like a diamond, but to those who knew, those who it really mattered to, they would recognize the Tear. As Amy debated how to cut the scale, the wing's outer edge took shape in her grandmother's skilled hands, tapered and flared, shaped in arcs like riverbones and wind lines. Each pass of the tool shed dust like old stories falling away, revealing only what needed to remain.

By midnight, the wing had taken shape. Sue held it up to the light. It was elegant, protective, and grounded in something older than her hands. She sent it gently on the leather pad.

"My part in this is done. The rest is between you and the spirits that guide you."

Sue got up and walked down the hall towards her room. The tapping of her cane stopped briefly. "Thank you for letting me be part of this."

"Thanks, Grandma. It was important to have you as part of this. But we still have to talk about sweaters."

Amy heard the tap of the cane again, then the bedroom door shut. "I know you heard me, Grandma," she yelled. "I know how thin the walls are."

Amy was sure her grandmother was in there, wearing the same grin she always did when she instigated trouble. Amy reached across the table for the rotary tool, switching out the tip for a new diamond cutting blade. She took a deep breath before setting the tool against the scale. She was surprised how easily the tool followed the lines she had sketched. As the shape of the tear fell away, Amy decided to cut one more small piece, but when she placed the rotary tool against the larger piece of scale, it didn't even make a dent, the tip turning shades of blue as it heated up. It was as though the scale itself knew exactly what Amy needed, and it wasn't to give up anything else.

Amy set the larger piece of the scale down and focused on lining the facets of the tear. It went quickly, though she knew it would have gone quicker if she hadn't dulled the bit trying to get a second piece. As she worked, she sang. Not for anyone to hear, but because it was the song she could hear in her head. Part memory, part hope. A thread through time.

It was early morning when she picked up the wing and began the next part slowly, carving the setting that would hold the Tear of the Dragon cameo. She continued to sing as she did. "Songs are how the land remembers," her grandmother had once said. "And the land never forgets, if we carve it carefully."

Amy's last task before going to bed was to set the Tear of the Dragon, carved from the scale of Earth's protector, given to her by the most powerful of the dragons, within the piece of Mother Earth, formed in the heat and pressure and changes of time, and polished by the cleansing waters. As she set the tear on the wing, she was overwhelmed with emotions.

Her grandmother found Amy asleep, her head on the table, the carved pendant, fully assembled, still held in her hand. Sue reached for the dragon wing, then drew her hand back. It was sacred to her granddaughter in ways that she did not understand, but she respected. Until Amy handed it to her, she would not touch it. Working quietly, she put the tools away and wiped away the stone dust that had now settled. She smiled as she did this, knowing that others would have lost their minds at a mess like this in their homes, especially their kitchen, but to Sue, doing this work here was part of what made her house a home.

As Amy woke up, Sue went quietly to her bedroom. She wanted to let her granddaughter wake up gently, but she also wanted to get something out of her jewellery box. It took her a while to find it, not having opened her jewellery box in a very long time. When she got back to the kitchen, Amy was up, making breakfast. Sue sat down.

"You have been up for a while," said Amy. "Sorry about leaving the tools out."

"If you had woken up, they would have been put away. You had a late night."

"I did, but I don't feel tired."

Amy set a toasted blueberry bagel smothered in cream cheese down on the table. This is what her grandmother had every morning, along with her mug of instant coffee, which Amy also brought to the table. Before Amy could pull her hand back, her grandmother grabbed her wrist, dropping what she held into Amy's palm. Amy sat down across from her grandmother and tipped her hand so the item she was given fell onto the table. She spread it out with her finger as she recognized the shape of a chain. It was silver, tarnished with age.

"We never had much," said her grandmother. "But somehow your grandfather found a way to buy me that necklace. It wasn't for a special occasion. It wasn't cause he was in trouble. He said it was because 'I would make the chain look beautiful.' Only romantic thing that old man ever said to me. I think you will make it look beautiful too, and you need something to hold that new pendant."

Amy reached for her pocket, pulling out the carving, running the chain through the single hole that had been left for that purpose. "Do you want to see it?"

"Yes, please," said Sue.

Amy slid the pendant, with its new chain, across the table. Her grandmother reached out and ran her fingers over it.

"You can pick it up," said Amy.

"No, I don't think I can."

Amy knew her grandmother had a reason for everything she did. If she didn't want to pick the wing up, there was a good reason for it.

"I do think that boy of yours should be the one to hang that around your neck," said Sue.

When Sue mentioned Kai, Amy's mind focused on him, and when it found him, she felt Kai's pain.

"I have to go, now," Amy said.

Her grandmother didn't say anything. Amy was out the door without another word.

Chapter 25.

As soon as Amy let Kai know she was home, Kai had made himself comfortable in his room and reached out for Uranus. He found the dragon, and he watched what Uranus was watching. In the darkness of night, no light filtered into the depths of the ocean, yet the waters around the dragon were filled with small, glowing particles, like a sky full of fireflies. Instinctively Kai knew this wasn't life he was watching, but death. The radioactive particles that had been part of the mining waste, now released into the oceans.

"The time has come," muttered the dragon.

"If we don't act, they will shut down the fishery," said Kai. "It is already killing off life in the ocean."

Uranus pushed himself from the ocean floor, a cloud of silt rising around him. He swam effortlessly towards the three containers leaking the mining waste. Kai heard the dragon's warning to all near him to leave, and he felt a power gathering within the great beast. With a single swipe of his massive tail, Uranus split the three containers of mining waste wide open, the contents instantly forming a massive, dense cloud. Before Kai could react, a massive ball of flame exploded from the depths of the dragon, the bloom of orange-peach flames roaring from the dragon's throat as though the flames were alive themselves. It pulsed outwards in slow-motion arcs, not consumed by the sea but burning with it, a superheated breath that boiled the water around it. The blaze shimmered like molten glass, coiling and twisting, carving a path of furious light. This is why he kept returning to the auroras, not just to re-energize himself, but to charge the fires within.

When the flame met the waste, the ocean writhed.

The heavy metals flashed silver and black as they ignited, reacting violently to the heat. Plumes of iridescent smoke burst upward, curling like ghostly fingers toward the surface. The sludge hissed, fractured, and shattered into particles too fine to hold form. Bubbles exploded like thunderclaps in the deep.

Uranus pressed forward, fire lashing again. It was more controlled now, carving a safe corridor through the death-cloud. His scales caught the light of his own fire, glowing like polished jade. The water steamed around it, a thunderstorm trapped beneath the ocean. As the poison thinned and the shimmer of danger scattered into silence, Uranus paused.

He hovered amid the chaos he had calmed, flame fading from his jaws, surrounded by heat and ash and the slow swirl of a cleaner tide.

But it wasn't clean. Not yet.

Above Uranus, the coast guard vessel cut quietly through the still water, running lights casting thin halos that barely pierced the gloom. It was just a routine patrol. A graveyard shift that all expected to be quiet as they ensured no one entered the controlled zone. Then the sea began to glow, and the crew quickly realized that there was not going to be anything routine about this shift.

At first, they thought it was a natural bioluminescence, perhaps from an algal bloom. But the light was wrong. Too alive. It pulsed, slow and rhythmic, a peach-orange shimmer rising from the depths like a heartbeat.

Then the ocean moved.

The water beneath the hull swelled without warning, not in waves, but in pressure, something immense pushing up from below. The ship groaned and rose with it, tilted off-kilter as boiling water erupted around them. Steam shot up like geysers, blinding white against the black sky. The surface buckled and hissed.

"Brace!" someone shouted, too late.

The ship lifted suddenly, bow rising like it had struck a submerged whale, only hotter. Beneath them, the water shimmered with fire. Not flickering like flame, but rolling, contained, burning under pressure, bright as a sunrise trapped beneath the waves.

From the bridge, an officer squinted through fogged glass and caught sight of it, just for a second. A shape. Long. Glowing.

A line of scales like polished jade, vanishing into the depths.

The deck lights flickered. Radios whined. The metal underfoot thumped, like something massive brushing past from below. And still the ocean rose, lifting the vessel on superheated water, foam bursting like fireworks around them.

Then came the noise. It was deep and resonant, almost like a roar, but muffled by fathoms. It wasn't sound. It was a sensation that rolled through their chests.

The crew stood motionless as steam curled around them, staring into the night-lit inferno boiling the ocean, knowing they'd seen something they weren't meant to.

And below, Uranus turned, his fire dimming as it sank once more into the black.

"It's done," said Kai.

"No, it is not," said Uranus. "Fire doesn't destroy. It transforms. But everything that was released, and everything that has transformed, remains in this ocean."

"But how do we clean it up?"

Kai watched as Uranus swam, wings wide, at a slow, steady pace.

"My scales will attract and bind most of the poisons. The radioactive particles. The arsenic. All that has escaped from those containers and more will bind to my body, no longer part of the ocean, but part of me."

The dragon switched directions, going back in the direction he came from.

As his dragon swam, Kai pieced together this conversation with the others he had with Uranus.

"No! That is why you were tired. You were sick. This will make you sicker!"

Uranus didn't respond. He continued swimming back and forth. With every turn, Kai could feel the filth as if it were on his own skin. He knew what Uranus was doing now. He was swimming a grid, intent on cleaning the entire area.

"This will kill you!"

The dragon didn't respond. Kai raced out of the house, finding his bike, and raced to the beach where he had met Uranus. It was a cold night, and Kai didn't bother to grab a jacket or sweater. He pedaled so hard that he didn't notice the cold until he stopped, only then noticing it all the more because of his sweat-soaked clothes.

"You should not have come," chided Uranus. "The world needs you. Amy needs you."

"The world needs you," insisted Kai.

"Dragons never die unless they choose to," said Uranus. "Because of you, and Amy, and the Tear, I choose not to."

"I don't believe you," screamed Kai, not in his head but in his real voice, the sound of it competing with the waves pounding against the shore.

"You may choose life, but shedding a tear of your own is not choosing this life."

Uranus knew that Kai understood more than he thought. There was a good chance that this action would end the life of the body he was in. His own tear might carry him to the next life, but yes, his death was possible. This is why there was a meeting of the dragons. Someone had to be there to collect and protect his tear. And if he did survive, he would not have the strength to return to his home for hundreds of years. But that would mean the others could leave, and he would remain to protect Nessie's tear.

"I am not going to deceive you. There is a possibility that happens."

"No," said Kai. "Come talk to me."

Uranus didn't answer. Kai walked toward the ocean.

"Come talk to me," Kai demanded.

Kai continued walking out into the water. A wave slammed into him and threw him back onto the shore.

Kai struggled back to his feet. He walked back into the water.

"Talk to me, damn it!"

He got further this time before the ocean spit him back out on the shore.

"You can't. You can't. You can't," repeated Kai as he dragged himself up to his knees. "I can't do this without you."

He made it to his feet one more time, walking back out into the water. This time the ocean wasn't just angry. It was grieving, too. And it hurled him, not in rage, but in sorrow, against the waiting cliffs. Kai fought to remain conscious. Then he saw dragons, and they saw Uranus. There was a voice, not words, just a feeling, then blackness.

Chapter 26.

Amy practically slid down the narrow path to the beach, the ground damp from the ocean mist. She didn't see Kai at first, but she did see the red dragon land on the other end of the beach. She paid it no attention.

"Kai," she called out. "Kai"

Amy stopped and took a breath. She reached into her pocket, feeling the cameo on the dragon's wing, and closing her eyes. When she opened them again, she walked straight to the boulder they sat on that first time they were on this beach together. She found Kai wedged between the boulder and the cliff wall. She reached for him, but his limp body was being lifted by the red dragon.

"You must be Mars," said Amy. "We need to get him warm."

Mars wrapped Kai up in the folds of his wings, leaving just his head exposed. As he held Kai in that cocoon, the red dragon watched the waves nervously.

241

"I did not think there were any more stubborn than my dragon-bound. I was wrong," said Mars.

"I heard that," Amy heard Kyle say. "Is he all right?"

"I don't know," said Amy. "He is not moving."

Amy saw something move in the corner of her eye, turning to see a blue dragon. Jupiter bowed her head to Amy, acknowledging her before approaching. Hannah and Jacob came down the trail, just as Mars handed Kai to Jupiter. As soon as he did, Mars flew off.

"Mars is not a fan of water," said Kyle. "I am surprised he came to help at that spot."

Amy understood how the dragon felt. She was holding back her own rage against the ocean at the moment.

"Set him down, make a fire, cover us," Hannah directed Jupiter.

Jupiter set Kai down gently in the sand and covered the four of them with her wings, closing the top of the tent-like structure with her head. With a very controlled breath, she heated the sand not just near Kai, but under him as well. Jacob checked Kai, but other than a large lump on his head, Jacob couldn't find any other problems.

Amy was used to being in control in emergencies. She was always the one who was calm and collected, but she wasn't now. "Is he going to be okay?"

"Can you feel him?" asked Jupiter.

Amy held her pendant tightly in her hand. With her other hand she reached under Kai's shirt and rested her hand on his turtle pendant. She felt him, but he was moving away from her. He was walking out into the ocean.

"Call to him," said Jupiter. "You are his anchor to the shore."

Amy called Kai's name and she saw him stop and look back.

"I have to help Uranus," she heard Kai say faintly.

"You can't help him from out there," said Amy, pleading. "Out there is where my father is kept, and he never helped me."

Kai stopped and turned around this time. Amy had his attention.

"Kai there are four of us bonded. I am bound to you and without you am less than whole. You are bound to Uranus, and without him, you are less than whole. If any one of us moves on, none of us survive. If none of us survive, hope dies too. Come back to me, and we can call Uranus back together."

Kai looked out to the ocean, then back to Amy. He tentatively took a step towards Amy, then another, and another, each step getting quicker. As he ran back in their minds, his body began to expel the salt water from his lungs as he coughed and hacked. Jacob rolled him onto his side. When he opened his eyes, Amy was looking down into them. He smiled faintly, then noticed the face of the dragon above him.

"You're not my dragon."

"No, Jupiter is mine," said Hannah. "You jerk"

"Whoa," said Jacob. "Take it easy on him."

"I am just saying what Amy wants to say," said Hannah.

Kai didn't seem to notice the chatter.

"Can you save Uranus?" Kai asked Jupiter.

"I don't have to, Kai. You set the example. Uranus will travel as far as you just did, but the bond to those that love him most will pull him back from those last steps. You made him understand."

Kai forced himself to sit up. He could feel the warmth radiate from the ground underneath him. He looked at Amy as

243

Jupiter's words, "those that love him most," echoed in him mind. He could feel her fear and anger swirling in her like a toxic cocktail. He was going to have to do something to replace those emotions with better ones.

They sat there for some time, talking between each other. With the emergency over, Jacob and Hannah took the opportunity to enjoy their time with Jupiter. Both of them had worried that heading in different directions for university might change things, but Jupiter reassured them that was not the case.

Amy got up from the ground, brushing the sand from her pants. She reached out and placed a hand on Jupiter's chest, realizing how much smaller she was then Uranus. "Thank you for being here."

"May I see it?" Jupiter asked

Amy understood. She opened her hand, which was still clenched tight around her dragon wing, and showed the pendant to Jupiter. Jupiter looked at it as though she was watching memories in the dragon scale cameo. Amy knew it wasn't just the memories that Jupiter was revisiting but the intention that was also carried in that carving. The dragon bowed her head to Amy, and Amy realized that Mars had done that as well when they first saw each other on the beach.

"Mars, if you can hear me, thank you for your help too."

Mars didn't respond, but Kyle did. "He heard you, Amy. He is not the most talkative. I am glad Kai is safe."

Jupiter left them quickly, the bright sun part way up the sky surprising them. It was barely rising when they had got to the beach. Jacob helped Kai up the trail. He was okay, but still a little unsteady on his feet. He stuck with him until Kai was sitting in Amy's car. Amy gave them both a hug.

"You still have lots of time to get out in your Kayaks, but don't launch from here," Amy said as she looked at the sky.

The sky had turned that soft, heavy blue it only wore when the sea was ready to rise. Not dark, not yet, but dulled, as though someone had scraped the shine off the morning. The clouds stretched low and flat, and the light felt strange on her skin, silvery, a little sour, like the storm had already touched the edge of the day.

"I would head out now, if I ever went out," said Amy. "I am guessing a storm this evening so don't go too far. Won't be a clean-up either so tell your families that dinner is at Kai's, since it's your last night here. Hope you like seafood."

Amy got in her car and headed toward town. She held Kai's hand as she drove, but she didn't talk to him. Jacob noticed Kai's bike before they left so he loaded it up on their bike rack. They went to a spot Amy had recommended to launch their kayaks, and spent several hours out paddling and taking in the views.

As they stepped in the door of Kai's, Kai stopped Amy.

"I am sorry. I didn't mean to scare you, or leave you behind. I didn't know how far I'd gone until I heard your voice. I just needed that reminder of that rope that ties us together."

Amy looked at Kai. With some time to process everything that had happened that morning she believed what he was saying. She took his hand and led him down the hall.

"We need to close this loop," she said, as she opened the door to Kai's parents' bedroom and pulled Kai in.

"Ummmm…."

"Really! Your mind goes in the gutter now?

Kai blushed in obvious embarrassment.

Amy pointed at the painting. "Your grandmother painted that."

"Really!"

"Yes. When your grandfather was out on the water, which scared her. She found comfort, in paintings and dragons. I think she heard the dragons' song, and I think your mother does too. Not like you do, but they heard it."

Amy took her dragon wing out of her pocket and placed it in Kai's hand.

"This is amazing. You made this in one night?

"Grandma helped. She found the dragon wing in the stone. She has heard the dragon's song and others in my family before her. That's why I think your grandmother heard it to. That is why I want to do this here, so your family is part of it."

Amy carefully unclasped the silver chain on her pendant. "You and I were bound together through one dragon. Now we are bound through two. We are bound to the past, and we are bound to the future." Amy paused, considering her next words carefully. "We are bound to each other, but we have never spoke that directly, ourselves. My grandfather once put this chain around my grandmother's neck. My grandmother carved the dragon wing on that pendant. My family is here. Your family is here," she said as she looked at the painting.

"Hang this around my neck please. Let's not let it hang out there, unsaid."

Kai understood what was happening now. She was right. Sure, he had told Jacob that he no problem with being bound to Amy, but if Amy had asked him to do this before he chased Uranus into the ocean, he would have hesitated. He didn't hesitate now.

"Turn around."

Amy turned around, reaching back to lift her long hair out of the way. Kai reached around her, then fumbled with the clasp of the necklace for a moment before he got it right. As the dragon wing pendant settled on Amy's skin, they both felt a vibration in their pendants as if they synced together.

Amy turned back around and kissed Kai deeply.

"Now let's get out of this room before your parents kill both of us."

Kai laughed. He didn't need to be told twice.

"I have to give my mother a call. They need to retest the water and stuff."

"Can you tell her you invited a dozen people over for supper?"

"What!"

"Maybe I will do that," said Amy. "It's going to rain later so I invited everyone to have supper here. It's their last night here."

"You better hope my mother loves you more than she loves me."

"She does," replied Amy, laughing.

Kai texted his mother. "Re-test the water and the fish. Trust me"

Mei looked at the message. They had already gathered new water samples and fish and shellfish to test. She had heard rumors that some kind of explosion had happened over the wreckage. Mei had already determined that there were no problems to be found, but she had to wait for the official tests to come back from the DFO. She was curious about how her son knew. That was when her phone rang. It was Amy, and it wasn't a text, so Mei prepared for the worst.

"Mrs. Chen, you know how you were saying Kai should have more friends?"

"Yes," Mei said cautiously.

"Well, his friends from Ontario are coming over for supper tonight, along with their parents. I didn't want them cooking out in the rain at their campsite."

Mei did a mental calculation of just how many people that was. The pause worried Amy.

"Sorry, I should have asked."

"You will be in charge of cooking and cleaning," said Mei. "Come by here. Pick up some fish and lobster. Pantry is full. Lu's mother made me do this as a test before she would let him marry me. I had to feed twenty people. Let's call this your test."

Amy laughed. "Yikes! We will be by soon. Thank you."

Mei hung up the phone. She was kind of pleased that Kai's friends were coming over, despite the short notice. She had been on his case about meeting them, and it looked like Amy solved that problem for her. Now she just had to tell Lu. He was not a big fan of company at the house.

Amy's next call was to her grandmother. "Get dressed. You are helping me cook for fourteen people tonight?"

Kai could hear grandma's laughter through Amy's phone from across the room.

Amy hung up and before she put it away, she typed one more message in it. Before hitting send, she showed it to Kai. "I am cooking dinner for family and friends at the Chen's tonight. I would like you to come."

"To your mother?"

Amy nodded. Kai hit send for her.

Amy's mother was the first one to arrive. "I hope you don't mind. Mei is telling everyone at the plant she is putting you through the same test her mother-in-law did. I figure she is joking, but thought maybe you could use a hand."

"I am not so sure she is joking," said Amy, trying to sound serious. "Thanks for coming though."

"I got just the job for you in here," called out grandma.

Amy saw her mother roll her eyes and laughed.

Mei arrived next, dragging Lu with her. He was none too happy about leaving work early, or about having company. Mei offered several times to help in the kitchen, but Amy kept chasing her out. She was at a bit of a loss at what to do with herself, feeling quite uncomfortable with everyone else working in her kitchen. It was Amy's mother that rescued her.

"Amy said no cooking. Doesn't mean you can't set out dishes and everything for everyone."

Mei instantly relaxed as she got to work. Lu hid in the office with Kai, both of them playing games on their phones to fill their time. When everyone else showed up the rain was just starting. The house got loud as everyone talked and introduced themselves. Kai could not remember ever having that many people over before. It was a very informal dinner as Mei filled plates and handed them through the passthrough. There was fresh fish chowder, and fish cakes. A fricot, and bannock. Salads, lobster, fish, and more. Blueberry grunt and lassy buns were on the dessert menu along with apple tarts. Amy had gone out of her way to make sure they got to experience some real homemade Cape Breton food.

Mei called Amy away from the stove at one point, wanting to show her what was happening in the living room. Anne's little brother had latched onto Lu and was talking his ear off. Mei took a video of it, laughing the whole time.

Kai's friends didn't stay late. They wanted to be on the road early in the morning so they could drive the Cabot Trail. Everyone had offered to help clean up, but neither Mei nor Amy would let them. When the last of them was out the door,

249

Mei made a bit of a show walking around her husband as though she were looking for something.

"Just want to make sure you sent your little sidekick home with his family."

Lu looked at his wife, a little grin on his face. "Amy," he said, sticking his head through the pass-through into the kitchen. "Do you know that when my mother put Mei through this test that she didn't cook enough rice, the dumplings were cold, and she spilled a plate of food? She won't tell you, but you passed."

Lu stuck his tongue out at Mei, then retreated back to the office, leaving everyone else to clean up.

"We have so many leftovers," said Amy. "What can we do with it all?"

"There are a couple of crews living on their boats at the pier," said Lu, who had come out of hiding to refill his tea. "If you pack it up, Kai and I will bring it down there. It won't go to waste.

His father was right. They found one of the crew members, and the food was quickly distributed, and probably gone just as quickly. Kai wasn't sure why his father had brought him along, but he found out shortly.

"Noticed you left early this morning. Real early."

"Sorry," said Kai. "You were asleep. I should have left a note."

"We just figured it was rescue stuff or something. Saw your bike was gone too."

Kai didn't say anything. He didn't want to lie to his father.

"Also saw your bike come home on the back of your friend's car, and that lump on your head."

Kai instinctively reached for the lump on his head. He had forgotten about that in the excitement of having everyone over. He wondered how to explain it to his father.

"Do you know what your friends have attached to their bikes that I never see you with?" Lu didn't wait for a response. "Helmets. You have one in the garage. Start wearing it."

"Yes, Sir."

Kai breathed a quiet sigh of relief, happy that he did not have to explain what happened to him that morning. When they got home, things were cleaned up, and the last load of dishes was in the dishwasher. Amy's mother had already left, and Amy and her grandmother were just sitting in the living room with Mei. It took a few moments for Kai and his father to notice that the dragon painting that had hung in the bedroom now hung on the living room wall.

"Amy said it shouldn't be hidden away, so…that's its new home."

Lu looked at it. He wanted to object because he thought it created an instant opinion of them to anyone who came into the house. That is why he had hung it in the bedroom. Something told him he wouldn't win that argument this time. "Amy, thank you for arranging that great supper and introducing us to Kai's friends. Next time, we will just ask you first instead of debating with my son about it." Kai made an obvious show of rolling his eyes. "I am off to bed. Morning comes quickly."

"We are going to go to," said Amy, helping her grandmother up from the couch. "I promise I will give you more warning next time," she added as she hugged Mei.

Amy gave Kai a quick hug as she and her grandmother left. There were words said between them, but no one else in the room could hear them. Grandma gave Kai a hug as well. There were words exchanged there to, but just through the gentle look of the old woman. Kai closed the door behind them and turned to see his mother standing in front of the painting. He joined her.

"Did grandma really paint that?" asked Kai.

"She did. I watched her. Everything Amy told you about the painting is true."

"She told me your mother painted it. Would you like to tell me the whole story?" asked Kai.

Mei looked at her son. The boy was gone, but the man beside her now was a good man, with a big heart.

"I would," she said quietly, putting her arm around him as she did when he was a child. "Your grandmother..."

Chapter 27

Kai slept to dreams of swimming, back and forth, never changing pace, never diverting from the path. This was the path Uranus was taking, moving like a machine on a track to scrub the waters of man's destruction. But he was a beautiful machine, cutting through the water like a planc cutting through clouds. His movement was silent, but every creature in the area heard him just through his presence. Some joined him out of appreciation and respect.

Kai watched through Uranus' eyes as a North Atlantic right whale joined him. He could see the texture of the callosities and the wrinkles of the whale's dark skin, mottled with lighter patches that contrasted with the dark waters around it. It moved with a slow, graceful power, its massive body gliding effortlessly through the deep blue. The whale's broad, arched back rose and fell rhythmically, its massive head highlighted by the ghostly whisps of ivory that were the baleen plates that hung from its upper jaw. Its eyes seemed small against the

253

sheer size of the whale, but they seemed almost contemplative, reflecting the ancient nature of the far too rare creature. The whale left a time or two, ascending to the surface for another breath before returning to join the dragon, and then Uranus changed directions, and the whale continued on its own path.

A school of fish joined Uranus like a flash mob arriving on scene, moving as a synchronized mass, shimmering like liquid silver. There were hundreds of thousands of them, but Uranus saw each one individually. He admired their long and slender bodies built for swift and efficient movement through the water. He appreciated the artistry of color as their deep, iridescent blue topside faded to a pale, almost silvery white on their belly, making them look like pixels of light dancing across a computer screen, every second a different image seen in the pattern.

They were minute creatures next to Uranus, each one barely the length of one of the dragon's scales, but as a school, the blueback herring formed a new creature that made Uranus seem small, and the dragon took joy in that. The fish darted and weaved in unison, an almost hypnotic dance. Each fish moved with precision, responding to the slightest shift in the group's direction, creating a near-perfect harmony. The school would undulate, then break and reform, a living organism shifting with the pulse of the deep, as though the entire group is one consciousness, instinctively guiding itself through the dark waters.

They, too, chose to maintain their path when Uranus changed his, following the invisible grid like a programmed machine. Many other creatures joined Uranus, but only one was brave enough to touch the dragon.

Uranus watched with curiosity as a leatherback approached him, gliding effortlessly despite the burden it carried. The leathery, dark-gray surface of its shell was marked by rough, ridged textures, but those textures were now speckled with clusters of barnacles, some small, others large and gnarled, firmly anchored into the turtle's shell. They formed a small, clustered city, their white and beige shells contrasting with the turtle's dark, mottled carapace. Tiny, flickering algae in shades of green and brown crept along the edges, creating an almost moss-like appearance that brushed against the water with each movement. A few sea sponges also clung to the shell, their soft, spongy bodies bulging in odd, organic shapes, while delicate, pinkish hydroids and other smaller lifeforms drifted lazily between the turtle's ridges.

Slowly, deliberately, the turtle settled onto the back of the dragon, resting there, blending into Uranus' massive expanse. It stayed there, anchored to its fleeting perch, like an ancient traveler finding respite in the immense, shifting world of the ocean it lived in. Uranus appreciated the company, understanding how his traveling companion felt, because he too felt the need for respite. His energies were draining, the poisons sapping him of life just as time had worn away at the gentle creature on his back. Time was running out for both of them.

Amy didn't dream that night, but as she slept, the song of the dragons played in her soul. It sounded like the hush of starlight spilling across a still lake, each note a ripple reaching the edges of her being; like the tide pulling against the moon—deep, sorrowful, and strong—as if the ocean itself were trying to remember the shape of love. It was a thousand wings unfolding in silence, the music of becoming, of belonging, of being more than one heart alone. And it was home—not a place, but a feeling threaded through every lifetime she had ever lived.

There was no single way to describe the sound, and no words that could capture its depth or beauty. Others had heard dragon songs before, but not like this. She was hearing it through the life within a dragon tear, absorbing every word of the dragons' collective memory.

Hannah and Jacob communed with their dragon as they slept. They were grateful to be in Jupiter's physical presence once again, but change was on their mind. They felt like they had handed off their roles to Amy and Kai, and that their return home may be a last as they packed once more and left again, only going separate directions this time. They were missing their home and their friendship already, and they hadn't even left for university yet. The weight of change was holding them both back. Jupiter understood, but she had lifetimes of change to relate to. Even with all that experience, change was never easy, but with change came room, space for growth, and the opportunity to become more than you already were.

Kyle wasn't dreaming. He sat in a forest, Mars as his backrest. He had missed his dragon, at times fearing Mars would never fully recover from the firestorm that had saved so many. He was here now, though, alive, well, and they had work to do. The time Mars had rested was a time of deep discovery for Kyle. He discovered lost family and lost heritage. He discovered the world outside the walls society had erected for him. But more than that, he discovered the world hidden in the walls he had erected around himself. He wasn't ready when Mars came into his life. He was now.

Anne also dreamed to the rhythm of the raindrops landing on her tent, falling through the tree canopy above. They weren't her dreams, though. They were everyone else's. She saw the dreams they were having. She saw the dreams they wanted. She saw the dreams that would be.

Lawrence Nault

Chapter 28

Kai sat in front of his computer. He had the office space to himself since Amy had to take her grandmother to the doctor. He offered to go along, though he really didn't know what he could do to help other than sit there and wait. Amy said it was just a regular check-up, but she appreciated the offer.

On the table around his laptop, Kai had sketch pads and graph pads, and random pieces of paper. The image of the school of blueback herring from his dream lingered, fragments of an idea swimming through his mind, just out of reach. One question kept bouncing around in his mind: What if students could work with their schools, and those schools with others, like a global network, all moving as one? In his research, he had already found several projects teachers were using with their students to understand water pollution, all using different filter sizes, depending on the age group, to filter out materials in the water. That led Kai to some training material for the rescue center that spoke about the different sizes of mesh that were used in nets to catch different fish. That led him down the rabbit hole of mesh sizes used for filtering water samples.

Kai had no idea how long he had spent searching the internet for mesh sizes and water pollution sampling, but when Amy came into the office, she found Kai scratching out numbers on a chart from that listed one to twelve in the first column. This was obviously not his first round of scratching out numbers, as this page was a mess, and the balled-up papers around the garbage can told her this wasn't the first page he had worked on.

"I don't even get a hello," said Amy.

Kai popped up out of his chair, and gave her a kiss. He hadn't noticed her come in the room, and he sat back down quickly enough, returning to his work, that Amy knew she wasn't going to get any attention from him. She reached in her bag and pulled out a plastic container, taking the top off and setting it down in front of Kai. Kai noticed the sandwich and realized he was hungry.

"Grandma insisted I bring you lunch," she said, pulling out a sandwich for herself and joining him at the table. She reached for the pad of paper he had been working on and pulled it closer so she could see what he was doing.

"What has all of your attention?"

Kai went on in detail about the concept he had to create a world-wide youth scientist program to collect water samples and maybe a database of the results, taking quick bites of his sandwich between words. "There are people doing this. Real scientists. But that data get's hidden or takes years to come out in peer-reviewed papers. I want something that is out there, in everybody's faces. Something the world has to notice."

"How did you get to the school idea?" asked Amy. She was invested in this idea now.

"Fish!" said Kai excitedly.

Kai got up, bumping the table as he did, then moved around the small room, his arms waving in the air, mimicking the movement of the school of fish as he told Amy about them. When he realized what he must have looked like, he stopped, feeling a little embarrassed. He quickly sat down and pointed at the pad of paper.

"These are grades, one to twelve," he said pointing at the first column. "The net column is mesh sizes for sample collection. I want something that gets smaller material each grade. The mesh sizes are good, but confusing. It's not scalable."

"What is this symbol?" Amy asked, hoping Kai would think it was his scratchy printing she couldn't read. She pointed at a 'μm'.

"Micron. Sorry my printing is messy."

"Does the mesh need to be exactly this size?"

Kai shook his head. "Just close."

"What if…" said Amy, grabbing a blank piece of graph paper and creating a new chart. The first line was the same as Kai's 'Grade 1 – 4000 μm'. "What if we divided that by the grade number, so grade two would be two thousand microns, and grade three would be one-thousand three-hundred and thirty-three, and…"

Kai already had a spreadsheet open and entered some numbers and Amy's formula. He looked at the results wide-eyed, comparing them with his scribbled notes. "I have been working on this for hours, and you come along with the perfect solution in minutes."

"Ummm, sorry?"

Kai laughed. "No, its perfect! But if my father asks, I did the math. It's so simple which makes it useable."

"You could build a whole theme around that number," said Amy.

Kai thought for a minute. "4000 students per country."

Amy liked that. "4000 schools around the world," she tossed out

Kai typed that into his spreadsheet. They continued to toss out ideas between each other. Some were wild and out there, but others they debated seriously. In the end they agreed that the four thousand could also be applied as the number of pieces of data per year, and the number of actions taken, and the standard water sample size in millilitres.

"Project 4000," said Amy.

Kai ran that through a search engine. "Already taken," he said, a little disappointed, running his hands through his hair in frustration.

Amy handed Kai the container the sandwiches had been in. "You need a break. Go put these in the dishwasher and get a couple of clean coffee mugs. I will make coffee."

Kai thought about arguing with her for a moment, but she was right. He hadn't moved from his chair all morning. When he got back from the kitchen he could smell the fresh coffee, the scent more noticeable as it was accentuated by sound of the last bits of water being pumped through the machine into the carafe. All the papers on the table were neatly stacked as well, and his laptop pushed back. There was a clean notepad in front of each chair.

"Thank you," said Kai.

Amy shrugged. "Grandma would have had my hide if I left my workspace like that. I can hear her now, 'How do you get anything done in that mess?' "

Kai laughed. "Grandma sounds a lot like my dad."

They sat and drank their coffee, and while they did, they bounced ideas off each other for a name. They had close to twenty different names between their two pads and they eliminated them one by one. Some got scratched off because they were already in use. Others were too complicated, and others just weren't catchy enough. In the end they settled on WAVE 4000. Wave was actually an acronym for Water Awareness Via Education, which Kai thought would help get schools to adopt it, but with the periods out of the acronym, it was also a word that could work around the world without translation, and it referred to water. Kai thought it was perfect. Amy wasn't so sure, but this was Kai's project, so she supported his choice.

"I would have been working at this for a month without your help. You're good at this. Now what can I help you with?" As Kai asked that question, he realized he had totally forgot the doctor's appointment Amy had just taken her grandmother to. "How did the appointment go? Is grandma okay?"

"I think so," said Amy. "She doesn't let me come in. But she said it was just a check-up"

"Oh good," said Kai, relieved and embarrassed he didn't ask sooner.

"Now my world project," said Amy with a smile on her face.

Kai wasn't sure he believed the smile. She had changed the subject far too quick. He noticed her smile waver just a second before she changed the subject, but he didn't push. Not yet.

"Kyle and I talked while I was waiting at the doctor's office. He wants to organize a beach clean-up out there."

"That would be wild. Coast to coast clean-up."

"That's what got me thinking," said Amy. "Things are slowing down here. There is still stuff washing up, and will be for a long time, but looking at the messages from young dragons, all beaches are like this. Doesn't matter if it is an ocean, a lake, a stream, or a sea?"

"How do you coordinate that kind of clean-up?"

"I don't think I do," said Amy. "I didn't realize that until we worked through your project."

Amy pulled Kai's laptop closer to her, and she brought up a picture of the globe.

"You are using citizen scientists, student scientists," said Amy. "What if we used citizen…young citizen coordinators. Each of them adopting a section of shore along a water body, and taking the lead for an annual clean-up. We could create a database like yours and record how much stuff everyone picks up. No big organization. No structure that has to be financed. Just young people saying, 'this is my section of shore, come join me in a quick clean-up.' Nice and simple."

"Wait a sec," said Kai, clicking through the tabs open on his computer. When he found the one he was looking for he handed the computer to Amy.

Kai watched as she read through the website, taking notes and screenshots as she did. He realized that, even if he had paid attention before they met on the hill-side, he never would have realized just how smart she was, or how pretty.

"I see you watching me, Kai."

Kai laughed. He had been caught. Amy set the computer down and smiled softly at him.

"That is kind of what I am thinking, but this is a United States government program. Given the site is about an environmental project, I am surprised it is still up."

Amy wasn't wrong. Every day the news was filled with stories about changes in the U.S. and it seemed all environmental projects were on a hitlist to be defunded and eliminated.

"Can you get more help from some of the young dragons?"

"There will always be young dragons that will help, but I think this will take one person a little more committed," said Amy.

Kai knew what Amy was leading to. This was her thought process. She wanted to be in the background and supportive and she would be content to support and lift up someone else who wanted to take the lead. If that person didn't exist, she would think about doing it herself, questioning her own ability to do so. The final step would be her doing what she thought needed to be done, and doing everything possible to be successful at it. Kai could have told her just to do it, but she needed to get to that last step on her own.

"I am going to add one more thing in here," said Kai, as he zoomed in on the satellite image of the earth until he could see the North Pacific garbage patch easily. "And I have no idea how to handle this."

"What are we looking at?" asked Amy.

"That is one of the four big garbage patches floating in the oceans. It doesn't look horrible from a satellite image, but through a dragon's eyes, they are like solid floating continents," said Kai seriously. "You have a plan to clean up what comes out of the water. My project helps to realize what is in the water. It is all no use without a plan to stop plastics and garbage from getting in the water to start with."

Amy zoomed in on the map, but it didn't have the effect she thought it would. Then Kai remembered their connection, and he took her hand and showed her the images of the garbage patch that Uranus had shown him. He felt her heart drop.

"I didn't realize," said Amy. "Now I understand why you feel like you carry the world on your shoulders sometimes."

Amy realized something else as she shared thoughts with Kai. Uranus was there, with him. The dragon was silent, but she could feel his pride and confidence in Kai. He had been there during the whole planning process they had gone through, but he was very near his end.

"I know," said Kai. "He is making his last passes, then he will…rest. It will be on me to keep him alive."

"On us, Kai. We are bound," said Amy quietly. Kai's focus on his project, then on hers, was not just concentration. It was his emotional control valve. She could feel the sadness backed up behind that valve, ready to burst forth.

"Grab a sweater and a jacket," said Amy. "You will want to be as close as you can."

Amy tidied the table and turned off the coffee pot. She found Kai waiting for her at the front door. They drove to their beach, Amy not entirely confident this was going to be a better experience than the last time they were here. Kai didn't wait for her when they parked. He was out of the car and almost sprinting for the trail. It was okay. Amy understood. She grabbed some blankets from the trunk of her car, then decided to also take her carving and tools down with her. They could be there a while.

Kai was standing at the water's edge, the waves lapping at his feet. Amy fought the desire to pull him back, spreading one of the blankets out and setting everything else on top of it. She went back up the trail, just far enough to find some pieces of wood to start a fire. Once the fire was going, Amy sat quietly, watching Kai, feeling Kai and Uranus, and finishing the details of her carving.

Lawrence Nault

Chapter 29

Amy placed her chisel in the pouch, rolling it tightly and tying it shut. The damp, salty ocean air would not be kind to her tools. She set the driftwood down, and watched the creatures she had released from the wood dance with each other, the flames their music. There was nothing left to take away from the wood, but there was something to add. Amy looked at Kai. He had followed the tide out.

She reached into her backpack and pulled out the remaining piece of Nessie's scale. Carefully she slid it into the center of the V, the cradle formed by powerful necks of each of the dragons as they looked down on the turtle, a slot on each side designed to hold it secure. Amy saw the flames reflect in the scale, and in the midst of those flames she saw herself, though she didn't recognize the woman she saw. That was when she felt Uranus.

"It reflects back what the dragons see, Amy. That beauty. That strength. That confidence. That woman you see looking back at you, is you. We found her, and with Kai's help you will to." Amy could see the dragon examining every detail of the carving, and watching his own reflection in the scale. She felt a tear well up in the dragon, and she heard Kai's voice on the wind as he called Uranus.

"No Uranus, you cannot. It is not your time," said Amy. "Rest. We will prepare for your return with what is to be."

It took the last of Uranus' energy to quell the tear, and hang on to the small spark of life that remained in him. At the water's edge, Kai cried, as he watched his dragon sink to the ocean bottom. He would have stayed there, not noticing the tide turn back, if he didn't feel Amy pull him back. He turned and walked back, his feet moving him across the sand while his heart remained with his dragon, sinking in the dark.

Kai sat down beside Amy, close to the fire, letting the flames warm him, but it didn't matter how close he sat to the dancing colors and hot embers, he could not get warm. He wondered if this was what Uranus was feeling. The warmth escaping from his body, a breath of ice taking its place. Amy threw one of the extra blankets she had brought down over Kai's shoulders. He could hear her humming as she moved closer to him, deep but quiet tones that resonated within her chest. He did not recognize the music, and neither did Amy, but she knew it meant something to her. It stilled her and she hoped it did the same for Kai. The dragons listened to her song as well. They did not recognize it, but they knew it was a song of Mother Earth, and that brought stillness to them because if Mother Earth was singing, there was hope. Uranus and his dragon-bound had succeeded where even the dragons had wondered if they would not.

Above the flames of the fire a bright light streaked across the sky. Those on the ocean that saw it would all swear they saw a meteor crash into the water. Some quietly celebrated the good omen, a powerful sign from the universe signalling change, reminding them to seize opportunities and telling them good fortune was on its way. Others quietly cursed at the anger of the gods, the meteor a sign of impending disaster. They were all right. And they were all wrong. They saw only what their own thoughts would let them see, and not the dragon at the center of the ball of flames.

Anne watched as her dragon bolted straight to the ocean bottom, sharing her sight with the other dragon-bound. Mercury settled on the ocean floor gently, barely disturbing the sand, despite the speed he approached at. As he walked around Uranus's motionless frame Kai they noticed the deep color had faded from his scales, and his massive body looked small. Kai noticed the leatherback still on Uranus' back, lifeless, its time coming to an end in the peaceful company and caress of a friend.

Mercury was small compared to Uranus, but he still lifted his limp body out of the silt onto his back and headed south. He struggled to move fast, the water not as free as the sky, and the burden he carried slowing him down, but he found strength from the others as they watched him. A journey of five days for the ships that moved on the water above him was only five hours for Mercury. At the edge of the abyss, Mercury floated with Uranus draped across his back, gazing down into the yawning maw of the Puerto Rico Trench. This was where Uranus' journey would end this night, but Mercury himself could not accompany him to the depths. His form was not suited for the crushing pressures of the underwater world below.

With a gentle motion, Mercury eased away from beneath Uranus, letting his still form fall freely into the abyss. He watched as the current, though faint, took hold of Uranus, pulling his form in the wrong direction. For a moment, he feared the limp body might drift off course. But then, he saw them—silently appearing from the depths, their ghostly forms barely visible in the darkness. Several deep-sea octopuses, their pale, translucent bodies barely discernible against the inky water, wrapped their long, sinuous tentacles around Uranus. Their touch was delicate yet firm, guiding him with uncanny precision. The current that had threatened to pull him away was no match for the octopuses' coordinated strength. With a subtle, fluid grace, they moved the dragon's body deeper, navigating him through the waters toward the heart of the trench.

When the first octopus finally released its hold, others took its place, their tentacles extending and curling around Uranus, gently nudging him along the ocean floor. As he sank lower, deeper into the trench, the sea became more alien. Snailfish, their bodies soft and gelatinous, swam in and out of the shadows, passing by and occasionally brushing against the dragon's body. Bioluminescent jellyfish pulsed faintly with an ethereal glow, their drifting movements illuminating the dark waters like ghostly beacons. The creatures moved in unison, guiding Uranus with an almost ceremonial precision. Some of the creatures here were unlike anything mankind had ever cataloged, and their existence remained a mystery.

Finally, the body of Uranus settled into the deepest reaches of the Milwaukee Deep. The ocean floor rumbled, a low, persistent tremor that seemed to echo through the vastness of the trench. It was a common occurrence in this place, where the Earth's tectonic plates wrestled in a constant, unseen struggle beneath the surface. But today, the tremor felt different—almost like a greeting. The water around the dragon grew even darker, as if the abyss itself were swallowing him whole.

Yet, despite the impenetrable darkness, life found its way to Uranus. Bioluminescent creatures, those strange and glowing organisms of the deep, approached, their flickering lights creating fleeting moments of illumination. They danced around his still form, their lights casting surreal shadows across the dragon's body. Near the ocean floor, the superheated water from the hydrothermal vents surged, mixing with the cooler depths. The currents from the vents caressed the dragon's form, their warmth contrasting against the cold stillness of the deep, while the creatures continued to swirl around him, their bioluminescence providing the only light in this darkened world.

The dark oxygen-rich waters washed over Uranus, as if the abyss were breathing him in, welcoming him into the eternal silence of the ocean's deepest realms.

"It is time to rest, Kai. You must carry the flame alone for a time."

Kai looked at Amy, sitting close beside him. "Not alone," he said quietly to his dragon.

Anne quietly praised Mercury as she drifted off to sleep, a sketchpad at her side. She had drawn Uranus' resting place long ago. What she had seen through her dragon's eyes was exactly what was in her drawing.

Kai shifted, backing away from the fire, no longer feeling cold. "It is you and me, on our own for a while." He took Amy's hand and told her what Uranus had told him.

Uranus, unlike the other dragons, had the ability to absorb heavy metals. As he swam in that grid he collected toxic elements like arsenic, cadmium, and rare earth residues. There were so many of them in the water that his body's natural ability to purge the toxins was overwhelmed. Uranus knew this when he started. Where he was now, would provide the warmth needed for the symbiotic organisms that existed on him, to consume those toxins. There were also creatures down there that would help with that process. In time, Uranus would heal, and the dark oxygen would re-energize him. But it would be hundreds of years before he would have the ability to return home. He would be the one to be with the Tear of the Dragon when the new life came forth. By then, the others would have returned to their home. Only the four of us, the bonded, would remain.

They fell asleep by the fire, holding on to each other, keeping each other warm long after the fire went out. They woke up to a gentle rain. Laughing they quickly gathered their things and raced up the trail to the car.

"We are in so much trouble," Kai said as he looked at the clock. Amy had texted Kai's mother when they left the house, letting her know they would be home very late, but as she noticed the time, she expected there would be questions. They let themselves into the house as quietly as possible, heading straight for the office. Kai had decided he would rather get in trouble for staying up all night working on his project instead of hanging out all night on a beach with his girlfriend. That would just lead to so many embarrassing questions.

They were working quietly when Kai's mother tiredly stumbled by the office door, reaching to turn off the light switch as she grumbled about the kids not having to pay the light bills. As her hand reached the switch, she realized Kai and Amy were in there.

"Did you two sleep at all?"

"We are trying to finish something up. Lost track of time," said Kai.

Mei looked at them sternly. Kai tried to figure out if she believed him or not, so he could prepare for what came next.

"You playing detective now?"

That question was no where on Kai's radar. He looked at Amy who just stared blankly back at him. Mei pointed at the computer.

"You have a fingerprint on your computer."

Kai looked at his screen, his eyes opening wide. Amy could see something switch on in his mind. He zoomed out to show his mother it was just a satellite image. Mei just shook her head as she came further into the room, putting a hand on Amy's shoulder as she looked at what Amy was working on.

"Everything okay, Amy?" Mei asked quietly.

"Yes, Mrs. Chen," said Amy, looking up at her and seeing only kind eyes that said a lot, but also said there wouldn't be anymore questions.

"Good. I will make you two some breakfast."

Kai zoomed back in on the satellite image, seeing exactly what his mother saw. a distinct, spiral shape near the center of the Atlantic. It was unmistakable. The swirling pattern was almost hypnotic, the debris concentrated in a perfect spiral, looking eerily like a fingerprint. The ridges and loops of the pattern stood out against the darker water, each curve accentuating the movement of the ocean currents. Kai's breath caught in his throat.

The image was of the North Atlantic Garbage Patch, but there was something about it, something he'd never noticed before. Something... different. The way the debris circled and converged, the way the lighter patches of floating plastic traced out a loop, a perfect spiral—he could almost see the whorls, like the lines of a fingerprint etched into the sea. It was both beautiful and horrifying, like nature itself was branding the ocean.

He ran a hand through his hair, his thoughts racing as he studied the image. His fingers instinctively brushed the keyboard again, zooming in on the central point where the debris seemed most concentrated.

The currents. It had to be the currents.

Kai leaned back in his chair, his mind piecing the puzzle together. The North Atlantic Gyre... The way the ocean currents moved in a circular motion, pushing the water and everything within it into that perfect, spiraling shape. The Gulf Stream, the North Equatorial Current, all of them feeding into the rotating motion that trapped the debris in the center. The debris was accumulating in the convergence zone, where the water slowed down and everything got caught in the whirlpool of the gyre's powerful rotation.

It was like the ocean had made a fingerprint of its own, created not from a human hand, but from the currents, the debris, and the relentless motion of the water. The gyre's rotation was pulling everything into the center, trapping it, creating those ridgelines that cut through the surface like the loops of a fingerprint, curling in upon themselves.

Kai picked his laptop up and rolled across the room in his chair. He set it down in front of Amy. "What do you see?"

Amy looked at the screen. "Can't quite put my finger on it," said Amy.

Kai started to explain, then he realized what Amy said and knew she saw exactly what his mother had, and what he was seeing now. He shook his head as Amy giggled, taking his computer and rolling back to his desk. He was carefully saving images and taking screenshots, looking for similarities in the other ocean garbage patches.

"Wait, what did you say?" asked Kai.

"I didn't say anything," replied Amy.

"No, before, when I showed you the picture."

Amy thought for a moment. "Can't put my finger on it?"

"That!" exclaimed Kai. "Can you put your finger on it? What if we asked everybody that question? Can you put your finger on it? On the problem…"

Amy turned in her chair to look at Kai. She could see his brain going at hundred miles an hour with this idea. It was a good one, but she was going to have to slow him down to put it together. She could smell bacon and knew breakfast was almost ready.

"Write it down, on paper, and pin it up so we don't' forget it. Then let's go eat breakfast with your parents."

Amy held up a finger. "Breakfast, then I am going home to check on grandma. We both are getting some sleep, and then we take your idea and turn it into something."

Kai's mind was racing, but he couldn't argue with her. He was hungry and tired.

Lu was surprised to see Amy and Kai seated at the kitchen table when he sat down. "Early start?" he asked.

"Yes," said Mei, giving Amy and Kai a look that said be quiet."

"Did you hear the good news?" Lu asked, looking at Kai.

Kai shook his head, not sure what his father was talking about. "You need to get out and away from that computer more often. The DFO is opening the entire area back up to fishing. They say water tests are actually coming back cleaner then they have been in years."

"That's good!" exclaimed Kai.

Lu looked across the table at his son, thinking he heard sarcasm in Kai's voice. He could see that Kai actually was as excited about it as he sounded.

"It is. One day they are ready to shut us down, and the next, everything is perfect," said Lu. "Someone must have screwed up."

"What about all those containers and stuff. Won't nets and gear get caught on it?" asked Amy.

"Good question," said Lu, getting up and putting his dishes in the sink. "I'll be in the car."

"We will clean up," said Amy. "Thanks for breakfast."

Mei rushed out the door after Lu. Amy and Kai, cleaned up the kitchen and put the dishes in the dishwasher.

"FYI, you ever put dishes in the sink when the dishwasher is empty, there will be a fight," said Amy.

Kai laughed. "Did you see the look my mother gave him. He didn't even notice."

Amy gave Kai a quick kiss. "I am going home. You are going to bed."

Amy found her grandmother asleep in her chair when she got home. The chill of the morning air that followed Amy in woke her up.

"Did you spend the night there?" asked Amy, concerned.

"I must have nodded off," said her grandmother, not quite answering Amy's question.

"I have something to show you," Amy said as she pulled up a TV table in front of Sue. Amy set the large item she was carrying on the table, and unwrapped the blanket from it. She watched her grandmother's face closely.

Sue reached out and touched the driftwood. She traced the lines and grooves with her fingers, almost caressing it. She fought the tears that were welling up for so many reasons. Amy had not asked for any help with this project. Sue took pride in that independence, but felt a loss as well because she loved working on projects like this with her. There was also a beauty and a spirit in the carving that spoke to her. There were elements of her culture and other cultures that combined to give it a power. Then there was the scale. Sue didn't know it was a dragon scale, but whatever it was made from reflected back an image of a young woman, full of energy, ready to take on the world. That was her, though her body had been telling her different lately.

"There are no words," Sue said softly "There are so many stories in there that I could sit forever and look at it, and never see them all."

"You like it then?"

Amy's grandmother struggled up out of her chair, Amy giving her a hand. Her grandmother wrapped her arms tightly around her.

"I have seen no better. This is an heirloom for the next generations of our family."

Sue reached for her cane.

"I am off to sleep in a real bed. You should do the same.

Lawrence Nault

Chapter 30

It took a week for Amy and Kai to work through their ideas. Hours and hours had been spent researching, debating, planning, talking with others on the young dragons site, and putting all the pieces together. In between all this there were shore clean-ups and the other demands of life. Amy felt pulled between her home and Kai's, so Kai spent a couple days at her house, even sleeping on the couch one night. It was late a night on a Sunday when Kai handed Amy a binder and memory stick, then made a show of closing his computer.

"It's ready. I can't do the next part."

"You could," said Amy.

"Maybe, if I had to, but that is not my role in this," said Kai. "I am Uranus. I will work quietly, unseen, and I will give everything I have to make sure it succeeds. You are Nessie. The internet is full of stories of her sticking her head up, wanting to be seen."

Amy wanted to smile, but she had other things on her mind.

"You know if this works, I will be here when you move away for university. We will be going in separate directions like Hannah and Jacob."

"No," said Kai. He had thought about this a lot. "Same direction, but a wider path. The path will narrow in a short time, and we will be moving side by side again."

Kai placed the palm of his hand over the dragon wing that hung at the nape of Amy's neck.

"We can be on opposite sides of the world and never be apart, and even without our draconalia, I know I would still carry a part of you with me wherever I go."

Amy smiled, resting her hand over Kai's turtle. This had become their way of sharing a moment. Stronger than words, more passionate than a hug or a kiss.

"Your words don't sound like those of a fifteen-year-old boy," said Amy.

"Maybe it is because I share a soul with a thousand-year-old dragon, or maybe because, as of yesterday, I am sixteen."

"Oh my god! How did I not know it was your birthday?" said Amy. "You mother never said anything."

Kai laughed.

"It's not funny. Turning sixteen is a big one!"

"You didn't know. We haven't stopped working on this project for days. And my parents have been so busy, I think they forgot too."

"But I didn't get you anything."

Kai placed the binder in her hands. "Go get me this."

Amy smiled, kind of sad, kind of nervous.

"Go home. Tomorrow is a big day."

Kai almost ushered her out the door. He didn't want her to feel bad about his birthday. He had just tossed in in there because it seemed kind of humorous at the moment. He laughed though when he pictured his father's response to asking to take the car for his driver's licence test.

Amy checked in on her grandmother when she got home. Sue was already asleep. Before going to bed herself, Amy checked the back of the miscellaneous drawer in the kitchen. This was where her grandmother had been hiding the bottles of medication she had recently acquired. The only reason Amy knew they were there is she noticed her grandmother quickly stashing them when she came home early one day. Amy checked the bottles to see how many pills had been used. The first thing she had checked after discovering the pills was what they were for. They were all heart medication, and that was why she had been making an effort to be home more.

The next morning found Amy sitting outside of Lu's office at the fish plant. Gone were the casual clothes she always wore. She wore a blue pant suit now that Mei had helped her find at a local thrift shop. Mei had offered to help her buy something new, but Amy wanted to do this on her own.

"You ready?"

Amy looked up to see Mei. "I think so."

"He doesn't know it's you coming. Use that element of surprise," whispered Mei.

Amy had asked for Mei's advice in approaching Lu with an idea. She never told Mei what the idea was, but she didn't need to. Mei took Amy out for coffee, and gave her some suggestions, including dressing professionally, and she scheduled this appointment.

"This is your nine A.M. appointment," announced Mei, opening the door to Lu's office.

Lu stood up behind his desk, ready to shake the hand of the person behind Mei, his jaw dropping a little when Amy stepped in. Amy didn't pause. She went straight to the desk and reached out to shake Lu's hand. Lu reached out and shook her hand, more out of natural reflex than anything.

"Sit down," said Mei. "You too Lu. And close your mouth."

They both sat down at her direction.

"Sir, I am here about a job."

Lu relaxed. This was an easy thing to deal with, though Amy wouldn't like the answer.

"I know you have no jobs. I want you to create a new role, just for me."

Lu was intrigued now, curious if this was a joke or Mei had put her up to it.

"And how much would I pay you?"

"I think the question about what the return for your company will be is more important."

Amy placed her binder on the desk. Lu cleared some papers away so he could open it.

"The numbers on that first page are the water test results when the DFO was about to shut you down, and beside those, the most recent results."

Lu gave his wife a side-eye look.

"Not to worry. Those numbers are all internal…now. But eventually, the DFO will have to release them, and when they do, we need to be prepared."

Amy didn't pause. She reached forward and flipped the page in the binder.

"In the next few pages you will find news stories about fish plants and other food processing plants that were the subject of theories, often conspiracy theories, around problems with their product. I have included sales data so you can see the results. Some…"

Lu held up his hand. "A moment please."

Lu flipped through the pages, paying attention to the details. He looked at Mei. "How will these numbers get out?"

"Requests for information. Reports. Leaks. We can't stop it," said Mei.

"And unfortunately, because there is such a large and unexplained change, there is going to be a lot of conspiracy theories about the numbers being fake, the good numbers, not the bad ones."

Lu looked across his desk at Amy. "Do you think they are fake?"

"No," said Amy, "but truth and facts don't win when it comes to social media."

Lu sat back in his chair. "Okay, you have my full attention now."

"There is a lot to go through. In addition to what is in the binder, you will find a flash drive with more information and details on it.," said Amy. "I want you to take the time you need to go through it all, and when you are done, hire me to coordinate the project. Take me on for the first year as part of my school's work experience program, so no cost to you except the incidentals that are outlined in the budget in the appendix."

"You have a budget."

"Yes sir. Years two through five include a salary."

"I will take a look at it. A serious look. But I have a few questions before you go."

"Okay. I will try and answer them," said Amy. her nervousness increasing with Lu's serious tone.

"Question one. Did you do this all on your own?"

"No, sir. Kai and I did it together, and we got help from others where we needed."

285

"So you were the brains, and he was the brawn."

"We switch," said Amy. "He is brilliant, and today, I am the brawn."

Lu laughed. "Yes, you are. Question two. You have a five-year plan. What about university or college?"

"Lu," Mei chided. "This is a business meeting."

"It is. But this is family too."

Amy's shoulder's slumped a little, as though the wind had been knocked out of her sails. "I know you said there is money for my school, but..." Amy collected herself. She did not want tears. "My grandmother has heart problems, that she is hiding from me. I can't go away to school. I need to stay and make sure she is cared for."

Lu stood up, offering a handshake. "I can respect that answer. Give me a couple days to go through all of this and then we will talk."

Amy stood up and shook his hand firmly, remembering Mei's caution to not give a limp handshake. "Thank you for your time. Is this business meeting over now?"

"Yes...," said Lu, not quite sure what she was asking.

"Good. Can we plan something for Kai's birthday, not now, but maybe later? We all missed it."

"Huh.." Mei exclaimed, sucking in a breath. "We did it again. And he is sixteen! We are horrible parents."

"His fault for being born at our busy time of year," said Lu. "You make plans Amy. We will be there."

"What do we get him for a gift?" ask Mei. "I have no idea what a sixteen-year-old boy wants."

"Get him driving lessons," said Amy. "So I don't have to drive everywhere."

"That is a good idea," said Lu. "And Amy, no matter how this turns out, I want you to know you did a very professional job and handled yourself well. I appreciate the respect you showed by treating it like business and not family or friends."

Mei walked Amy out of the office, closing the office door behind her. "Lu is not big on emotions and stuff so you might not have noticed, but you really impressed him."

Amy sat in her car for a while, collecting her thoughts. There was an emptiness she felt at the moment that was new to her. She had put so much time and energy into putting the presentation together, and stressed the entire night about how she would handle the meeting with Lu. Now that it was done, she felt like she had some breathing room. That was what she was feeling, not emptiness, but space to breathe in. She smiled and started the car. Now she had to make up for Kai's missed birthday.

Two days later everyone sat around a table at a restaurant in a nearby town. This was a rare treat for all of them. Aside from the local café, eating out was something unusual. Everyone apologized for missing his real birthday except for Amy's grandmother.

"I didn't miss it. How can I miss what I don't know is happening," she said, the restaurant filling with her laughter. "But I already had your gift ready anyways."

Sue reached into the shopping bag she carried with her and pulled out a sweater. "This is what I have been knitting, and bonus," she said, pulling another sweater out of the bag. "They are a matching set."

Amy rolled her eyes. She appreciated the sweater, but having a matching sweater with Kai seemed, a little much. Kai loved his though. He looked at the intricate design of a turtle carrying the world on its back at the center and a dragon on either side of the turtle, and it reminded him of Amy's carving. That was too much to be chance. Mei took the sweater from Kai, admiring it as she folded it neatly. She knew that Amy's grandmother sold similar sweaters for hundreds of dollars. She would be reminding Kai of what he received many times. It he treated it well, it would last a long time.

"This is my gift," said Lu, sliding an envelope across the table. Kai opened it eagerly, and he wasn't displeased when he saw what was inside. It was a certificate for driving lessons, which surprised Kai. He thought he was going to have to beg to get a chance to drive so he could get his license.

"Thanks, Dad," said Kai. "Maybe now I won't crash your car."

"Not my car," said Lu. "Driver's ed car, and then Amy's car, and maybe some day your own car."

Mei elbowed her husband. "Here," she said., sliding a piece of paper across the table. "This is the real gift from us."

Kai unfolded the paper and stared wide-eyed at it for a moment.

"Amy said you are doing some big projects on your computer, and the laptop you have needs more power or memory or whatever. We didn't know what would work, so that store credit will let you pick out what you need."

"Wow…Thank you."

"Speaking of projects," said Lu. "I saw what you did with Amy. You put a lot or work and thought into it and I kind of thought you were just playing games or something. Good work. I have another gift. Not really a gift though. It was earned."

Lu slid a large manilla envelope across the table to Amy. "Before you open that, there are strings attached."

"May I ask what they are, Sir?" asked Amy.

"You keep your grades at A or better during your work experience. I won't have this work detracting from your school."

"Oh, I like that string," said Amy's grandmother is. "I have no idea what this is about, but I like that string."

"I think you will like this one too," said Lu. "The contract is for five years, like you proposed, but those last four, you agree to finish University. You can do it online. Never have to leave the community."

Amy had never thought about doing university online, but it really was a good compromise.

"I get to choose my study?"

"Of course," said Mei.

"One more thing."

"Oh, oh," said Kai, recognizing his father's tone.

"In one week is the big celebration the town holds every year. I want to announce this, and I want you to launch this during that celebration. I looked at it all. You are ready."

Amy reached her hand across the table. Lu shook it.

"What is happening?" said Sue. "I feel like I missed something."

"We will explain on the way home," said Mei. "You can ride with us. You two stop by the house and have some cake, then you can go and spend some time on your own."

As they drove away from the restaurant, Mei lowered her visor, pointing at the mirror. In the mirror they could see Amy jumping up and down and doing a little dance. "I am surprised she held on long enough for us to pull away."

Lawrence Nault

Chapter 31

The birthday cake was cut and waiting for them when the got to Kai's. They were just settling down in the living room when Amy and Kai came in the door.

"There you are," said Sue. "I thought you might still be dancing your little jig in that parking lot."

"Oh no! You saw that?"

"I was wishing I had one of those camera phones so I could get it on video."

"It was kind of funny," said Kai.

Amy elbowed him. "My grandmother doesn't need any help from you."

Mei handed them each a plate with a piece of cake on it, and told them to sit down for a while. "We didn't tell her why you wanted her to stay," she whispered in Amy's ear.

"We are going to leave soon and drive Sue home. We thought you two earned some time alone, not working on your projects and stuff. Let's call this another birthday present," said Mei.

"But Amy wanted us all together here to give you her present I think."

Kai looked at Amy. He had no idea she had got something for him. Amy set her plate down, and took a moment to finish the bite she had in her mouth.

"I kind of had a speech prepared, but I have totally forgot it, so you will have to be very patient with me." Amy took Kai's hand as she spoke. "A lot has happened this summer for all of us. Kai and I meeting through a carving. The shipwrecks and the garbage and the clean-ups. That whole crazy, man I rescued off the beach thing. In the background of all of that so many people came together, but none more than the five of us here." Amy stopped to take a sip of her water. Kai squeezed her hand reassuringly.

"Kai and I came together, just like you and Mr. Chen did at our age," said Amy, looking at Mei.

"We were younger, I think," said Lu.

"Well, like the two of you, Kai and I will be together when we get to your age still. We aren't playing games. This isn't a summer fling. I wanted you to know that."

Kai's parents looked at him.

"She is right," said Kai confidently.

Lu started to say something, but Amy interrupted him. "He is going away to school still. His education is still a priority."

"See, the brains of the operation," said Lu.

"I also came together with this family. You took me in like I always belonged, as I found out that in many ways you have always treated me and my grandmother as part of the family. And Mei, you went out of your way to help me connect with my own family."

"I could go on and on," said Amy, "but I don't think I need to. Turning sixteen is a big thing for most teenagers. A line crossed over from one stage of life to the next, and we have all crossed our own lines this summer, so…."

Amy got up, and went down the hall, returning with something large and covered with a towel. She placed it on the mantel under the painting of the dragons. Kai just noticed the mantle had been cleared of the stuff that was usually on it.

"I think you have all seen this already, at various stages. And Mei, like you said about this painting of your grandmother's being handed down in the family, I think this should be as well, and grandma agrees with me. I think these two things belong together from us to our children to…"

"Your children!" Kai's father exclaimed.

"After he is done school and has a good job," said Amy.

Lu made a dramatic show of wiping his brow with the back of his hand.

"Any way…" Amy pulled the towel off to reveal the carving. She stood back to look at it. Sitting beneath the painting, it took on a whole new life.

Kai's father was the first to get up and approach it. He reached to touch it, but pulled his hand back, not sure how delicate it was. "Did you help with this?" he asked, turning to Amy's grandmother.

"That is all her," said Sue proudly. "Her skills have passed mine."

Amy watched as Lu bobbed his head from side to side in front of the scale. She wondered what he was seeing in the reflection. Whatever it was, he liked it, and she wasn't surprised. As hard and strict as he came across, he had a heart of gold. It was a shame that he never got to practice as a doctor in Canada, because he would have been so good with his patients. Fate had its reasons though.

Mei joined her husband in front of the carving. She touched it and turned it, describing exactly what she was seeing as she did. She paused quietly for a long time staring at her reflection. "I don't like that part. It makes me look like my mother." Her words said one thing, but her tone, and the tear in her eye said the opposite."

Amy turned to Kai and noticed his lost look, and red eyes. Mei noticed as well.

"I think it is time for us to take Sue home," she said, grabbing Lu's arm.

"Yup, it's past this old woman's bedtime," said Sue.

The three of them were quickly out of the house.

"Did I say something wrong?" Amy asked Kai, who had gotten up when his parents left, and was now standing in front of the carving.

Kai put his arm around her gently. "I was just reminded of the first time I saw this complete. It brought back memories."

"Oh, I didn't think about that. I was worried when I talked about us being together for good, or joked about children, that I said something wrong. I didn't think of the bad memories it might trigger."

"Not bad," said Kai. "Difficult, but what I remember most is you being there for me, with me. I could feel your fear as I stood by the water, and still you supported me. And then we got to fall asleep by the fire together, and the rain that woke us up."

Kai shifted the carving so he could see both of them in the reflection of the dragon scale. "You were right about us being together for a long time. I didn't know how to tell my parents how serious I was. I am guessing, like Uranus and Nessie, it won't be just this lifetime, but many."

Amy watched Kai stare into the scale. "What do you see?"

"A future," said Kai quietly.

Amy was pulling out of the driveway when his parents pulled back in. He was putting away the dishes and trying to fit the cake in the fridge when they came in. "You two head to bed. I got this. Thanks for everything. This was a good birthday."

The conversation Amy had with her grandmother when she got home was a little different.

"You had a secret you didn't share with me," her grandmother said, not unkindly.

Amy walked calmly into the kitchen and opened up the junk drawer. She pulled out the bottles of pills and set them on the kitchen table. "We should probably talk about the secrets in this house lately," said Amy. "There seem to be a few."

Sue sat down in her chair and motioned for Amy to join her. Amy sat on the floor at her feet, leaning against her grandmother's legs. She felt her grandmother's fingers run through her hair. It had been a long time since they sat and talked like this.

"You're right," said Sue. "I should have told you, but you graduate this year, and then you can get out of here to university and see the world. I know you. I knew you would think you have to take care of me."

"So how bad is it?" asked Amy.

"Who really knows?" said Sue. "Doctors never really say. They just want to run more tests. But I am no spring chicken anymore."

"Kai's father would flip if he heard me say this, but I want you to meet your great-grandchildren, and teach them our ways like you taught me."

Sue laughed. "Lu's head would explode if he heard you talk like that. I thought it was going to happen when you mentioned children at the house."

"Yeah, that was kind of funny."

"You don't have to stay for me, Amy. There is a whole world out there. I will be okay."

"Here is the thing, though," said Amy. I don't want to go anywhere. I have found my place in this world. I know my purpose. Even if you weren't sick, I wouldn't be going anywhere."

"I believe you," said Sue. "Lu never talks, but tonight he went on and on about how you came into his office, and your report, and your plan. Oh, and about how you motivated Kai to do some real work."

"I think Kai has always done that, but never had the confidence to show his father. His mother knows."

"Oh, they both know," said Sue. "Parents are just like that sometimes. They want their children to succeed."

"You don't do that," said Amy.

"Never had to. And I think happiness is more important than success."

"Now hand me my knitting needles. I am going to wind down a bit before bed. You should get some rest."

Amy pulled the knitting basket closer and handed her grandmother her needles and a ball of wool. She got up off the floor and gave her grandmother a hug. "Love you."

"Love you too, my girl."

Amy grabbed the pill bottles to put them back in the drawer. Her grandmother stopped her.

"May as well leave them out. At least that way I won't forget to take them."

Sue watched Amy walk away, the bottles now out in the open. She didn't like being seen as fragile, but somehow, Amy's love made it feel like strength.

Lawrence Nault

Chapter 32

The entire village was a hive of activity. Every year, on the second-to-last weekend of August, the village hosted the 'Line and Lore' celebration. It was a combination of celebrating the end of another fishing season, the end of summer, and just celebrating community in general, though people travelled from all over to be part of it. Oral traditions were as much a part of Cape Breton as fishing was, and several years ago, after a long night of swapping stories in the local pub, one of their councilmen came up with the idea of the Line and Lore celebration.

Like many celebrations happening on the East Coast, it had a blessing of the fleet where a local minister blessed the boats and the people who worked them. This was followed by the Wharf Walk as locals and visitors walked the wharf, admiring the boats that had been decorated with flags and lights, chatting with fishers, and taking part in mini-tours. Then there were the chowder suppers and fish fries held by various groups around the community under tents, outdoors, and in community halls. There was more lobster, scallops, mussels, chowder, and fried fish than anyone could imagine. Wherever a person went, there was live music with fiddles and guitars. Gaelic and Acadian songs filled the air. Step dancers put on shows to the delight of onlookers.

The events that many travelled for though, were the storytelling events. Under a gazebo in the main park elders shared tales of the sea, lost boats and local legends. At another, youth performed spoken word, and did readings from their own works. Beside a bonfire, Mi'kmaq elders told their legends. The main event though, was the "Fishermen's Tales" competition. This was what people travelled to hear and to compete in. It was a competition where the "wildest tale wins." The prizes were getting bigger every year, and they were offering prize money in four categories this year. The Gold Hook Award was for the best overall tale. The Silver Oar award was for the best delivery. The Knot of the Night was for the most outrageous but well-tied-together lie. The audience vote chose the winner of the last prize which was the Fishwife's Favourite.

Amy stood off to the side of the stage that was set up in the local hockey arena. The arena was full to a sold-out crowd. Lu stood with her, and she took comfort in the fact that he looked more nervous than she did. This year, they had a well-known comedian taking on the role of the host. He stepped on stage and quickly had everyone's attention.

"Good evening, everybody. I am the Bosun of the Mic for this year's Fishermen's Tales competition, and I am perfectly suited for this role. Let me tell you why"

"Years ago, I was out in a dinghy no bigger than a bathtub, trying to catch mackerel with a line made from my shoelace and a bent safety pin. The sea was calm, the fog was thick, and I was three sandwiches deep with no luck. Suddenly—bang— something hit the bottom of the boat so hard, I nearly lost my fourth sandwich."

"I looked over the side, and there, I swear on my Aunt Margie's banana bread, was a halibut the size of a dining table, staring up at me with one lazy eye and what I can only describe as… disdain. Before I could react, it thumped the boat again—out of spite, I think—and swam off with my entire tackle box in its mouth like it was collecting tribute."

"Now, that's not why I'm qualified. I'm qualified because, two weeks later, that same halibut was spotted off Louisburg dragging three tackle boxes and what appeared to be someone's sandal collection."

"Folks, if I can survive a passive-aggressive halibut and still spin a yarn, I can certainly guide you through tonight's storytellers."

"But first—before the wild words start flying—let's give a big round of applause to one of our generous sponsors. Everyone, this is Lu Chen!"

Lu made his way onto the stage to applause. He held up his hand and waited for the sound to go down.

"Our fish plant, and the jobs in this community wouldn't exist without the fishers of Cape Breton, so we are proud to be a sponsor of this amazing event, but that is not why I am here. I have a story too. It's about ships sinking and garbage washing up on our shores, and the things in our waters that make it hard for people to survive."

The arena went even quieter as Lu continued to speak.

301

We faced a tough and scary time this summer, but we got through it, together. We catch the best fish and shellfish in the world off our coast and we process it right here, but like everywhere else, we increasingly face the challenges of pollution in our pristine waters. That is why we are launching a program that promotes our clean waters and clean fish, and encourages the world to help us preserve that."

There was a small round of applause.

"But that isn't my story tonight. My story is about the person we have hired to lead the program. Many of you know her already. Our shores are clean because of this one young woman who worked tirelessly to get people together and clean up the debris, keeping our shores and waters pristine and wildlife safe. You all know her by her first name, so please join me in thanking Amy for everything she has done."

Amy stepped on the stage, and the applause erupted, many people standing and calling her name. She pinched the bridge of her nose to hold back tears.

"I need to correct something," said Amy, "Mr. Chen said the shores are clean because of one young woman, but that is not accurate. They are clean because a community cared and worked together. Can you play the video, please?"

The lights dimmed, and a video montage played on a large screen. Men in the restaurant coloring the map, people on the shores picking up garbage, before and after pictures of the shores they cleaned, people enjoying food afterwards, and bins of garbage being hauled away.

"Cape Breton really has the best people," said Amy as the lights came back up. "Every single person who helped in the smallest way should be acknowledged for their effort. I applaud you all."

Amy clapped, and everyone joined in.

Now, before I go, I have a story of my own," Amy said, pausing. "Let's dim the lights one more time."

The lights faded. On screen, the camera began a slow descent — from the stars above Earth, down through the clouds, and into the heart of the Pacific Ocean. The water darkened. Suspended within it was a swirling mass of debris — the Great Pacific Garbage Patch.

A voiceover began, steady and low:

"In the middle of our oceans lie massive islands of garbage — drifting with the currents, sinking below the surface, breaking down into billions of invisible pieces. Microplastics. Out of sight, out of mind... right?"

As the words echoed, the garbage patch on screen shifted shape, forming a human fingerprint — the same pattern Kai had once glimpsed from the satellite image.

"So what's the problem?" the voice asked, as a hand rose from the ocean. The swirling debris aligned with the fingertip.

"Can you put your finger on it?"

The forefinger, now marked with the garbage-print, descended onto a map of Earth — pressing over North America. The fingerprint remained, a smudge of waste superimposed on the land.

"What if it was here?"

The finger moved — Australia. "Or here?"

Europe. "Or here?"

As the fingerprint moved across the globe, it shrank into a corner of the screen. In its place came vibrant footage of students — collecting water, examining samples, working in classrooms.

"That's why we're launching W.A.V.E. 4000 — a global initiative empowering students from Grades 1 through 12 to test local waters for waste and microplastics."

The image transitioned into a patchwork of faces — students and families from around the world holding crayons, coloring in maps of coastlines and rivers.

"That's why we're supporting the International Adopt-a-Shore Program — inviting everyone, everywhere, to grab a crayon and claim a stretch of shoreline to keep clean."

The scene darkened. Floating plastic shimmered under a beam of light, slowly sinking.

The voice returned, quiet now:

"But if we can't stop the plastics from entering the water to begin with..."

A single finger — the same one marked with the garbage fingerprint — reached toward the screen, growing larger, until it filled the frame.

"Help us put a finger on the problem of water pollution."

Fade to black.

As the lights came back up, the claps started quietly, and got louder and louder and louder.

Amy set her microphone on the stand and walked off the stage. Letting the video speak for itself. The host was quickly back on stage, but it took him several moments to get the audience's attention back on himself.

Amy left out the back entrance, Lu following closely behind, both relieved to be out of the spotlight. As they stepped out into the evening chill, they heard someone calling Mr. Chen's name and turned to see who it was. They turned to see someone running towards them with a television camera. Amy recognized the reporter close behind him from the first beach clean-up.

"Mr. Chen, can you tell us more about the video and those projects?" the reporter asked.

"No," said Lu smiling "But Amy can." Lu turned and walked away, leaving Amy to handle the media.

"Did you make that video?" asked the reporter.

"It was done by a group of young people from around the world," said Amy, reaching into her pocket and grabbing a card. "You can download the video here, and it has full credits, and there is also a making-of video on the same website."

The reporter looked at the card.

"Can I find the project details there too?"

"You can. And More."

"You are really doing this all yourself?" asked the reporter.

"I am just the person that is here," said Amy. "I have help from people of all ages from everywhere, and that is the only way we are going to find a solution to these problems, if everyone helps."

"Thanks for this," said the reporter. "We're going to get back to the show."

As the reporter disappeared back into the area, Kai came around the corner, a large group of people with him. Every one of them had the phone or some small video device in their hands or on a gimble.

"These are the people you want to talk to," said Kai. "They were all out here doing social media content today, so I had Mom stream your presentation in there and told them all to meet me here to talk to you."

"Your mother knows how to stream?" said Amy.

"She does now," said Kai.

Kai quickly removed himself from the scene, staying just close enough to keep an eye on Amy and make sure she was okay. For three hours, she talked to people, posing for pictures and videos, handing out her cards, and telling everyone to share the video and adopt a shore. By noon the next day, the video was viral in Nova Scotia. In another twelve hours, it was viral across Canada. And then it hit the world.

Chapter 33

Amy and Kai wished they could say their video changed the world, but it didn't.

It attracted a great deal of attention, good and bad, for a short while. Change, they discovered, wasn't a single wave. It was a tide that came slowly, pulled back often, and sometimes left behind wreckage before anything new could grow. In a world driven by clicks and shares, getting noticed was easy. Staying noticed? That was the hard part.

Especially when your story threatened people's comfort.

In the unfiltered churn of the attention economy, where neither fact nor moral compass seemed to matter, Amy quickly became a target. Not just for her ideas or her actions, but for who she was. She was young. She was indigenous. She was a female. And that made her a lightning rod for the kind of hatred that had nothing to do with her work. The comments about her body, the inappropriate messages, the constant undermining—not of her argument, but of her existence—cut

307

deeper than she expected. What she faced wasn't random. It was part of a larger pattern. A pattern that sought to silence voices like hers, not because they were wrong, but because they were right, and that frightened people.

She hadn't been fully prepared for that. Who could be?

More than once, she considered stepping away. Just disappearing. Letting it all go.

But she didn't.

Because she wasn't alone.

She had Kai. She had the other dragon-bound, who understood more than most. She had her family, Kai's part now part of that word. And she had her community, and the global network of the Young Dragons. More than that, she had the song.

The tear's song.

It pulled from within her a strength she hadn't known she had. It reminded her that dragons don't flee from storms, they ride the wind above them. And so, she stayed.

Not for the spotlight.

But for the oceans.

From their sanctuaries across Earth, the dragons watched, not just over their dragon-bound, but over Amy as well. There had been a change, when the tear bonded with Amy, and when the four became one. They had returned to Earth at Nessie's death calls, and working to save the planet was their gift to her, a fulfillment of her final wishes. Up until now they had remained and continued on that path out of a sense of duty. Now, it was with a flame of hope the gave them strength.

Pluto returned to the cavern she had created for herself, deep in the ice of Antarctica. She listened to the dragon's song and waited patiently. She felt a loneliness being so far away from the life-force of her home, and despite searching, she had not found her dragon-bound yet. She questioned if there was even a human bound to her. Had the connection forgotten about her existence, the way the humans had minimized and forgotten about her planet, relegating it to something far less than they could ever understand.

In the Himalayas, Neptune watched over the boy bound to him. It would soon be time to introduce himself, but not quite yet. While he waited, Neptune communed with the animals of the Himalayas. To most humans, the Himalayas was Mount Everest, an obstacle to be conquered. The people who lived there knew better. It was so much more than just a mountain. It was a region of diverse ecosystems and even more diverse wildlife. So many of those animals were at the end of their lines, the last of their kind, and Neptune sought these rare creatures out to commune with them. Snow leopards, Tibetan wolves, Himalayan musk deer, black bears, and griffon vultures, all rare and elusive species, sought the dragon out as Neptune looked for them. Kashmir Stags and Chiru were more difficult to find, even for Neptune, their kind barely hanging on to continued existence.

And then there was the Yeti, a legendary ape-like creature said to inhabit the Himalayan region. To the humans, the Yeti was a creature of myth, but then so was Nessie. Yeti were almost as old as the dragons, and like the dragons, once abundant, but now only a few. They were tied deeply to the lives of the creatures in the Himalayas, and as those creatures disappeared from existence, so too did the life force of the Yeti. They were very few, but they too found hope in the dragons' songs.

Saturn was not resting. Zara, her dragon-bound was being offered a way out of the refugee camp. With the support of an uncle and his church in the United States, Zara and her family were being processed to be sent to the U.S. under a sponsorship program. That only seemed like a better alternative than the refugee camp. Saturn and all the dragons had been paying attention to the U.S. as its most recent government was not only undoing environmental protection, but also instituting programs that would make things much worse.

Saturn knew that if Zara entered the U.S., not only would her voice, the voice of the dragons, be silenced if she was to remain safe, but that she would likely end up detained in one of the modern-day concentration camps and shipped back to her home country, putting her in danger again. There was no way the dragons could interfere with that process other than taking physical actions to redirect the transportation.

Saturn was considering this choice as she tracked the truck carrying Zara and her family from the Nakivale Settlement to Kampala, then the plane to Nairobi. She could feel Zara's fear and hope, their mixture enough to unsettle the stomach of the dragon, herself. The family got on yet another plane that flew from Nairobi to Amsterdam. Saturn followed the flight from high above it, pleased to be able to stretch and use her wings, but debating with herself the entire time on what she would do to prevent Zara from going to the United States. As the plane crossed the skies, Zara's fears were left behind.

Fate stepped in, and Saturn did not have to take the risk of exposing her existence. Zara found herself standing next to her mother, helping to translate the words of the International Organization for Migration officer, who was delivering some difficult news. During the flight, an executive order had been issued by the President and the U.S. was no longer accepting refugees from their region.

Zara's mother started to panic, worried they would be returned to the refugee camp and never get out. Zara tried to calm her mother, fighting her own fears at the same time. The IOM officer understood, having been through this same scenario several times recently. This time, she was prepared, though.

"You are not going back," the officer said kindly. "We have already worked with another group, and you are going to Canada now."

"Canada," Zara said, trying to conceal her happiness at the change. That had always been her hope, that they would go to Canada.

"Canada?" Zara's mother questioned?

Zara explained to her mother, who, in her panic, hadn't understood what the IOM officer was explaining to them. Her mother was relieved and grateful.

"I do have some more bad news for you, unfortunately," said the IOM officer. "Your uncle and his family have been detained by the U.S. and are being held to be deported."

Zara wasn't sure how to respond to this. She didn't know her uncle, and her mother showed little emotion over the news. Exhausted from all the travel, they sat and waited quietly for their flight to Canada, Zara keeping her two younger brothers entertained while her mother rested.

Jupiter rested in the depths of Algonquin Park. She talked often with Jacob and Hannah, trying to understand the stress they were feeling, but also to calm them. This was a new phase of life for them, and Jupiter understood that. Until now, they were like the tear Nessie had left behind, sheltered from the world by their family, absorbing as much information as possible, and taking everything in. They thought they knew it

311

all, but with all the facets falling off their protective barrier, the world would have many more lessons to teach them.

Hannah would do just fine, Jupiter knew. She was a strong woman, and even if Jupiter had never come into her life, Hannah would have achieved amazing things. Jacob, Jupiter was not so confident about. Jacob had strengths of his own, but he did not see them in himself, and the separation from Hannah left him exposed and vulnerable. Jupiter could do nothing to help, but listen to him, and his tears that he hid from others.

Mars had returned to Chara Sands to rest. He was much more talkative with Kyle now. While he had recovered from the fire tornado, Kyle had found something in himself, and that new-found confidence boosted their bond. Mars didn't quite understand the change, because as a dragon, he remembered everything from his time, and from the dragons before him. Kyle's boost in confidence seemed to come from his new connection to his roots. Perhaps that was the problem with humans—they forgot too easily, not because they didn't care, but because they didn't know how to carry memory the way dragons did.

Mercury was bold. He ventured out often from his sanctuary in the waters off Bermuda. Usually, it was to spend time with Anne, and occasionally he would let Murray just catch a glimpse of him. It was a game. Anne chided Mercury for teasing her brother, but she found joy in the way Mercury set Murray's imagination on fire. That would serve her brother well when he stopped talking so much and started putting his words on paper. Anne knew her brother was destined to be a writer. She had seen it in the way it seemed only she could.

The young girl that Jacob met and opened her world with pencils and a sketch pad was transforming into something else.

Some would call her ability to see the things she did magical or fantastical, but she knew that wasn't the case. She spoke little and noticed everything, taking in information like a sponge. That was one of the reasons Mercury visited her so often, to share his new discoveries and information. Anne could never get enough. Her mind freed her from some of the things that would distract others, and her profound sense of empathy helped her to understand the information she took in, and how it would and could affect others.

Venus kept the tear safe, wrapped in the coils of her tale. Since the bonding ceremony between Uranus, Kai, and Amy on that Cape Breton beach, the tear grew brighter every day. Venus sang the song of the dragons to the tear, but she could hear the tear singing its own song to Amy. The energy in the tear was hope. The dragon-bound that had been joined, with Uranus, Jupiter, Mars, and Mercury, were hope. Was that hope enough to counter the fate of the humans or would karma have its revenge, leaving Earth as barren as her home world? Only time would tell, and there were more dragon-bound to be found, including hers.

At the bottom of the ocean, Uranus lay unmoving. The silt carried by the currents now covered his hulking body in a thin layer. Creatures of the deep watched the ocean floor move violently from time to time, not from an earthquake, or the thermal vents under it, but from the pain that wracked the body of Uranus. The dragon never cried out or called for help. Instead, he retreated into his mind, and the minds of those bound to him. He listened, only rarely talking, a skill he wished he would have learned long before he left Earth the first time.

Kai would often find his way to the shore, letting the waves lap at his legs, as he spoke to Uranus. He felt that ocean water gave him a more direct connection to his dragon. In recent days he had seen the weight on Amy's shoulders, that hate fueled by the anonymity and distance of the digital world, empowering the voices of anger and quashing the voices of hope. He wondered if helping Amy had been the right choice. "Do you have any regrets, Uranus?"

Uranus seldom responded these days, knowing that Kai's questions and words were more just streams of thought that he had to work through, and Uranus was confident that Kai would find the right path through those thoughts. This question, Uranus felt a need to respond to, not just because Kai had asked, but in his convalescence, he, too, had been asking himself that question.

"I am a flawed dragon, Kai. Too often, my desires clouded my empathy, and I put myself ahead of others. Those choices caused pain—and real harm—and for that, I am truly sorry. But to say I regret them would be dishonest. At the time, I believed they were necessary. I can't undo them. I can only carry the weight of what I did and try, however late, to be better."

"My only true regret is leaving behind the one I truly loved, and returning too late. But even that regret is selfish, born of my own sense of loss. The truth is, they thrived in my absence. It was my leaving, not my staying, that gave them space to grow. And perhaps that's the hardest truth of all."

"I am not leaving her," said Kai.

"No, you aren't," replied Uranus. "You are a better man than I will ever be a dragon. I once believed I had to choose between love and duty. Now I know that choosing one at the expense of the other was never strength—it was fear disguised as wisdom."

Uranus drifted off to sleep, a welcome reprise from the pain, and as he slept, he dreamed. This confused him because

314

dragons don't dream, but he had seen Kai do it often. Uranus found himself back in his youth, dancing through the skies and the waters with Nessie at his side. He breathed in clean air and watched creatures partway around the world through crystal clear skies. Through the dreams, twinges of pain poked, but he fought to remain asleep and stay in this world, even for a short time.

More dreams would come. Dreams of the past, and dreams of the future, where the tear had opened and his love returned to him, and the world found its new path led by those who followed the paths of dragons. Perhaps that was the beginning—not of a new legend, but of a future that remembered.

Lawrence Nault

W.A.V.E. (Water Awareness Via Education) 4000

1. Introduction: From Fiction to Action

W.A.V.E. 4000 began as a student-led initiative in the pages of this story, imagined by the characters as a way to confront the growing crisis of water pollution. But like all good ideas, it didn't stop at fiction.

This appendix offers a real-world version of the W.A.V.E. 4000 concept, designed to be freely adopted, adapted, and shared by educators, environmental organizations, and communities around the globe. It is both a classroom science framework and a call to collective action, rooted in the belief that education and environmental stewardship must go hand in hand.

317

2. Core Concept

At the heart of W.A.V.E. 4000 is a simple idea:
Mesh Size (in microns) = 4000 ÷ Grade
As students advance through the grades, the mesh they use to collect water samples becomes finer. This progression mirrors their growing understanding of the invisible threats in our environment, such as microplastics.

From larger visible debris in Grade 1 to microscopic fibers in Grade 12, W.A.V.E. 4000 scales science education with age-appropriate, hands-on exploration. The combination of data collection and real-world action encourages young people to become informed stewards of their local environments.

3. Educational Framework

W.A.V.E. 4000 is structured to grow with students, offering a 12-year scaffold of increasingly sophisticated science learning. Here is how the program works by grade level:

Grade	Mesh Size (microns)	Sample Focus
1	4000 μm	Leaves, wrappers, visible trash
2	2000 μm	Straws, candy wrappers
3	1333 μm	Small plastic fragments
4	1000 μm	Bits of packaging, soft plastic
5	800 μm	Synthetic fibers, glitter
6	667 μm	Film plastics, organic debris
7	571 μm	Textile fibers, paint flakes
8	500 μm	Small microplastics, fragments
9	444 μm	Microbeads, deteriorated particles
10	400 μm	Fine microplastics, synthetic fibers
11	364 μm	Transparent microplastic fragments
12	333 μm	Near-invisible plastics

This framework is inclusive and adaptable, making it suitable for urban, rural, and Indigenous communities. It can be integrated into curricula tied to science, math, geography, social studies, and civics.

4. Global Vision

W.A.V.E. 4000 envisions a youth-led environmental science network across the globe:
- **4000 students per country** participating in water testing and shoreline observation
- **4000 schools worldwide** adopting the grade-based model
- A **shared open-source database** where students upload their findings, photos, and insights
- Contributions to citizen science and alignment with **Sustainable Development Goals (SDGs)**, particularly:
  - ○ **SDG 6**: Clean Water and Sanitation
  - ○ **SDG 13**: Climate Action
  - ○ **SDG 14**: Life Below Water

The project supports global youth participation, environmental education, and hands-on science learning that transcends borders.

5. Sample Activities by Grade

Grade 2: Students visit a local stream and collect water using a kitchen strainer (2000 μm mesh). They sort visible trash into plastic vs organic and record what they find in a simple chart.

Grade 5: Students use fine mesh and tweezers to separate synthetic materials from organic particles. They create posters to show how plastic breaks down over time.

Grade 9: Students dye samples with Nile Red and use a UV light to identify microplastic particles. They compile data in a shared spreadsheet and write short reports comparing sample sites.

Each activity builds on observation, classification, data collection, and communication, developing both scientific literacy and environmental empathy.

6. Action & Advocacy Component

W.A.V.E. 4000 is more than observation. Students are encouraged to take local action:

- Organize or participate in shoreline or community cleanups
- Share findings with local councils or water stewardship groups
- Partner with Indigenous communities to learn about traditional water knowledge
- Host school science fairs or town hall events about water pollution

The project also supports the **Adopt-a-Shore Program**, where students and families choose a local shoreline to symbolically color in and keep clean.

7. Join Us: A Call to Educators, Scientists, and Organizations

This project was born in fiction but designed for the real world. We invite educators, youth groups, scientists, conservation organizations, and policymakers to bring W.A.V.E. 4000 to life.

Whether you run a classroom, a lab, or a lake stewardship group, you can join this global initiative. Use it, adapt it, expand it. All that matters is that we empower the next generation to understand their water, protect it, and lead us toward a cleaner future.

Author's Note

In real life, our dragons aren't massive, scale-covered beasts with powers we don't understand. They are those that came before us and led the way, their march of resistance and persistence creating the paths we follow in. Their wisdom shared... Their understanding that they may have come from a different time and place but that doesn't stop them from sharing and passing on their knowledge, and their mistakes, as the next generation builds new inroads off those trails, ever working towards a sustainable future.

This book is fiction. While it introduces elements from various cultures and traditions, those elements are included to celebrate the diverse world we live in and to encourage readers to seek out stories written by those within those cultures. I have done my best to treat every culture, story, and tradition with respect, but I have also taken creative liberties to support the fictional world of the novel. Please consider this book a starting point, not a source. The most meaningful knowledge always comes from lived experience, and I encourage readers to explore authentic voices, especially from Indigenous, Black, and other historically underrepresented communities.

To the young readers: You don't need to be bonded to a dragon to make a difference. Every beach cleaned, every question asked, every conversation started, and every small act of care ripples out into something bigger. The future isn't waiting for someone else – it's waiting for you. You already have everything it takes to start shaping it.

This book is also a quiet thank-you to the elders – mine, and those I've been lucky enough to listen to along the way. The ones who taught with their hands, with their stories, and with their patience. The ones who reminded me that tradition isn't something locked in the past, but something living, breathing, and evolving with each generation.

Fiction can inspire, but real change comes from listening, learning, and acting. As much as I've imagined here, I hope it drives you toward real voices, real facts, and real action. I hope it encourages you to explore science, environmental stewardship, and storytelling from many perspectives.

If parts of this story felt heavy, it's because the world can feel heavy, too. That's okay. You're not alone in that. Just like the characters, we all find strength in each other – in community, in family, and in the stories we choose to carry forward. That weight becomes lighter when it's shared.

Lawrence Nault

www.ingramcontent.com/pod-product-compliance
Lightning Source LLC
Chambersburg PA
CBHW021447240626
47153CB00001B/337